2000

"You can't hide out forever," *Shane murmured, folding Gigi* *gently into his arms and* *rocking her.*

She buried her face in the side of his neck. He smelled clean and strong.

"I don't want to," she said. "I don't want to live looking over my shoulder anymore, wondering if someone is behind me with a gun, but I don't ever want to go back to being the woman I was."

When her breath had steadied, she asked, "So what do we do now?"

He pulled his head back until he could look at her. "Now we're going to fix it so that you can be whoever the hell you want to be."

His smile warmed her from the inside out. She felt her own lips curve in answer. A few more days—that was probably all they had left together.

So why did she feel like he'd just promised her forever?

Dear Reader,

Once again, Silhouette Intimate Moments has rounded up six top-notch romances for your reading pleasure, starting with the finale of Ruth Langan's fabulous new trilogy. *The Wildes of Wyoming—Ace* takes the last of the Wilde men and matches him with a pool-playing spitfire who turns out to be just the right woman to fill his bed—and his heart.

Linda Turner, a perennial reader favorite, continues THOSE MARRYING McBRIDES! with *The Best Man,* the story of sister Merry McBride's discovery that love is not always found where you expect it. Award-winning Ruth Wind's *Beautiful Stranger* features a heroine who was once an ugly duckling but is now the swan who wins the heart of a rugged "prince." Readers have been enjoying Sally Tyler Hayes' suspenseful tales of the men and women of DIVISION ONE, and *Her Secret Guardian* will not disappoint in its complex plot and emotional power. Christine Michels takes readers *Undercover with the Enemy,* and Vickie Taylor presents *The Lawman's Last Stand,* to round out this month's wonderful reading choices.

And don't miss a single Intimate Moments novel for the next three months, when the line takes center stage as part of the Silhouette 20th Anniversary celebration. Sharon Sala leads off A YEAR OF LOVING DANGEROUSLY, a new in-line continuity, in July; August brings the long-awaited reappearance of Linda Howard—and hero Chance Mackenzie—in *A Game of Chance;* and in September we reprise 36 HOURS, our successful freestanding continuity, in the Intimate Moments line. And that's only a small taste of what lies ahead, so be here this month and every month, when Silhouette Intimate Moments proves that love and excitement go best when they're hand in hand.

Leslie J. Wainger
Executive Senior Editor

Please address questions and book requests to:
Silhouette Reader Service
U.S.: 3010 Walden Ave., P.O. Box 1325, Buffalo, NY 14269
Canadian: P.O. Box 609, Fort Erie, Ont. L2A 5X3

THE LAWMAN'S LAST STAND

VICKIE TAYLOR

Silhouette®

INTIMATE™MOMENTS®

Published by Silhouette Books

America's Publisher of Contemporary Romance

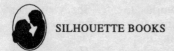 SILHOUETTE BOOKS

ISBN 0-373-27084-4

THE LAWMAN'S LAST STAND

Copyright © 2000 by Vickie Spears

Books by Vickie Taylor

Silhouette Intimate Moments

The Man Behind the Badge #916
Virgin Without a Memory #965
The Lawman's Last Stand #1014

VICKIE TAYLOR

has always loved books—the way they look, the way they feel and most especially the way the stories inside them bring whole new worlds to life. She views her recent transition from reading to writing books as a natural extension of this longtime love. Vickie lives in Aubrey, Texas, a small town dubbed "The Heart of Horse Country," where, in addition to writing romance novels, she raises American Quarter Horses.

IT'S OUR 20th ANNIVERSARY!
We'll be celebrating all year,
Continuing with these fabulous titles,
On sale in June 2000.

Chapter 1

Fight, or die.

The unspoken omen pierced the heavy cloak of semicon-sciousness clouding her mind the way a foghorn pierced a misty sea. It surrounded her. Reverberated inside her. Rallied her senses to consciousness.

She didn't want to die.

Forcing her sluggish eyelids to part, she found herself alone in the cold and the dark. Her first cognizance of where she was and how she'd gotten there came from the soft ping of ice crystals against glass. The windshield. The storm. The accident.

Or was it an accident?

Lying lengthwise across the seat of her old pickup, the woman the people of Pine Valley, Utah, knew as Gigi McCowan lifted her cheek from the frigid vinyl, uncurled fingers stiff from the cold, and probed her aching forehead. Wincing at the lump she found above her right temple, she pulled her hand away. Her aching head would have to wait, as would her throbbing knee. At the moment she had other priorities—like staying alive.

Outside, the wind that had howled earlier, driving a late winter storm before it, had diminished to a soft weeping. The creak of brittle branches added to its lament.

A footstep sounded somewhere above her, at the top of the ravine maybe, the light crunch of a boot on frozen ground.

Her nerves jangled, instantly clearing her pain-shrouded mind. Her senses went on full alert. Soundlessly she reached down to the floorboard and wrapped her fingers around the smooth, cold handle of the twitch. A fitting weapon for a veterinarian, she thought—an instrument designed to cause pain. The twitch was a baseball bat with a noose tied through a hole in the thick end. By pinching a horse's muzzle through the loop and twisting the bat until the rope bit into the tender flesh, she could coerce even the most agitated animal into standing still while she treated its wounds.

Sometimes you had to hurt them a little to make them better.

Tonight her motives weren't so humanitarian. She just wanted to hurt the man in the blue Mercedes who had run her off the road. Hurt him before he hurt her.

She tightened her grip on the twitch. Despite the cold, her palms were sweating. Her breath clouded in front of her face the way the mist had hung over the mountain peaks that morning. The sight had made her heart swell, and despite the chill in the air, she'd taken her coffee out on the porch, settled down in a weathered Adirondack chair, and just sipped, and stared.

Dawn bloomed against a backdrop of violet-and-peach-pastel mist many a morning in this part of Utah. Color Country, the locals called it. Paradise was a better word, to her mind. That was why she'd stayed so long. Too long. She'd fallen in love with the forested hillsides, the columns of rock that stood guard over the wilderness like Indian totems, the community that had taken her in as one of their own.

Now it was all gone to her, evaporated into nothingness, like the mist she'd watched that morning. Paradise lost. Even if she survived the night, she would have to leave Utah.

A twig snapped outside. A barrage of pebbles skittered down a slope.

Tears jammed up behind her eyelids. She blinked them back, fighting the need to sniff, not wanting to give herself away to the stalker nearby.

"Dammit," a muffled voice rumbled.

Her sawmill breath and the pounding of her heart almost drowned out the word. From the sound of it, the stalker was trying to negotiate the steep wall of the ravine, and having trouble. With any luck, he'd fall and break a leg. But luck was fickle tonight. The uneven footfalls righted themselves and crunched toward the truck.

Too late, she noticed the driver's side door was unlocked. *No time. No time.*

Stretched out across the truck seat, her heels against the door handle, there was no room to swing the twitch. She would have to go for a punch. She hid the bat alongside her thigh and lay perfectly still.

The handle clicked. Hinges creaked. A gust of cold air rushed over her prone body.

And she struck.

She punched the bat out the door as hard as she could, sitting up and throwing her weight behind the blow. The rounded end of the bat hit bedrock in the midsection of a man. For a second, victory thrilled through her. Her attacker toppled backward, the breath whooshing from his lungs.

Her victory was short-lived, though. Before his backside hit the ground, he grabbed hold of the end of the bat and yanked, his weight and momentum dragging her out of the truck before her panicked fingers could release their grip.

She wound up in a heap on top of him. Instinctively she raised her fists to fight, but strong hands locked her wrists in iron grips, staving off her blows. She opened her mouth to scream—

"Gi-gi?"

The wail died in her throat.

He had spit out her name in two short gasps, like he didn't have enough air for words with multiple syllables—which he probably didn't, given the way she had planted the bat in his gut. Still, the voice had sounded familiar.

A new chill raised along her spine as she put a name to the voice. Shifting her gaze down, she groaned.

Familiar, silver-plated eyes shone up at her. Odd that the cloud-muted moonlight should give his eyes such a cold sheen. In the daylight, she knew, his eyes were warm and soft, and blue as cornflowers. *Trust-me-baby* blues, she and her girlfriends had called those kinds of eyes as teenagers, for all the innocent girls eyes like that had lured into the dark recesses under the high school bleachers. But Gigi knew better than to fall for trust-me-baby blues.

Or at least she thought she did, until she met Shane Hightower.

"Are you...all right?" His breath warmed her cheek.

No! She was definitely not all right. She was splattered across a man's chest like spilled paint. And not just any man, but Shane Hightower—*Special Agent* Shane Hightower, of the DEA—a man she'd spent the better part of the last two months avoiding. Even before she had known he was DEA, she'd known enough to stay away from him. He'd been introduced to her and everyone else in town as the interim sheriff when the old geezer who used to run the county had retired suddenly. Shane's true identity as an undercover agent, sent to Pine Valley to ferret out a narcotics ring run by a couple of local deputies, had been revealed just three weeks ago when he'd made a dramatic arrest on the mountain.

Looking down, she saw he still wore the Washington County Sheriff's badge pinned to his leather bomber jacket— helping out until a new interim sheriff could be named, she'd heard. But sheriff or federal agent, the difference didn't matter much to Gigi. One kind of cop was as dangerous to her as another.

Yet here she was, lying as intimately with him as two people could lie without...well...being intimate. Knee to breastbone, not a molecule of air wedged between them. Her softness molded to his hardness. Her curves pressed into his hollows. She should move, but she couldn't. She felt frozen in place, frozen in time.

"Dr. McCowan? Are you all right?"

His words lifted her stupor. She couldn't afford to have this man worried about her. She couldn't afford to have him think about her at all.

She lurched away from him, disengaging tangled arms, legs, and knees, as she rose. "I'm fine," she assured him.

He followed her up slowly, eyeing her all the while. "You're sure?" He twisted right, then left, methodically brushing slush and wet leaves from the sleeves of his coat and the back of his khaki trousers.

"I said I'm fine." Regretting the snap in her voice, she crossed her arms over her chest and took a deep breath. She did not need to pick a fight with a federal agent, but she was scared, tired and cold. And her head hurt.

"Good." Very slowly, very precisely, he turned toward her. When he looked at her, his gaze pulled her pulse to her extremities. She could feel her heartbeat in the soles of her feet. The pounding made her head ache even worse.

"Then what the hell did you think you were doing coming at me like that?" he asked.

Her jaw fell slack. So much for not picking a fight. "Coming at you? What were *you* doing sneaking up on *me?*"

"I wasn't sneaking. I thought you might be hurt. Your truck is twenty feet off the road in a ditch!"

His words hit like tom-toms inside her skull. "You could have called out. How was I supposed to know who was out there?"

"I did call out." He swung his hand up the ravine toward the roadside. "Up there. Why didn't you answer me?"

She reached for her throbbing forehead, squeezing her eyes shut. "I might have—" all this shouting was making her woozy "—if I'd been conscious." The drumroll in her brain built to crescendo and she swayed on her feet.

"Whoa, there." He reached out and steadied her elbow. "I thought you said you were all right." Just like that the ire was gone from his voice, replaced by concern.

"I'm fine."

"Sure you are." She tried to step away, but his grip on her elbow tightened, preventing her escape. "That idiot could have killed you."

A surge of fear jolted her. She jerked as if she'd touched a live wire. "How did you know?"

"I was above you on the switchback curve. I saw that car sideswipe you. Did you get a look at him? A license plate?"

Her heart fluttered, and she told herself to stay calm. He didn't know anything; he was just curious. *Cop curious,* a voice in her head warned. *Not good.*

"No, nothing," she told him, hoping he would drop the interrogation.

A heavy pause hung between them. Shane's brows drew down in to a frown. "The sorry pissant didn't even stop.

Least he could have done was come back and made sure you were all right.''

A shudder that had little to do with the cold and everything to do with a sorry pissant in a midnight-blue Mercedes racked her body. If Shane hadn't come along, the man would have come back, all right. But it wouldn't have been to help.

Had he really left? Or had he sneaked back while she and Shane had been arguing?

She peered into the darkened woods surrounding her. Her mind twisted tree trunks into burly bodies, gnarled limbs into outreached arms, the glitter of moonlight off wet leaves to the gleam of a cold steel barrel trained on her, or Shane.

She wrapped her arms around herself and squeezed.

Shane's scowl deepened. "Let's get you out of here," he said.

"But my truck—"

"Is not going anywhere tonight. You can call a tow in the morning." He smiled, even white teeth flashing in the darkness. Gigi didn't see what he found to be so happy about. "Guess you'll have to bunk with me for the night."

She caught her gasp before it escaped her throat.

"Figuratively speaking, of course," he explained. "The roads are nasty and getting worse by the minute. I only live a few minutes from here. We have a lot better chance of getting to my place safely than we do of making it all the way to your house."

Suspicion honed by three years on the run kicked in her stomach. "You know where I live?"

Surprise registered in his eyes. "It's a small town."

"And you're a cop."

"Something wrong with that?"

"No. It's just—"

Her mind suddenly changed tack. She knew where he lived, too. A woman like her kept tabs on men like him. And even taking into account that they had both been coming from the same place tonight—their mutual friends Eric Randall and Mariah Morgan's engagement party—Shane shouldn't have been here, on this road.

"What are you doing this far east?" she asked.

He paused, looking as sheepish as a teenager caught fingering a beer in his dad's fridge. "The roads are slick and you left Mariah's in a hurry. I wanted to be sure you got home okay."

"You were *following* me?"

The guilty look on his face quickly turned to stubbornness. "And it's a lucky thing for you that I was." He nudged her forward. "Now let's go."

Her panic surged. This couldn't happen. She couldn't be anywhere near him, much less spend the night with him. "I—I can't. Really."

"Why not?"

He turned those trust-me blues on her, and for a moment she considered telling him the truth. About New York. Her father. The man in the Mercedes. But that would be foolish. Shane was a cop, the last person she should confide in.

But what choice did she have with *him* out there somewhere?

She glanced into the woods, and then up the ravine toward the shoulder of the road.

Shane looked at her quizzically. "What are you gonna do, walk home?"

"Maybe I should wait with my truck. You could call a wrecker."

Shane shook his head, disbelief settling on his face, and let go of her elbow long enough to poke at the welt on her forehead. "Just how hard did you hit your head, anyway?"

She brushed his hand away.

"Forget it, Doc. I'm not leaving you out here."

One look at the square set of his jaw and she knew resistance was futile. He wouldn't leave her here, alone. He was a cop, and he obviously took his job very seriously.

But then, so did the man who was after her.

She held her breath and listened. Other than the slow patter of sleet on rocks, all was quiet. No one was there. No one except Shane, whom she couldn't afford to make suspicious with unreasonable protests.

Maybe his cabin was the safest place for her to be tonight. She couldn't go home. The man in the Mercedes undoubtedly knew where she lived by now. But he wouldn't know about Shane.

She hoped.

Her heartbeat gradually slowed. "I guess you're right," she said. "Thanks for the rescue."

He smiled again. Gigi tried not to notice the dimple that dented his right cheek as he swept his arm grandly toward the hillside. "M'lady..."

She turned toward the open door of her truck. "I need my bag."

Shane dodged around her and leaned across the seat. "I'll get it." He reached to the floorboard and pulled out her tapestry handbag.

"Thanks," she said, taking it. "But I didn't mean this one." She tried to keep her voice light, not to arouse suspicion. "There's an orange backpack, behind the seat."

He looked at her, his blue eyes brimming with curiosity.

"Sometimes I'm out all night on emergency farm calls. I keep a few...essentials...in the truck." She forced herself to smile. The things she carried in that bag were essential all right. To survival. Which is why she called it her survival bag. But she had to think of some other excuse for Shane. "Believe me, by morning you wouldn't want me around if I didn't. A woman's got to have her stuff in the morning, you know?''

He retrieved the bag. "I'd want you around in the morning," he said, his voice grown suddenly husky. "Stuff or no stuff.''

He passed her the bag, and their hands brushed in the exchange. She retreated, and her sore knee buckled.

He caught her before she realized she was falling. Giving her a look that dared her to protest, he helped her up the slope to the road, where blue and red lights strobed over the icy pavement. He was still driving the sheriff's Blazer. No wonder the guy in the Mercedes had left. He must have made Shane as a cop right away.

He steadied her as she stepped up into the cab and then he walked toward the front of the truck. Her fear redoubled for a moment. She half expected to see the Mercedes come gunning out of the darkness.

Relax, she told herself, studying the sparkling ice on the road. *Breathe.* No one was gunning anywhere tonight. Not without hockey skates. She was safe.

Shane circled the hood of the vehicle, moving with the natural grace of an athlete, despite the slippery footing. Watching him, she had the same funny feeling in her chest that she'd had the first time they'd met. An acute awareness.

Safe, huh? Safe from the man in the Mercedes, maybe.

Shane Hightower was another matter altogether.

He climbed behind the wheel. With the vehicle's interior lights on, he switched the heat on full and turned all the vents toward her.

As he worked the knobs, a few strands of damp hair fell across his forehead. The hair on the sides and back of his head was trimmed short. But on top, where the sun had bleached dark blond to shining gold, a longer, heavier layer swept to one side. Brushed back, the cut appeared very conservative, very law enforcement. But when those locks tumbled forward, like now, they gave him a much less civilized look. Rugged. Careless. And very sexy.

She wished she could reach up and push those troublesome locks back in place. It would be easier to remember he was a cop that way.

"Buckle up," he said.

When she didn't move, her attention still captured by a silly lock of hair, he reached across her and pulled the shoulder harness over her chest. Her nostrils flared at the sudden scent of damp leather and understated aftershave.

He pushed the metal buckle into the fitting. "There. All set."

She waited until he'd straightened up to breathe again.

He smiled at her. A very male, knowing smile like he knew what she'd been thinking. She would have called him arrogant, if he hadn't been right.

Her fingers curled, tightening until her fingernails dug into her palms. As if being rescued by a cop wasn't bad enough. Did she have to be so unbearably attracted to him, too?

"Sit still."

"It stings."

"It's supposed to sting. It's good for you."

"What kind of logic is that?"

"The kind that keeps people from getting infections?"

"It's not going to get infected."

"No, it's not, because you're going to sit still and let me put this stuff on it."

"I'm the doctor here."

"You're a veterinarian."

"You didn't seem so particular when you were the one bleeding to death."

Exasperated, Shane rocked back on his heels where he

squatted in front of the toilet. Gigi—Dr. McCowan, he reminded himself—sat on the porcelain lid wearing an old flannel robe he'd loaned her so she could get out of her damp
clothes. She was wriggling like a trout on the line.

"I was not bleeding to death," he said. "And neither are
you."

He had been wounded, though, thanks to a couple of local
drug dealers, even if the injury wasn't as serious as she made
it sound. And Gigi McCowan, the first on the scene once all
the shooting had stopped, and the only one around with any
medical training, had provided first aid.

Shane had been hurt before in his eight years with the
DEA, but never had he enjoyed being doctored—even if it
was by a vet—as much as he had that day. She'd been his
angel of mercy, sent from heaven to stanch the flow of blood
with a gentle touch.

Then she'd turned her face up to him, and one look into
her eyes turned his thoughts polar opposite of angels and
heaven. Images more congruent with what was sure to be his
ultimate fate sprang to mind. She'd made him think of fire
and brimstone. A scorching desert sun and a sea of sand.

Sin and sweat and sex.

Even now, her eyes intrigued him. They were blue, like
his own, but a shade wilder in color. Indigo, like a pair of
jeans not quite broken in.

And mysterious. Those eyes held secrets.

She squirmed on the toilet seat and he realized he'd been
staring. Pulling his gaze away, he found his attention captured by her feet instead. Her toes were wiggling, like the
rest of her. Bright-pink paint adorned her toenails. He smiled
to himself, finding that small vanity endearing. And suiting.
Gigi was all movement and bright colors.

At least she had been until tonight. Tonight she was different. Still busy, but with a nervous, restless kind of energy.

"Why are you still in Utah?" she asked.

He glanced up. He'd been asking himself that question for days. The docs had cleared him for duty, and he sure as heck didn't have anymore leave coming. He'd used that up months ago. "I was planning on leaving in the morning."

At least he should have been planning on leaving. But the rent on the cabin was paid through the end of the month, and somehow he'd never gotten around to packing. The truth was he liked it here. The mountains were peaceful and frankly, small-town law enforcement was more his speed after what he'd been through the last couple of years than the fast-paced world of drug enforcement. He liked it that people here waved to him on the street and knew his name. And then there was Gigi…

Sometimes he wished he didn't have to go back at all. But wishes weren't horses, and sooner or later he had to leave. Most likely sooner. "I just wanted to stay for Eric and Mariah's party."

The party to which he would never have accepted the invitation if Mariah hadn't let it slip that Gigi would be there. He wished the best for Eric and Mariah in their marriage and new life together, but he felt out of place at social events like that—family gatherings. Having grown up in a county youth home after being abandoned as an infant, family was a mystery to him.

Almost as much of a mystery as Gigi McCowan.

He went to the party hoping for a chance to prove that the electricity that had crackled between him and Gigi on the mountain had been a fluke. Nothing more than nerves on edge.

After all, he'd just busted a drug operation and nearly gotten himself killed. He'd been hurt, and high on adrenaline. He'd told himself it wouldn't be like that when they met again.

But it had been. He'd clinked his wineglass against hers in a toast to Eric and Mariah, they'd locked eyes, and the energy had coursed between them. It had built more slowly—less like a lightning strike and more like a bank of circuits, their breakers thrown on one at a time—but it hadn't stopped until the power to light a city flowed freely between them.

She had to be the source of the energy. Lord knows, his soul was dead as an old battery.

She recharged him.

Then Eric had called her over, given her something, and she'd left, in a hurry. Left Shane standing there with the burgundy he'd been drinking burning a path to his gullet and all his lusty imaginings about taking her out of there himself, taking her home, ending on a cold gust of wind and a slamming door.

And he didn't know why.

Unsettled, he dabbed at her forehead with the cotton ball. "Ow." She swiped her hand out. "Give me that."

"Fine. You finish your forehead," he said, handing her the antiseptic and cotton ball. "I want to see that knee."

Rebellion charged through her eyes before resignation set in. Slowly she slipped one leg out of the slit in the front of the robe. His irritation dissolved in a wave of masculine appreciation. He cupped one hand behind her calf and slid the other down to her ankle for support. Her leg was slender, firm and smooth to the touch. Very attractive.

He flexed her knee gently, carefully supporting her lower leg. "That hurt?"

She shook her head.

Even more carefully, he leveraged her lower leg sideways. Her stifled gasp stopped him.

"I'm sure it's just bruised," she said tightly.

"Uh-huh." It was more than that, and he knew it. He suspected she'd wrenched it pretty good, but he didn't press the issue. At least it didn't seem to be swelling. He set her heel on the floor and rested his palm on her good knee.

She lowered her head. "I'm sure it will be fine."

"I'm sure it will be, too. If you stay off it tonight."

Before she could protest, he scooped her off of the toilet seat and into his arms. She planted her palms against his chest and pushed. "What are you doing?"

"Helping you stay off that leg."

He paused in the hallway. A turn to the left, and he could settle her in his big bed, instead of the sleeper sofa he'd made up while she changed. But she was bound to argue. And having her in his bed for the night while he tossed and turned on the sleeper might be more temptation than he was ready for.

He turned to the right, toward the great room. Hell, it was the nineties. *She* could sleep on the couch.

When he deposited her carefully on the cushions, he didn't have to turn to know what had gathered her attention over his shoulder. The entire east wall of the great room was glass.

He straightened, following her gaze to the midnight void. "The view is a lot nicer during the day," he explained self-consciously. Not everyone appreciated sitting on the edge of the world the way he did, especially at night.

She looked down into the dark valley below. "It's beautiful, even in the dark. It's like the whole world doesn't exist. Never existed," she whispered. "But it's so...lonely."

"Yeah, well. I guess growing up in a home with thirty other kids taught me to appreciate solitude."

She smiled wanly, pale in the near darkness. "I know what you mean."

"Grow up a ward of the state, too, did you?" He wouldn't have believed her if she'd said yes. She didn't have the look about her. She hadn't always been alone.

"No," she confirmed. "Boarding schools."

"Ah, the life of the privileged."

"Privileged, maybe. But also crowded."

She surprised him, finding that small common ground between them despite their obviously different backgrounds.

"I like the view better at night, myself," he admitted.

Her expression brightened as she angled her head up. "Look at all the stars."

Yeah. Look at the stars, shining in her eyes, Shane thought. And he knew, with as much certainty as he knew his name that he'd make love to her some night, with the starlight glancing off her eyes like that.

But not tonight. Tonight he just wanted to make whatever had put the tension in her body and the raw, disturbing look on her face go away.

He cleared his throat, turning his attention to making her comfortable. He got her a blanket and pillow, then when she was settled, he rubbed his hands together. "How about a fire? It's chilly in here."

Soon he had a blaze building. He held his hands up to it, feeling the warmth of the flames on his palms. "How's that?"

He sat on the edge of the couch, next to her thigh. Firelight danced across her cheeks, giving her fair skin a tone more like ruddy honey. She tossed her head and her short, blond curls gleamed, catching the flickering light.

She eased the blanket up to her chin and tucked her arms underneath. "It's nice. Thanks."

Her words were sincere enough, but that was no cozy tone of voice. "You're welcome," he said, wishing he knew what else to do for her. To help her relax.

Outside, the call of an owl mingled with the whisper of wind through the trees. Pupils dilating, her gaze flew to the window, and the sound, straining to see through the darkness.

Watching her reaction, he wondered if the edge on her

nerves might be due to more than just the accident. She should have shaken off the effects of the wreck by now.

Three loud knocks sounded above them like footsteps. She jumped visibly beneath her cover.

"Easy. It's just limbs on the roof. I've been meaning to cut those trees back."

Still, worry lines creased her forehead. She breathed in shallow, silent gasps, and he felt the lack of oxygen as if it were his own. He hated the vulnerability marring her otherwise flawless features. "Do you want me to sit with you awhile?"

She jerked her head toward him. "No, that's not necessary."

Her wide eyes said differently. Unable to resist, he reached out and stroked a springy yellow curl back from her forehead, wishing he could brush away her fear as easily. She'd said she didn't want him, but he couldn't leave, not with her so out of sorts.

And himself so out of sorts, as well. Damn she was beautiful in the firelight. In any light.

Forgetting his manners, he searched the depths of her mysterious eyes. Searched beneath the surface of whatever was bothering her to see if she felt what he felt.

And he found it.

Buried deep, the answering call to his cry. A spark of attraction. He studied it with the same awe that early man must have studied fire. She turned her face up as if she might say something, and without thinking he lowered his mouth to hers.

Her lips were incredibly soft. Incredibly warm. He kept his touch light. It was meant to be a kiss of comfort. At least at first. But when her initial shock faded and she leaned into him with a soft sigh of acquiescence, comfort became need. Then need bordered on greed.

He touched his fingertips to the graceful arch of her cheek and slid his hand down, past her jaw, until his palm splayed around the fragile column of her neck. Holding her, he raised over her, slanted his head and probed at the entrance to her sweet mouth. He wanted to feel her, taste her. All of her. He'd wanted her from the moment she'd pushed her way through a dozen armed DEA agents and ordered him to sit still and shut up while she tended his wound and he hadn't dared do anything but comply.

He surged against her, long-denied desire curling in his blood. Her lips parted, and for an instant he felt the moist slip of her tongue against his.

Then she reared back, pushing at his shoulders with fisted hands. "No!" Panic laced her eyes. She braced against the back corner of the couch and clutched the blanket to her chest with both hands.

He lurched to his feet and took two steps back. The sight of her fear soured his stomach until he had to turn and stalk away. That reaction hadn't been caused by any accident. It was much too sudden, much too intense. Only one thing could have caused it.

Him.

Whatever had possessed him to kiss her? He'd known she didn't want him. She'd proven it often enough since that day on the mountain. Her medical training had kicked in during the crisis, but afterward, every time he'd tried to get a word with her in town, she'd made a hasty escape.

If he turned north on a street corner, she turned south. If he walked in someplace, she walked out. Just like she'd left Mariah's tonight almost as soon as he'd arrived.

In a moment of stark self-awareness, he realized that was why he'd followed her. He'd wanted to see her safely home, yes. But he'd also wanted to find out why she was avoiding him. Why she got such a trapped look in her eyes whenever he got close.

In the darkened doorway to the great room he stopped, his back still to her. The spit and hiss of the fire mingled with a barrage of curses heard only in his mind.

"Are you afraid of me?" he asked, his jaw tight.

"Of course not. You're a cop."

"You say it like it's a dirty word."

She didn't respond for a long time. "I'm sorry. I've had a long day."

An apology, or a hint for him to make himself scarce? He had no idea. Still wondering, he left the firelight behind and let the darkness of the hall devour him.

Long into the night, Gigi stared at the fire, dreading the moment the last ember would flicker out. Quietly she reached over the side of the couch and picked up her handbag, the tapestry one with horses galloping gaily across the side. From it she drew a folded square of newspaper. The golden glow of the fire shed light across the banner at the top of the page—Oil Exec Returns to Scene of Crime—For Wedding.

Eric had given her the clipping at the party just hours earlier. How quickly her life could change.

The story had run in the business section of a major Los Angeles newspaper. It described how Eric Randall—an oil executive and now Mariah's fiancé—had helped the DEA—Shane—bring down a drug operation here. And how in the process Eric had fallen in love with Mariah and resigned from his position with the oil company to return to Utah to marry her.

But the article wasn't what bothered Gigi. That right belonged to the accompanying picture. A photographer had caught all four of them—Eric, Mariah, Gigi and a wounded Shane unloading from the DEA helicopter that had carried

them off the mountain. She'd never even seen the camera-
man.

That was how they'd found her. It had to be.

Why she had to leave.

In a way, leaving Utah would be a relief. Her life here
was a lie. A necessary one, but still a deception. The more
she came to care about this place and its people, her friends,
the harder the deception became. And the worst lie of all was
the lie she had told to herself. That she was safe here. That
they wouldn't find her, this time. What a fool she'd been.

Feeling the thrum of fear strike up a new beat in her breast,
she put the news article back in her handbag, set the handbag
on the floor, and picked up her survival pack. She hadn't
been without the bag since she'd left New York, three years
ago. The bag was her safety net.

Whether he knew it or not, tonight it was Shane's safety
net as well. If the man after her somehow did manage to find
her, he wouldn't hesitate to kill one unsuspecting DEA agent.
He'd killed federal agents before.

Guilt struck a sour chord in her head. She really didn't
believe anyone would find her in the next few hours, but she
still should have told him. Her silence—her very presence—
put him at risk.

Glancing down the darkened hallway, she thought about
telling him now. But he was probably long asleep, and she
couldn't knock on his door in the middle of the night wearing
nothing but her bare feet and a soft flannel bathrobe that
smelled like him. Not after that kiss.

Not after the way she'd treated him after the kiss. She had
no right to ask him for anything, least of all to watch over
and protect her. Besides, he was a cop. He would ask questions she couldn't answer. So tonight, like every night, she
would watch over and protect herself.

And she would protect him, too.

Digging past the assorted getaway paraphernalia in her backpack, Gigi wrapped her hand around a solid shape folded inside a cotton T-shirt.

She'd never loaded the gun before. Didn't want to do it now. But she had no choice. By letting him bring her here, she'd taken Shane's life in her hands. She had to be prepared to defend it.

With the pistol on her lap, she unzipped an outer pocket of the pack and pulled out the ammunition. Carefully, just like she'd been shown in New York, she inserted the shells.

By sheer will, she kept her hands from trembling. All she had to do was make it to morning, she told herself. Then she would leave Utah forever. Because she'd stayed too long. Because she'd let a cop get too close.

And because somewhere out there, a cold-blooded killer was looking for her.

Chapter 2

After a chilly morning at his cabin—one due more to the frosty demeanor of his houseguest than the unusually cool spring weather—Shane dropped Gigi off at John Lane's scrap yard. She'd called John not thirty seconds after sunrise, the moment the ice on the roads began to melt, and talked the tow truck driver into going after her truck. Then she'd banged around the kitchen under the pretense of making coffee until Shane couldn't stand the noise and got up to see what the racket was about. She'd seemed so desperate to leave that Shane had joked that if she was in such a hurry, she needn't have bothered to wait for him to take her to town. She could have just stolen his truck and driven herself.

Gigi hadn't laughed.

Shaking his head, he pushed his way through the door to the Washington County Sheriff's Office with one hand, carrying a cup of coffee from the diner in the other.

Bailey Henrickson, the young state trooper sent to keep an eye on things until a new sheriff was appointed, greeted him. "Hey, Agent Hightower."

"Hey yourself."

He hurried past Bailey, hiding his grin. Shane couldn't help it. He liked Bailey. The kid seemed to be a fair enough lawman, but his ears were just too damned big for his head. Especially when he put on his smoky hat and it pushed them out to the side.

Keeping his head lowered, Shane sat at the desk in the corner. The one with the computer. He felt Bailey watching him, but he didn't look up.

"Something I can help you with?" Bailey finally asked.

"Nope."

A minute, maybe two passed while the PC booted up.

"Something you need?" Bailey said.

"Just a little information."

He heard the kid shuffle some papers. "You know, you aren't officially supposed to be using that equipment anymore. You're supposed to be headed back to Phoenix and the almighty DEA today." He grinned. "You can leave the sheriff's badge and the keys to the Blazer with me."

Shane smiled into his coffee cup. "You kicking me out, Trooper?"

The paper shuffling stopped. "Well, no sir. But..."

"Good. Because I'll be done before you could call for backup."

"Ha!" Bailey barked. "State Trooper needing backup to handle one sissy DEA agent. That'll be the day."

Shane grinned wider, tapping out a few commands on the keyboard.

A chair scraped back and Bailey's footsteps echoed across the wood floor. Shane looked up, and raised his hand to his mouth, coughing to cover his laugh. The kid had put on his hat.

"If you're going to be here a few minutes, would you mind catching the phone if it rings?" Bailey asked. "Think I could use a cup of that slimy diner coffee myself."

"Sure. You go ahead. I'll keep an eye on things."

The deputy left. All the better. Shane could do what he needed with Bailey here, but it was best if he wasn't. Accessing people's private information for personal reasons wasn't strictly legal, but Shane had questions that needed answering.

He didn't know why Gigi's reaction last night bothered him so much. He'd been rejected before. It wasn't like he was any great prize. He was leaving town today, anyway. Even if he weren't, it wasn't like they had any future. It wasn't like he was dreaming of blond-haired babies with wild blue eyes. Shane wasn't family material. Never had been, he guessed.

But Gigi had responded to him—hell she'd electrified and incited him—at least at first. Until she'd remembered what she was doing. Or who she was doing. A cop.

He'd lain in bed after he'd left her, thinking about her. His nose had wrinkled, catching a scent eight years in the DEA had taught him never to ignore. He smelled trouble—a wispy tendril, like the first curl of smoke from kindling—but trouble nonetheless. He just wasn't sure what kind.

From here, thanks to the wonders of the Internet, he had access to every database available to law enforcement, as well as a few that weren't supposed to be available to anyone, law enforcement or not, courtesy of many hours in the computer lab at Arizona State. He'd worked the night shift to put himself through school, and in those long stretches before dawn, he'd learned a great deal about computer systems that wasn't in the textbooks. In half an hour, maybe less, he'd know everything there was to know about Gigi McCowan. Then he could head back to Phoenix.

His fingers laced together, he cracked his knuckles and set to work. Sixty-five minutes later he sighed, rolled his head around his shoulders and admitted he'd been wrong.

Hunched over the flickering screen, he pinched the bridge

of his nose, then scanned the text again to be sure he'd read it right. "Well I'll be damned." He definitely wouldn't be going back to Phoenix today.

He didn't know who the woman who'd spent last night in his cabin was, but he did know one thing—

She wasn't Gigi McCowan.

Gigi took one last look around as she waited for John Lane to dig out his paperwork. Her pickup truck was still strapped to his wrecker in the drive.

She spun slowly, her gaze skimming over the junkyard to the mountains beyond, trying to memorize everything from the piney smell of the mountain air to the calls of birds in the treetops. She had to memorize it, because soon memories would be all she had left of Utah.

She took a deep breath and turned, hearing Mr. Lane walk up behind her.

"You're sure you want to do this? Trade your pickup for my old Jeep?" John Lane asked. "Damage on your truck doesn't look too bad. I can have her good as new in a day or two, and it's bound to be worth twice what my heap is worth."

She put on a false smile. She loved her old pickup. It was worn in all the right places. But she couldn't afford to wait a day, much less two, for him to fix it. "I've been thinking I need something that eats a little less gas," she said. "And after that ice storm last night, four-wheel drive sounds pretty good, too."

"All right then." He handed her the keys and title.

"You'll be sure to take the rest of the veterinary supplies out of the back and give them to Mariah Morgan out at the Double M?" She'd already taken the few supplies she might find useful and boxed them up in the back of the Jeep. The remaining supplies weren't much to offer Mariah in the way of goodbye, but they were all she had to give. Besides, it would be a shame to let them go to waste.

"Yes, ma'am."

Nodding, she turned to survey her new vehicle.

Once, the Jeep had probably been fire-engine red. Now it had faded to the color of weak tomato soup. But the motor sounded fine and it had a full tank of gas. It would do.

The road blurred in front of her as she headed south, out of town. She tried not to think about never coming back here. She'd always known she would have to leave one day. She just hadn't thought it would be in a run-down Jeep with nothing except her survival bag and the clothes—dirty clothes at that—on her back.

She wished she could have risked stopping by the house, just for a minute. Besides her clothes, she'd like to have picked up the few prizes she'd gathered on her frequent mountain hikes—a pine cone as big as her forearm, a smooth, round stone with grain in it in the shape of a peace sign, and a walking stick. Not much to show for twenty-eight years of living, but it was all she had.

Used to have. Even those few treasures were gone now. It was time to move on to a new life.

Except she liked this life.

Her eyes stinging, she pulled into a small rest stop fifteen miles outside of town. In the women's room, she pinned her hair back and slipped on the wig from her emergency bag. Dark contacts came next, coloring her eyes from blue to brown. She studied her new image in the cracked mirror over the sink. Not bad for two minutes' work. She didn't look anything like herself.

That random thought almost brought her tears back. She couldn't help but feel she'd finally given up the last vestiges of her true self. There was nothing left of the person she used to be. But that couldn't be helped.

A new life was better than no life at all. Better than death.

Squaring her shoulders, she slung her pack over her back and stepped out of the washroom.

And stumbled into a broad male chest.

Shane.

He steadied her elbow, setting her back on her feet. Her hand brushed the fine, crisp hair of his forearm as she pulled away. The sensation shot up her arm like a jolt of static electricity.

His head tipped a fraction, and she felt his gaze peruse her slowly, even if she couldn't see it behind his reflective sunglasses. She burned under his scrutiny, from the tips of her ears to the ends of her curling toes.

Shane.

He straightened, his jaw set perfectly square, and stood with his hands behind his back, his feet shoulder width. He looked very tall. Very disciplined.

Very cop.

"This is a new look for you, Doc," he said, reaching out to finger her shoulder-length fake hair. He let the wig go and folded his sunglasses into his shirt pocket.

Being able to see his eyes heightened the effect of his gaze. She felt her face heat.

"A girl gets tired of same ole–same ole." The quaver in her voice didn't sound too convincing, even to her. She swallowed hard. "Did you need—I mean, is there something I can do for you?"

"You didn't mention that you were leaving town today."

"No, well, yes…it was sudden. My aunt is…sick."

"I'm sorry to hear that."

"Thank you." She jangled her keys in her hand. "I hate to run like this, but I really should get going."

Shane moved himself between her and the Jeep. "You know, all this time I thought you were avoiding me because you just didn't like me."

Her heart leaped. "Of course not. I mean, I haven't been

avoiding you. And I—'' Her mouth suddenly felt like she'd been lost in a desert for days. "I like you."

"Yeah, I figured that out last night when I kissed you. That's what finally tipped me off."

"Tipped you off to what?"

"That it's not me you're afraid of." He thumbed his badge off his chest. "It's this."

"No, it's just—"

"I *know*," he said, the challenge in his words clear despite the dead calm in his voice.

Her heart bucked. "Know what?"

"That Gigi McCowan, D.V.M., is sixty-two years old and lives on the thirteenth hole of a nice retirement community in Ocala."

She'd thought her plan was perfect. The forger from whom she'd purchased her false identification in New York was reputed to be the best. The real Gigi McCowan, her mentor in vet school, had even gone along with the scam, providing authentic diplomas and transcripts so that she could apply for and receive a real veterinary license from the state of Utah. She didn't see how anyone could have figured out she wasn't the real thing.

But then Shane Hightower wasn't anyone.

Knowing it was the wrong body language to send, but unable to stop herself, she crossed her arms over her chest. "There must be some mistake."

"No mistake. You lied to me. You've been lying to everyone. The town, your customers, your friends."

Her throat bobbed, grasping for words and finding none. She clenched her upper arms to stop her fingers from trembling. The lies that should come easily weren't there anymore. In their place, she found only deep, cutting remorse.

Shame.

The tremor in her hand became a full-fledged quake. Her keys fell and clanked on the gravel. She bent to retrieve them.

Without warning the Jeep's driver's side window exploded over her head. Before she knew what had happened, Shane tackled her and rolled along the ground, cradling her against him as tires squalled.

Over Shane's shoulder she glimpsed an arm holding a pistol out the window of a midnight-blue Mercedes—the same Mercedes that had run her off the road the night before.

How had he found her? Had he been following her all morning, waiting for his chance to attack, or had Shane brought him?

Fire flashed from the gun's muzzle. He was shooting at them! But there hadn't been any noise. No shots.

She didn't have time to decipher the meaning of that, as Shane tucked her head against his shoulder and rolled again, this time propelling her behind the bumper of the Jeep. With the vehicle as cover, he raised up and pulled a weapon from under his jacket in one fluid movement. Gigi sat up beside him, and he pushed on the top of her head with his free hand. "Get down."

She took his advice as another volley of bullets skittered across the hood of the Jeep. Still no gunshots. They must be using a silencer. But then, they were pros, she knew that.

Shane returned fire. He certainly wasn't using a silencer. The explosions from the muzzle of his gun pounded her eardrums. The Mercedes sped past the rest stop, and Shane grabbed her hand and pulled her into the Jeep, snagging the keys off the ground as he went.

He shoved her into the driver's seat, handing her the keys, and then climbed in the back. "Drive," he shouted as the Mercedes did a one-eighty a few yards down the road.

"Me?" She yelled, stabbing the keys into the ignition. "Why me?" He was the DEA agent; she was just a civilian. She wasn't trained for this sort of thing.

"Because I'm going to be busy shooting." To prove his point, he leveled his weapon and squeezed off two rounds at

the approaching Mercedes. A slug from the sedan clinked off
the roll bar, convincing her that starting the Jeep's engine
was more critical than arguing at this point.

The Jeep roared to life and she slammed it into reverse so
hard that the lurch almost sent Shane flying into the front
seat. He grabbed the roll bar for support. "Go! Go!"

She blasted onto the roadway, turning the Jeep so that she
faced the attacker head-on. She stomped on the gas, and this
time Shane was nearly flung out the back of the Jeep. They
flew by the Mercedes before either Shane or the other driver
could regroup and get off another shot. The unwieldy luxury
car squealed into another one-eighty, giving Gigi and Shane
a few seconds' lead.

"That way. That way." Shane waved with the gun in his
hand to one of the county roads that wound down the mountain.

Gigi complied, bringing the Jeep around in a screeching
turn. In the rearview mirror, the sun gleamed off the polished
hood of the sedan, too close behind them.

Shane clambered into the front of the Jeep then turned
around, kneeling backward in the passenger seat, his gun arm
braced on the seat back as he squeezed off another shot at
the sedan. "Faster!" he yelled. "He's gaining on us."

The wind whipped through the Jeep's open canopy. "Faster? We're on a mountain. That's a sheer cliff over there. If
we skid over the side, we're dead!"

"And if that guy catches up to us in the open, we're dead!
Take your choice."

Holding her lip between her teeth, Gigi pushed the accelerator to the floor. Briefly, the Jeep pulled away from the
Mercedes, but the car soon matched the Jeep's speed, and
then some.

The driver behind her was firing again, but the bullets
weren't hitting the body of the Jeep. He was probably aiming

at the tires. Gigi said a silent prayer that he didn't hit them. Not with those cliffs so close to the side of the road.

Pointing at a break in the trees, Shane said, "Turn there, up ahead. On that gravel road."

Gigi slammed on the brakes and swung the Jeep into the narrow opening. She swung her head from side to side, not liking what she saw. Walls of trees hemmed them in, pushed them forward. They were trapped. The trees encroached so closely on the road that they had no maneuverability.

But neither did the car behind them. Even with its superior speed, the sedan couldn't pull alongside for a clean shot.

Shane checked the progress of the car behind them. "All right, scum. You wanna play, let's play."

"Play?" Gigi adjusted her clammy grip on the steering wheel. "You think this is a game?"

"Just keep driving," he ordered. "As fast as you can."

Gigi checked the rearview. The Mercedes plowed down the trail behind them, leaving a plume of dust in its wake.

The front right tire of the Jeep dropped into a deep rut in the road and then rebounded with a vengeance, catapulting Shane out of his seat. He grabbed the roll bar with both hands.

"Faster," he ordered.

"I'm going as fast as I can."

Gigi looked over her shoulder. The Mercedes was right behind them. The gun hung out the window.

"Duck!" Shane shouted. Several rounds dinged off metal. She couldn't tell where. Keeping her head as low as she could and still see over the dashboard, Gigi pressed the accelerator to the floor.

"All right, get ready," Shane called.

She glanced up warily. "Ready for what?"

He dropped into the passenger seat and climbed across the console until he was practically sitting in the driver's seat with her. "Ready to hit the brakes and make a hard right turn."

"Why?"

"Because the road ends right up there."

"What!" She raised her foot to stomp on the brake, but he quickly kicked her foot away. Then he stomped on the gas.

"Move over," he yelled.

Move? Move where? She crushed herself against the door, giving him haphazard control of the Jeep.

He pushed the accelerator to the floor once again and locked his fingers around the steering wheel. "Hold on! Five...four..."

The road ahead disappeared into nothingness. Gigi grabbed the door handle.

"Three..."

She let go of the handle and wrapped her arms around the headrest of the seat.

"Two..."

Her heart stopped, she let go of the headrest and, in a moment of sheer desperation, coiled herself around him. She buried her cheek against his chest.

"One... Now!"

Shane stood on the brake and yanked the steering wheel viciously around to the right, sending the Jeep fishtailing into a tight curve surrounded by a choking cloud of dust and gravel hail. Gigi ground her chin into him and held on.

He jerked the wheel back to the left, pulling the Jeep out of the spin within feet of the cliff and driving parallel to the precipice.

Over his shoulder, she saw that the driver of the car had finally seen the danger ahead. He was reared back from the steering wheel, elbows locked straight as if could push himself away from the cliff by physical force. The big sedan's brakes ground and groaned with the effort, but couldn't stop his momentum in time. Just as it slid to a halt, the nose of the Mercedes edged over the embankment. The car tottered forward, then back, coming to an unsteady rest with the front half of the car hanging precariously over the edge. A shower of pebbles clattered down the slope, then all went quiet.

Shane stopped the Jeep. Slowly Gigi uncurled her fingers from the front of his shirt and looked up at him.

He had the audacity to grin. "Antilock brakes aren't so nifty when stopping fast is more important than stopping straight."

"I can't believe we just left him there. Aren't you going to arrest him or something?"

Gigi glanced at Shane. His once golden tanned complexion had jaundiced. He hadn't said a word in the ten minutes since he'd ordered her to drive, leaving the man who'd ambushed them dangling off the side of a cliff. For an experienced federal agent, he wasn't taking a little thing like a shoot-out too well.

His eyes drifted shut. "You want to cross an open field in front of a man with a gun and try to take him down, you go right ahead, honey. Me, I prefer *not* to go out in a blaze of glory. At least not today."

"You could have kept him pinned down or something while I went for help."

"Yeah, I could have. Except the nearest help is in town, better than half an hour away, and I'm out of ammo."

"Out of ammo?"

"Well, not technically out. I've got one round left. In case of emergency."

"Don't you carry extra?"

"Sure. In the glove compartment of my Blazer."

The same Blazer that was twenty miles back in the other direction, at the rest stop, along with his police radio and his cell phone, no doubt.

Shane's lips curled into a weak smile. "Besides, I wasn't sure you'd come back for me."

Gigi didn't know what to say to that. She was desperate to get out of this town and away from Shane, but leave him one-on-one with an armed assassin... No, she wouldn't do that. Would she?

"I would have sent someone back, at least," she grumbled.

Shane sighed. "Well, I guess that's something." His eyes pulled open slowly, as if the small act required tremendous effort. "We'll stop at the first phone we see and call the deputy, although I doubt he'll find anything by the time he gets out to that cliff."

Gigi's stomach turned. The last thing she needed was more cops involved. "Then why bother?"

He scowled. "Because he'll want to start a search for the guy before anyone else gets shot at, so why don't you help things along by telling me who the hell that was and what he wanted."

Gigi steered the Jeep off the county highway and braked to a stop behind a stand of birch. With shaky hands she shoved the transmission into neutral and shut off the engine.

His head rolled toward her. "What are you doing?"

"I need to stop." Despite her best efforts at control, her voice cracked a little on the last syllable.

"We need to keep going."

"I said I need to stop."

He raised his eyebrows and cranked up one corner of his mouth. "You couldn't have gone before you left the house?"

She wouldn't dignify that with an answer. She reached up automatically to push her curly bangs out of her face until she realized she didn't have bangs anymore. She'd almost forgotten. She lowered her hand, yanked at the door handle on the Jeep and bounced out of the vehicle.

"Where are you going?" he called out behind her.

"For a walk."

"Lady, there's a man out there with a gun. And you want to take a hike in the woods?"

Everything she knew about Shane Hightower told her this wasn't going to be easy. He was smart, stubborn, and took his job very seriously. Some might say he was obsessive about it. So how was she going to talk him into walking away? Or letting her walk away?

The way she saw it, only one tactic had a chance of working. She stopped walking, but didn't turn around. "That man is exactly why I want to take a hike. A very long hike. Who knows where I might end up? California maybe. Or Seattle."

He snarled like a rabid dog. She heard the door on the Jeep open and close, and then his footsteps pounding up behind her. "Who is he?"

She faced him. "I have no idea."

"No idea? Really? He just showed up and shot at you for no reason. Just like you were all dolled up and sneaking out of town to see your *sick aunt*."

He reached up with his left hand and pulled on the fake hair. "Your wig is crooked."

She slapped his hand away and slid the hairpiece off. With the pins removed, her short curls sprang free. She bent over, shook her head and fingered through the tangled mass. When she looked up, his eyes had narrowed again, and faint, pinched lines had appeared at the corners of his mouth.

"That's better," he said, clearing his throat. "Now the contacts."

She blinked out the tinted lenses and shoved them in her pocket, oblivious to whether or not they'd be ruined. "Happy now?"

"No." She didn't doubt him. He didn't look happy. "Who was that guy?"

"I told you I don't know." She started walking again, and he followed, the hairpiece swinging from his fist.

"And I told *you* I'm not buying it," he said. "If you don't start talking quick, you're getting back in that Jeep and we're going to town. You can sit in a cell at the sheriff's office until your tongue loosens up."

"You can't do that!"

He caught up to her in one long stride and swung her around to face him. He loomed over her, purposely using every bit of his six-foot-one frame to intimidate her, she was sure. She searched his blue eyes—the same ones she used to think so soft—and found them hard as glaciers. A queasiness started in her stomach and worked its way up into her throat. He wasn't going to let her go.

She glanced at the Jeep, judging her chances of making it before he caught her. No way.

How had this happened? How had her carefully crafted plan fallen apart so quickly? *He's a cop, that's how.* And she'd let him get too close.

Numbly she backed up until her spine hit the trunk of a birch tree. Nowhere else to go, she stopped, her mouth dry and her heart and lungs fighting to keep up with her body's demands for blood, oxygen.

He must have sensed the raw panic racing through her veins. His voice gentled to a soothing tone, similar to one she'd use with some mistreated animal brought to her clinic. "Tell me, Gigi," he crooned. "Tell me what's going on."

She shook her head, her hair snagging on the tree bark behind her.

"You're in trouble. I can help."

"No."

"How bad is it? It must be pretty bad for you to be this scared." The glaciers in his eyes fractured momentarily, replaced by familiar concern. His words stretched out, low and mournful, like an old forty-five record played on thirty-three rpm. "Let me help you."

She swallowed hard. "You can't help me. No one can."

"Why are you running?"

"Because someone is trying to kill me."

"I mean why are you running from *me?*" His pale-blue eyes bathed her in sincerity, intensity.

She shook her head, panic and confusion clogging her throat. For the second time in twenty-four hours, she fought an almost overwhelming urge to tell this man—the last man she should tell—the truth. A truth she hadn't spoken in three years.

He lifted the wig in front of her. "Disguises can't protect you from men like that. But I can, if you'll let me."

He edged closer. The tree bit at her back.

"Let me take care of you," he said. He reached for her, and her panic reached full bloom, bursting forth in an explosion of movement that set the world back on the right speed.

She knocked his hand away, twisting his arm behind him and using her hip to throw him to his back as she pushed past him. He cursed as he hit the ground.

She almost made it. Almost got away. But she tripped over him as she tried to run. Her foot connected with his back and his gasp, sharper than it should have been from the light kick, made her turn instinctively. Already off balance, her sudden shift in direction brought her crashing to the ground facedown. Her chin hit the ground with a thunk, and she bit her tongue. The coppery tang of blood filled her mouth.

Before she could recover, he was riding her, his hands pinning hers to the ground above her head, just enough of his body weight grinding her chest into the dirt to effectively restrain her without crushing her.

"Get off!" she screamed. "Get away from me!"

She struggled mightily, but with little effect. Not against his superior size and strength. She resorted to mindless kicking and writhing, but facedown she had no leverage, no way to strike at him. He clamped one heavy thigh over hers and locked her legs in a vice grip between his.

Gradually, she went still. Everything but her heart, that is, which continued to pound so fast that she couldn't separate one beat from the other.

"Are you through?" He sounded as if he were talking with his teeth clamped together. Like he was in pain.

She hadn't thought any of her blows had connected. Or that they'd had the power to hurt him if they had. But maybe she'd been wrong.

She nodded, her cheek scratching in the dirt and decaying leaves beneath her.

"Good." He loosened his grip on her wrists and lifted a measure of his weight from her back, but didn't let her get up, or even turn over. She gulped in mouthfuls of cool, mountain air.

"Now what are you running from?" he asked. This time no sympathy, no sincerity tinged his voice. His words were flat and devoid of any emotion at all, except maybe disillusionment, if that could be called an emotion. "What have you done?"

When she didn't answer, something cold and metal scraped over her left wrist. Handcuffs! "What are you doing?"

"People don't live under assumed names or refuse to talk to the law after someone shoots at them. Not unless they have something to hide."

"I'm not a criminal."

He paused with the second cuff pressed against her right wrist. "Then tell me what's going on."

He didn't understand. He couldn't. And in his lack of understanding he would arrest her. He would take her to the pitifully defenseless sheriff's office in town. There, he and the deputy wouldn't have a chance against the man bent on getting to her, because getting to her meant getting through them. More good men would die because of her. Would the killing never end?

"It's not what I did," she explained, her voice sounding tinny. Trapped. "It's what I saw."

"What?"

She closed her eyes, and as always, the vivid images played out in her mind. Two men in the stable, talking in hushed tones. The squeal of car tires. Three firecracker pops. Blood and other matter sprayed on the wall across from where she stood, out of sight behind the wash rack.

The victims hadn't even had time to cry out. They'd died quickly, their screams stillborn in their throats.

"Murder," she whispered. "I saw a murder."

Chapter 3

*M*urder. The word bounced off Shane's chest like a stone flung by an angry mob. Hardly a fatal blow, but debasing, disparaging. A defamation of humanity, flying unfettered in the face of everything he stood for. A slur on the law he'd sworn his life to uphold.

It made him mad as hell.

But what had he expected? He'd known she was in trouble. Bad trouble. Any lingering doubt about that had vanished when she'd tried to fight her way past him. She had to have known she'd never make it. Only a desperate woman would even have tried.

That desperation had worked in her favor. The look in her eyes—terror, hot and unadulterated—had frozen him in that critical moment. By the time he'd moved, it had been too late to block her kick.

The throw that followed the kick had been smooth and practiced. She'd used his own momentum to take him down. Even scared half to death, she fought smart. He hadn't known she'd had self-defense training.

Shane swallowed a bitter laugh. Why should he have known that? Hell, he didn't even know her real name.

An odd feeling crept over him, lying so intimately with someone at once familiar and a complete stranger. Rigid as she held herself beneath him, she was still soft in all the right places. She'd fought hard, but the lush curves molding to the contour of his body made him well aware that she was no raw-boned tomboy. She was all woman, full and mature, he thought.

He also thought he had better get off her before he couldn't think at all.

Slowly he rolled to her side, grimacing at the pain in his back, and propped himself up on one elbow. He hoped she didn't run again. He wasn't up for another round of hand-to-hand combat.

Saying nothing, she turned herself over and fixed her gaze on the sky. Guilt blanched his mind as he took in her disheveled appearance.

Her forehead still bore the abrasion from last night's encounter with the steering wheel of her truck. Her indigo eyes were shadowed in deep sockets, her cheeks cherried with fatigue, her clothes rumpled. Her golden hair framed her head in a tangled halo.

But it was the single drop of blood clinging to the corner of her mouth that undid him.

No nameless gunman had done that to her. That was his fault. He'd pushed her too hard. He knew she was scared and he'd panicked her instead of talking her down, the way he'd been trained. Damn, but he found it hard to think around her instead of just...reacting.

Slowly his hand moved over her hair, honey-colored silk kissing his fingers as he teased a twig out of a gleaming curl. His palm slipped down to cup her face. Her breath enchanted his fingertips, called them to dance, to touch again. He held them poised just over the arch of her cheek.

Then his thumb rolled over her full lips, swept away the violent evidence of battle, and she quivered beneath his touch. The terror he'd seen flashing in her eyes before dulled to blunt acceptance.

"Tell me what happened," he said softly, not wanting to break the peace between them.

"I can't."

"Why not?"

"This isn't your problem."

"Someone tried to kill me. That makes it my problem."

She turned her gaze away.

"Fine," he said, reining in both his temper and the urge to pull her to him and rock away the despair in her eyes. How could he be so mad at her and ache to have her in his arms at the same time? Chagrined at his distraction, he gritted his teeth and continued, "You don't want to tell me about the murder, then tell me about the shooter in the Mercedes."

"I really don't know who he is," she said after only a moment's hesitation.

He ignored the restless shifting in his gut. Patience was the key to interrogation. Patience and relentlessness. Getting information was like solving a maze. There were lots of paths. He just had to keep trying until he found the one that led where he needed to go.

He turned down an alternate hedgerow. "Then tell me who *you* are."

She gulped in a breath of air, misery rising from her like steam off rocks in a sauna. "No."

Her sharp refusal popped his patience like a pin on a balloon. Frustrated questions exploded out of him. "What do you want to do? Run away again? What if next time he finds you, he shoots at you while you're crossing a crowded street or standing in front of a school bus? How many people will die because you ran away?"

Her jaw wavered and her eyes turned shimmery, but she held her tears back.

"You can stop this," he implored her, "Whatever it is, I'll help you. But you've got to trust me."

"I—I can't."

"Can't what? Can't stop it? Or can't trust me?" Impatience flared again. He already knew the answer. "Dammit, you know who I am. You know what I am. All I know about you is that you've lied to everyone in this town, and yet I still took a bullet to protect you back there. And *you* don't trust *me?*"

"I—" She stopped before her second word. "You what?"

Raking a hand—the one he could move without feeling as if someone was taking a razor blade to his back—through his hair, he struggled to his knees. The effort required more concentration than it should have. "Never mind," he said, hoping his voice was steadier than his hand, "Just—"

"You're hurt?" She looked him up and down, her tears suddenly pooled in wells of deep-blue concern. "Where are you hurt?"

He locked gazes with her as she grabbed the flap of his jacket and peeled it back. Resignedly, he shrugged it off his shoulder and rotated to give her a partial view of his back.

From the way his shirt was stuck to his skin—not to mention her startled gasp—he guessed there must be a fair amount of blood.

"Ow, sh-" Shane gasped, sitting in the passenger seat of the Jeep. He never finished the expletive. More because he ran out of air than because he was worried about insulting Gigi's—or whoever-she-was's—sensibilities.

She stopped whatever she'd been doing that set his back on fire and stepped around in front of him. A bloody gauze pad still in her hand, she peered at him like a specimen under a microscope, then without a word, cupped her hand around the back of his neck and shoved his head between his knees.

"Hey!" he called out, "What are you doing?"

"You're white as a ghost."

"I'm fine." He sat up, biting back a small moan at the dizziness that assailed him.

Rolling her eyes, she shoved his head back down. "Of course you are. Now take deep, slow breaths before you pass out."

"I'm not going to pass out." But he wasn't going to try sitting up again just yet, either.

Behind him, he heard her tear something. Looking back, he saw her soak a clean gauze pad in something out of a large brown bottle.

"This is going to sting a little."

He groaned again, figuring that if what he'd felt before was any indication, it was going to do more than just sting. "Just get it over with."

She steadied his shoulder with her hand. His muscles automatically bunched under her touch, anticipating what was to come.

"Try to relax. I'll be as quick as I can."

He tried, but his nervous system had other ideas. She was still holding that soaked gauze.

"You know," she said, "you weren't such a wimp last time you got shot, and that wound was a lot worse than this."

He clamped down on his tongue with his teeth as the gauze pad hit his ravaged back. He knew she was trying to distract him with her teasing. It wasn't working, but he'd be damned if he'd let her know how much what she was doing hurt.

She drew the gauze across the furrow a bullet had gouged across the middle of his back—far enough to the side to be well clear of his spine, thank God. His lungs burned with the need to draw a breath. He tried visualizing the skim of her fingertips—without the bloody gauze—across his bare skin, but that only succeeded in making other parts of him burn as well. He needed air; he couldn't seem to fill his chest. The heat got hotter. A sweat broke out on his forehead.

Thankfully, the cleaning and prodding ended.

"You okay?" she asked when the agony stopped.

"You tell me," he said, lifting his head cautiously.

"You'll live. The wound is fairly deep, but the bullet just grazed you. It may have nicked a rib, but nothing's broken, and the bleeding is stopped and it's clean." She snapped off her latex gloves as he sat up gingerly. "You're lucky I'm a doctor."

"You're a vet." He turned around, narrowing his eyes. "You *are* a vet, aren't you?"

"Of course I'm a vet. What do you think I am, some kind of quack?"

He frowned as she taped a bandage to his back. She was too good to be a fake. The ranchers around here would have seen through her ruse in a week if she wasn't the real deal.

He straightened up, studying the ruined shirt in his hands, then tucked it under the seat and slid his leather jacket on over his bare chest. It was torn too, but at least the dark leather didn't show the blood as much, and it was too cold to go without. "Tell me about this murder you saw." Now that the torture was over, the interrogation could continue.

"There's not much to tell."

He knew differently by the tensing of her shoulders, the way the chords of her neck pulled tight. "Humor me."

She shrugged, packing away her supplies. "I saw two men. Then I heard a car, and there were shots. Then it was over."

He clenched his fists, knowing there was a lot more to it than that. She had closed her eyes when she stopped talking. Deep lines carved themselves in a frown at the corners of her mouth. It was the same look she'd worn when she'd first told him she'd witnessed a murder. Like she was remembering.

Which she probably was, he realized. He'd seen enough violence to know the images stayed with you, like bad movies on videotape, playing over and over in your mind.

"Who was killed?"

Her eyes opened. "It's best if you don't know any more."

"Best for who?"

"You don't understand."

He hopped out of the Jeep and stood next to her as she fidgeted with paraphernalia in her first aid kit. "No, I don't. You walked away from a murder investigation. Left a killer on the street."

She was ignoring him. He grabbed her wrist. "How many more people do you think he's killed since you let him go?"

She wheeled angrily. "I did not let him go. I gave up my work and my home—life as I knew it—to do my part for law and order, to be a good citizen. And this is what I get in return. A life on the run."

He felt like he'd just been whipsawed. "You were a protected witness?"

"If you can call what they did protection. I barely survived it."

"Someone got to you?"

She nodded, torture swimming in her expression. "With a little help."

"Help from who?" She didn't answer, but her silence was telling. As telling as her lack of trust in cops. "Someone on the inside. A cop?"

She shook her head, her lips clamped tight. He didn't think he'd get any more out of her, but she raised her head, her lips thin and tight. "I wasn't even in protective custody two days. He got to me that quick."

"And you've been running ever since." He loosened his grip on her wrist and ran his hand up her arm in a long stroke. "You can't let whoever did that get away with it," he told her.

"I never saw him."

That didn't sound right. If she hadn't seen the shooter, why had she been put in protective custody? He would've liked to ask, but they were running out of time. If that guy was lucky enough to get his car back on the road in one piece, he could be on them any minute.

Besides, she looked like she was at the end of her rope. This wasn't the time for an in-depth interrogation. He needed to get her someplace safe. Someplace she could unwind without worrying about a blue Mercedes. Then he would coax some more answers out of her.

"Whether you saw him or not doesn't matter," he said. "Someone thinks you know something. And he's willing to kill you and anyone else who gets in his way because of it."

"So what am I supposed to do? Go back to New York? I might as well paint a big, red target on my back."

He paused a moment, trying to decide how best to present his plan. He decided straight out was the only way. "I have a friend in the Justice Department—"

"No!"

"This friend is straight as an arrow, you can trust—"

She jumped up, hands on her hips and defiance swirling like a cloud around her. "No. I'm not putting my life in anyone else's hands. Not again."

She crossed her arms over her chest as if to stop the shaking in her body. She wasn't going to trust anyone on his say-so; hell, she didn't even trust him. Someone had really worked a number on her. He planned to find out who, and then work a few numbers of his own on him for putting her through this.

For now though, he focused on calm. She needed his reassurance, not his rage. "Nothing will go wrong this time. I promise. I won't let anything happen to you."

Her head snapped up. "I don't want you involved. You

don't know what kind of trouble you're getting yourself into.''

A bemused grin tugged at the corners of his mouth. ''Honey, I'm DEA. I live for trouble.''

Her lips pressed into a grim line. She never laughed at his jokes.

''I can take care of myself,'' he reassured her.

She looked a little queasy, as if she didn't quite believe him. ''You're doing a great job of it so far, getting yourself shot.'' She eyed him narrowly. *''Again.''*

He feigned a mortal wound to the chest, then smiled. ''I do seem to attract bullets, don't I?''

''You think this is funny?''

''No. I don't think it's funny at all. But I do think we have to get out of here. So what do you say? If we hit the road now, we can be in Phoenix by dark.''

She paused, considering. ''Do I have a choice?''

He absorbed the petulant look on her face, the way her toe jabbed at the dirt. If anyone was just stubborn enough to survive this, it was Gigi. ''Yeah.'' He stood and stepped forward until he was toe to toe with her, chest to chest. ''You can go easy, or you can go hard. Which is it going to be?''

In place of an answer, she huffed and flounced around to the back of the Jeep, then rattled in her pack again. He sure hoped she didn't have a gun in there. If she did, he figured he was dead meat. He watched her a minute, but she just fussed with bottles and medical supplies.

He turned away. ''You've got exactly one minute to come up with your answer,'' he called over his shoulder.

''You allergic to anything, Hightower?'' she asked.

''No.''

''You sure? Penicillin, aspirin, nothing?''

''I'm sure, why do you as—'' He quit the question, the answer in her hand as she walked toward him. ''Oh, no. Don't even think about it.''

"What's wrong, Mr. I-live-for-trouble DEA? Afraid of a little needle?"

"A *little* needle, no. But that thing…"

"Sorry. I'm a horse doctor, remember? This is the smallest I have."

He scooted backward across the seat as she got closer. "You could knit a sweater with that needle."

"Quit whining."

"I'm not whining." He sulked a moment, then shrugged off his jacket not able to stand her mocking stare any longer.

"Sorry," she said, glee ringing in her voice. "Penicillin needs to go in deep muscle." She tapped the syringe and pushed the plunger, squirting a drop of liquid out the end of the needle. Looking down at him, she smiled evilly. "Drop 'em, Hightower."

He scooted an inch farther back on the seat. "No way."

"You don't want that wound to get infected while we're in Phoenix, do you?"

A mild infection didn't sound too bad, compared to that needle. How much antibiotic did it take to kill a few little germs, anyway?

Suddenly he realized what she'd said. She didn't want him to get an infection, "in Phoenix." She'd agreed to his plan.

"Well, what's it going to be?"

He eyed the needle again. "Do I have a choice?"

"Sure." She tapped air bubbles to the top of the syringe again. The morning sun glistened off her rosy cheeks and mussed hair, giving her a sleepy look. Like he imagined she'd look when he rolled over in bed in the morning after a long night of lovemaking and found her looking at him.

"You can go easy, or you can go hard," she said. "Which is it going to be?"

Fixing his stare on her seductively arched brow and wicked grin, he reached slowly for his belt buckle.

Oh, he would go hard, all right. All the way to Phoenix, if she kept looking at him like that.

Gigi woke unpleasantly, her mind full of dark images—two men whispering in a stable late at night, a faceless man in a midnight-blue sedan, and Shane, standing in a doorway, shadows and firelight dancing with the doubt and desire etched across his face.

Are you afraid of me? The memory of his words taunted her.

No, she would have told him, if she'd been honest. *I'm afraid of me.* Afraid she'd fall for those trust-me eyes. Afraid she'd find them looking up at her dull and lifeless one day because of it.

"Did you have a nice nap?"

Those words weren't echoes in her mind; they were real. She opened her eyes, feeling like someone had hung ten-pound weights on her eyelids, and found the very eyes she'd been dreaming about staring at her from the driver's seat.

She pulled herself closer to the door, wiping her face with the back of her hand. "How long have I been out?"

"An hour or so."

"Sorry, I didn't get much sleep last night."

"That makes two of us."

She wondered fleetingly what thoughts had held his sleep at bay last night, then when she felt his heavy-lidded gaze linger on her, she decided she didn't want to know.

They drove up on an exit. Shane put on his blinker, and let the Jeep coast off the two-lane highway. His hair settled sexily over his eyes as the wind that had been whipping it around his head diminished with their speed. She really wished he'd brush that hair back, before she gave in to the impulse to do it herself.

"We need gas," he said. His words cooled the heat of his stare, but did little to slow the clamoring beat of her heart.

Lord, what was she thinking? She had to get away from him, before she did something neither one of them might live long enough to regret, like trusting him.

The convenience store with the pumps out front looked deserted. Shane handed her a twenty-dollar bill and pointed at the See Cashier Before Fueling sign. "You pay, I'll pump."

Gigi took the money, but didn't move, holding her breath as he swung the door open and climbed out of the Jeep. The keys were in the ignition. This could be her best chance to escape before they got to Phoenix.

Shane pushed the door and it thunked closed behind him. Her heart lurched when he turned around and smiled at her, then dropped to the floor of her stomach when, never taking his eyes off her, he leaned into the Jeep and slid the keys out of the ignition.

For a moment she could have sworn he knew what she'd been thinking. A guilty flood of heat bloomed in her cheeks.

He jammed the keys in his pocket. "Why don't you get us some drinks while you're in there?" he said coolly, turning away to lift the handle on the gas pump. "You look a little hot."

She made a face at his back.

Walking out of the store with a brown paper bag of cool drinks and a package of peanut butter cookies, she couldn't believe her luck. A new-looking sedan pulled right up to the door. The driver, a well-dressed young woman, hopped out and left the engine running when she got out.

Gigi glanced out at the pumps. She could get away after all. Shane was nowhere in sight.

A different kind of adrenaline rush kicked her system into high gear. Where could Shane have gone? Had something happened to him while she was in the store? What if all the time she'd been inside plotting her escape, he'd been lying hurt—she wouldn't let herself think it could be worse than that—out here somewhere?

Seconds ticked away. The young woman still hadn't come out of the store, and there was still no sight of Shane.

Ugh. She hated herself. Her best chance to leave, and she couldn't go. She couldn't take off without knowing Shane was all right.

Hurriedly she reached into her pocketbook and dug around until she found a makeshift weapon. She considered going for the gun in the Jeep, but she wasn't Police Woman. She couldn't see herself running around a gas station brandishing a pistol.

All she could find was a metal fingernail file, but it had a long thin blade that would certainly hurt if it were jabbed somewhere strategic. With the file clutched in her fist, she crept to the corner of the convenience store and peaked around the corner.

Nothing.

She crept around the other side.

Bingo. Shane was there, but he wasn't lying hurt. The cold chill of fear she felt turned to a hot blast of anger.

He was propped against the side of the painted cinder block building next to a phone booth, his long, jeans-clad legs crossed at the ankles, the fingers of one hand crammed into his pocket, looking like he didn't have a care in the world.

He glanced over his shoulder, saw her and jutted his chin toward her to acknowledge her presence as he talked. Heat rushed up her neck as she marched to him. What was he doing? They'd called the deputy long ago, from the first gas station they'd come to.

He covered the receiver with his hand and opened his mouth to say something to her. Before he got a word out, she reached out and jabbed the hook on the phone down.

"Hey! What are you doing?"

"Who were you talking to?" Her throat was so tight she could hardly get the words out. Had he given her away already?

"What is wrong with you?"

"I told you, no warning anyone that we were coming. I don't want a reception party waiting for me when I get there."

He made a sound of disgust. "You are really paranoid."

Her temper rose to a boil. "If I'm paranoid, it's with good reason. I've been driven away from my home, forced to leave my friends and my job, chased, shot at—" The odd look on his face stopped her. "What are you staring at?"

He waved toward her hand. "That."

Looking down, she remembered the pitiful weapon still clenched in her fist.

"What were you going to do, hold a nail file to my throat and force me to give up the keys?"

"Now who's being paranoid?"

"Tell me that's not what you were thinking a little while ago. You were going to take off with the Jeep and leave me stranded in the middle of nowhere."

Damn him. He *had* known. And yet he'd said nothing. How did he do it? Stay so blasted calm, so indifferent? Years of practice, she decided. That, and not having any feelings to begin with.

She recognized that as a lie before she'd fully formed the coherent thought. He'd felt something last night, when he'd kissed her. And he'd made her feel it, too.

Double damn him.

He pried the metal file out of her hand. "How far did you think you'd get? If that guy in the Mercedes didn't chase you down, I would."

"You make it sound like I'm the criminal here."

"I'm still not sure you aren't."

"I told you I haven't done anything wrong."

"And I'm trying real hard to believe it—so hard that I just helped you cross state lines. Do you know how much trouble that could get me in if you really are a fugitive?" He dragged the hair off his forehead with his fingers and sighed. "I really want to believe you're an innocent victim in all this. But you aren't making it easy."

His argument threw her. He was risking his life and his career to help her without even knowing who she really was, with only her word as proof that she hadn't done anything to deserve the trouble following her, and all she could think of was getting away from him.

Well, maybe that wasn't quite *all* she could think of. She lowered her gaze to the file in her hand. He thought she carried it for him. In a way, she did.

To protect him.

The notion was foolish, she recognized. The only way to truly protect Shane was to get away from him.

But even that probably wouldn't work. She couldn't see him giving up that easily. If she escaped, no doubt he'd feel compelled to come after her. And that would put him in the path of a killer.

Gigi was cornered. Her only choice was to let him turn her over to his friend in the Justice Department. It was the only way he would leave her alone. The only way he would be safe.

And the one thing most likely to get her killed.

She hung her head. "I said I'd go to Phoenix," she said, watching numbly as he pulled the file from her stiff fingers and ignoring the tingle of sensation that erupted where he touched her. "I'll go to Phoenix."

"Damn right you will," he grumbled.

She glared at him. "I'll listen to what your friend has to say. After that, all bets are off."

"Fine by me."

"Until then, though, no more questions. I'm not telling

you anything until we've met your friend and I've made up my mind what to do.''

A muscle ticked in his jaw. "Still don't trust me, huh?"

She gathered her strength, meeting his gaze directly. The harder she could be on him, the better. She didn't want him feeling anything for her. The less he liked her, the more likely he was to leave her. "Don't take it personally," she said coldly. "I don't trust anyone. Especially cops."

"Great. You don't trust me, I won't trust you. We ought to get along just peachy."

They settled into the Jeep. "For what it's worth," Shane said, his expression unreadable as he pulled onto the highway. "I wasn't calling ahead to Phoenix. I called back to Utah to see if Bailey had caught the guy in the Mercedes."

"Did he?"

"No."

"I didn't think so." She dug her body into the unpadded seat of the Jeep. She hadn't thought about needing to stay in touch with the deputy, in case he found anything. She guessed it made sense to stay in touch. "Next time you're going to phone home, how about letting me know first."

He nodded. "Fair enough."

Two hours later, it hardly seemed fair. Standing in front of a large, expensive-looking brick home with high, arching windows and columns supporting the front veranda, Shane visibly relaxed, as if relieved to see the end of a torturous journey, while her nerves sparked more violently with every second that passed.

His nightmare was ending; hers was about to start. Or restart. She was about to relive the worst days of her life. Protective custody.

His hand reached out and pressed the bell. He smiled reassuringly, his irritation from the gas station forgotten somewhere in the final hundred silent miles they'd driven.

Footsteps sounded from behind the door, closer and closer. Gigi's heart thundered with each step. Promises or no promises, all she could think was *run*.

Run now, before it's too late.

Chapter 4

Shane rested his hand on the small of Gigi's back, feeling her tension mount as the doorknob twisted. She jerked as if she might bolt when the heavy oak door swung open. He stepped close behind her, blocking her path and, he hoped, reassuring her at the same time.

The broad face of his old friend, Bill Maitland appeared in the open doorway. Bill's thin brown hair, salted with gray, flowed over his shoulders just far enough to brush the top of the Bar-B-Q This! apron he wore over a button-down shirt and khaki trousers. Even on his days off, Bill looked like the nutty professor that he was.

He and his wife, Margo, had practically adopted Shane twelve years ago when he'd been a student at Arizona State. Since the first time he'd been invited over for dinner, he'd felt at home here. Almost like a member of the family.

Almost.

Bill's wide cheeks, rounded by years of perpetual laughter, puffed up in hearty recognition. "Shane, my boy. Good to see you," he said, waving the spatula in his hand. "I thought we were going to have to send a tactical team up to get you out of Utah." He laughed even more heartily and his gaze fell on Gigi. He quirked up one eyebrow. "Then again, maybe Utah is exactly what you needed."

Looking over her shoulder, Shane saw the blush creep onto Gigi's cheek.

"Uh, Bill this is—" he struggled for a name to introduce her.

She took the matter into her own hands. "Gigi McCowan," she said as if it were God's truth and glancing sideways as if daring him to deny it.

"Gigi McCowan," he repeated. Best to save the truth for later, anyway. "Gigi, meet my old friend Bill Maitland."

She nodded brusquely, notably skipping the usual "Pleased to meet you," part of the conversation. Shane nudged her inside as Bill opened the door to let them pass.

"Come in, come in," he said. "I'll throw another couple of burgers on the grill."

"That won't be necessary," Gigi told him hastily.

Shane squeezed her elbow. "Burgers would be great. We haven't eaten anything but peanut butter cookies all day."

"Well then, I'm sorry it's not steaks." Bill opened the refrigerator and took out a couple of raw patties. He nodded toward a window looking out over the backyard, where two children shrieked in laughter as they chased a golden retriever. "The grandkids prefer burgers, you know. Turn up their noses at T-bone." He shrugged. "The fast-food generation."

"Burgers sound great," Shane said, his mouth watering.

In minutes, two more places had been set at the kitchen table. When Bill turned his back, Gigi gave him a bug-eyed, get-on-with-it look. Coolly, he picked at the label on the beer bottle Bill had set before him. He watched the older boy outside, Bill's grandson Ben, throw a tennis ball and the dog charge after it. Gracie, the little girl, squealed after them both.

"So how are Ronnie and Michelle?" Shane asked, referring to the kids' parents, Bill's son and daughter-in-law.

"They're good. Off to Galveston for a weekend of parental nonresponsibility."

Bill turned to stir a pot of beans on the stove and Gigi waved her hand in a speed-it-up motion.

Shane ignored her. "And Margo?"

"Can you believe, our one weekend to spoil the grandkids without their parents watching us like hawks, and she gets called to D.C.?" Bill said over his shoulder.

Shane's stomach sank. Bill turned back to his pot. Gigi squirmed in her seat, her impatience palpable.

"What's going on in D.C.?" Shane asked. Gigi rolled her eyes.

Bill shook his head. "I know better than to ask."

Spreading her palm flat on the table, Gigi interrupted. "Mr. Maitland, I can appreciate that you and Shane haven't seen each other in a while and have some catching up to do, but our visit is somewhat urgent."

Shane crossed his arms over his chest and let her roll, holding his tongue when she paused and looked at him for support. He wondered how long it would take her to figure out she had the wrong Maitland.

"Oh?" Bill frowned at Shane, holding his ladle in the air until bean sauce dripped to the floor.

Shane sucked a long draft from the bottle, then looked to Bill. "When is Margo due back?"

"Thursday maybe."

"Thursday. *Maybe*." Shane let the words soak in with another hit of beer. "Damn."

"Excuse me!" Gigi said, standing now, her hands on her hips.

Shane gave Bill a long-suffering look. "Gigi is in a little bit of trouble."

"Shane seemed to think you could help us—me," Gigi blurted out. "Frankly, I doubt it, but he insisted on dragging me here to talk to you."

Holding his spoon in the air, Bill raised his eyebrows. "Just what sort of trouble are you in, young lady?"

"Someone is trying to kill her," Shane said, then took another swig of beer.

"Ah!" Bill gave Gigi his sage look, setting his spoon in the ceramic spoon rest beside the stove and hooking his thumbs around the sides of his apron. "That right?"

She nodded. How could this nice, strange old man possibly help her?

Bill rocked back from toe to heel. "I'm afraid I can't help you," he said as if he'd read her mind.

"I didn't think so." She stood to leave. "I'm sorry for wasting your time, but Shane said—"

He threw Shane a reproving look.

"All I said was that I had a friend in the DOJ," Shane said in self-defense.

Bill settled himself quietly in the chair next to Gigi and lifted one hand from her hip. Unfurling her fingers in his and giving the back of her hand a grandfatherly pat, he smiled up at her. "Ms. McCowan, should you need help with your operating system, a new computer chip, or a hard drive crash, I'd be glad to assist. But as for your other, ah, situation, I'm afraid I can't help you."

"You don't work for the Justice Department?" Gigi asked.

Bill's smile grew broader. "Me? No. I teach computer science at Arizona State University."

She turned a confused frown toward Shane. "But you introduced him as your old friend."

Shane shifted uncomfortably.

"So I am," Bill said. "I've known Shane since his first

semester at the university. He was my star pupil—'' Bill Maitland winked ''—until my wife seduced him.''

Gigi nearly choked. Her eyebrows flew up like birds taking wing.

Bill chuckled. ''Seduced him to the dark side of academia, that is—the criminal justice program.''

''Your *wife* is with the DOJ?''

''As well as a frequent guest lecturer in the CJ program at ASU.'' He made a clucking sound and shook his head. ''I should never have introduced them. But young Shane here had nowhere else to go for Thanksgiving and I felt sorry for him and brought him home for dinner. The rest is history.''

Shane took no offense, even if Bill's description made him sound more like a stray pup than a nineteen-year-old college student experiencing real life—life outside of a group home, that is—for the first time.

The Maitlands were as close as he'd ever have to blood relatives. Sometimes when he shared their home, their food, he could almost believe they were related—his aunt and uncle, maybe. Sometimes he wished they were.

Shifting uncomfortably in his seat, he locked those wishes away with all the others from years ago and asked quietly, ''Can you get in touch with Margo, Bill?''

''I'm afraid not,'' he answered, ''except by going through the DOJ and telling them it's a family emergency. I'm not even sure she's in D.C. any longer. You know the cases she works are classified.''

Shane nodded. The family emergency drill was not an option. Not only would it be unfair to Margo, scaring her with the possibility that something was terribly wrong at home, but it would alert too many others in the DOJ. Require too many explanations.

Gigi sank back into her seat. ''Thursday,'' she mumbled.

''I'm sure someone else in her office—'' Bill started.

''No.'' Gigi's head snapped up, her body came forward.

Bill's eyes slanted in question. Gigi looked imploringly at Shane.

"It'd be best if we dealt directly with Margo on this." Shane said, relieved when Gigi eased back into her seat.

Bill nodded. "She calls home every other day or so. I'll let her know you need her."

"I'd appreciate that."

Just then the two children and the dog burst through the door, and Shane was distracted for a few minutes with bear hugs and cries of "Unca Shane, Unca Shane," while Bill served up plates of hamburgers and beans.

Once the children were settled again outside, Bill brought the other burgers in on a plate. "In the meantime," he said as if their conversation had never been interrupted, closing the door behind him. "I hope you like your burgers well-done, Ms. McCowan."

"We really should be going." Gigi fidgeted with the bright-yellow place mat in front of her.

"You have to eat," Bill admonished. "And if you stay here, you'll be close when Margo calls in."

Gigi looked out the window, toward the two kids swinging their short legs under the picnic table as they struggled to control hamburgers too big for their little hands to manage. A moment of panic slashed across her face, and Shane could practically hear her recalling his earlier warning, *What if next time he shoots at you, you're crossing a street or standing in front of a school bus? How many innocent people are going to get killed?*

He swore as he imagined where her thoughts would lead her. The graphic images he knew would play out in her mind. He knew what she was thinking, and he knew she was right. That didn't mean he had to like it. "That's not a good idea, Bill."

Bill's expression darkened as he looked from his grand-children to Shane. "I'm not going to turn you out if you're in trouble. I can put the kids on a plane to Galveston. Ronnie and Michelle won't mind.''

Shane reached across the table and clasped Gigi's fingers in his, squeezing gently. He pushed down his awareness of her soft skin and the strength of her hand beneath it, grateful that for now at least, she didn't pull away. "You're not turning us out. We're insisting on leaving."

His scowl deepened. "Doesn't mean it feels right," he grumbled. "There's gotta be something I can do."

Shane mustered up a grin. "You can put those burgers in a bag to go," he said hopefully.

Two minutes later, Bill was handing him not one, but three bags, stuffed with what looked like half the supplies in his kitchen.

"Anything else I can do?" Bill asked.

"You wouldn't happen to have any nine-millimeter ammunition around, would you?"

"Now I really don't like this." His brows drew together as he stalked away, but he was back in seconds with a box of shells. "What else?"

"I could use a clean shirt."

"Right." Bill eyed Shane's bare chest beneath the bomber jacket. Shane didn't offer any explanation for what had happened to his shirt. He knew Bill very well, and he could tell his friend was getting close to the point of insisting they call someone for help. Showing him his bullet wound would undoubtedly push him right over that edge. His best bet was to keep Bill distracted, and helping.

"I'll get you a cell phone, too, so Margo can reach you."

"Thanks," Shane answered. "And are you still driving that gray Honda?"

"It's silver. And yes."

"Can I borrow it?"

"I suppose I can drive Margo's Jag for a few days." He dug a set of keys on a gold key chain formed like an old doubloon from his pocket, but hesitated before handing them over.

Shane smiled reassuringly. The Honda might not be as expensive as Margo's car, but Bill babied it just the same. "I promise to bring it back in one piece."

He dropped the keys in Shane's palm. "The hell with the car. Bring yourself back in one piece." He jutted his chin toward Gigi. "And your pretty friend, too."

Heat crept into Shane's cheeks. "I'll do my best." He piloted Gigi toward the door.

When Bill was out of earshot, Gigi said, "We can't leave the Jeep here."

He knew she was right. Only, getting the Jeep away from here meant splitting up until they could dump it. Asking Bill to help wasn't an option. He'd already involved his friend more than he should. If anything happened to Bill...

He wouldn't let himself think that way. No one would track him here. Not without having access to a lot of personal information on Shane Hightower. And access to personal information on DEA agents was hard to come by, even in law enforcement circles.

"We're going to have to leave it somewhere with an awful lot of cars if we don't want it to be found. It kind of stands out," he said.

"Kind of." She grinned. She was right, he thought. It looked like tomato soup. "The airport?" she asked.

"No. Too many security cameras. I'd rather not have anyone taking pictures of us coming and going. We'll leave it at the shopping mall."

Bill's returning footsteps echoed in the hall behind them.

"You're going to have to drive the Honda," Shane told her, holding the keys out to her. "Take the cell phone. I'll follow you. If the Jeep draws trouble, take off. Dial one on the speed dial and it'll ring here. Bill will get help to you."

She nodded and wrapped her fingers around the gold key

chain, but Shane didn't let go. His eyes narrowed. He'd driven Bill's Honda before. It was small, but it was quick. A lot quicker than that rattletrap Jeep if she decided to run. "You take off *only* if there's trouble, right?"

Her cheeks turned pink, but he couldn't tell if she blushed because she was embarrassed that he'd figured out what she was thinking again, or because she was mad that he thought she'd take off and leave him in a vehicle that drew killers like a magnet drew paper clips.

She yanked the keys from his hand. "Right."

Bill reappeared, handing Shane the shirt and phone.

"Thanks for the help," Shane said, not bothering to hide the seriousness of the moment behind a false smile.

"You're welcome," he said looking from Shane to Gigi and back. "I think."

He walked partway down the drive with them. Gigi walked a step ahead and Bill held Shane back. "Fitz is going to have a cow about this."

"I can handle Fitz."

"He's been calling here, making noise about booting you out if you don't show up at the office tomorrow."

Shane's gaze trailed over Gigi, who had stopped at the edge of the stoop. From the tilt of her head, he guessed she was listening to every word. He knew he should call his boss, let him know he was back in town. But Hugh Fitzsimmons would want some explanation why he wasn't at work. And Shane had promised Gigi—no one else involved in this.

Besides, he'd been having second thoughts about the DEA since long before he'd met the woman who called herself Gigi McCowan. "Don't worry about Fitz, Bill. If he fires me, it'll just save me having to type up a resignation."

"You're really going to do it, then? You're going to quit the DEA?"

"I don't know. Maybe. Tell Fitz I'll call him when I can."

Gigi stopped, her hand on the door of the Honda. Her gaze

darted up and down the street the way a person's did when she had something to be afraid of.

An ache settled in Shane's bones as he put a name to the look—the look of the hunted. He guessed she had good reason to look that way.

Bill must have seen it, too. "Just what kind of trouble is she in, boy?"

"You don't want to know."

"That bad?"

"Yeah."

"And you've stepped right into it with her."

Shane hiked up one corner of his mouth. "Hip deep."

"You ought not do this alone."

He followed Bill's gaze to Gigi. "I'm not exactly alone."

"Uh-huh," Bill said sourly. "That's what I'm worried about."

Shane knew what Bill meant. *Keep your head on straight and watch your back.*

He didn't need the reminder. He'd let a beautiful woman blind him to the truth once, underestimated what she'd do to protect her family. He wouldn't let it happen again.

"It's under control," he claimed, as much for his own benefit as for Bill's. "It's all under control."

And it was. But for how long?

An hour later, Gigi climbed out of the Honda in front of a long, low motel where Shane had rented them a room for the night. She jumped at the brush of something wet along her lower leg and turned in time to see a mottled black-and-white dog, hardly more than a pup from the look of him, but already as tall as her knee, dart behind the car beside her. When her heart restarted, she took a tentative step forward. One lopped ear and a nose poked around the bumper.

"Here guy," she called softly. "Here little guy."

Shane was at her side. "What's wrong?"

She felt the tension in his touch on her elbow. "Just a dog," she answered. "A stray, maybe." She'd felt the pup's bones through his loose skin. Poor thing was probably half-starved.

Shane relaxed a bit. "Let's go. We're in room 126."

He walked on, but Gigi hung back, looking for the pup.

Shane stopped. His shoulders sagged tiredly, but his voice was firm. "Gigi, come on. We have to get out of the open."

Regretfully, she followed Shane's echoing footsteps along the boardwalk porch that ran the length of the motel. She clutched her survival bag—the only thing that mattered if she had to make a run for it—to her chest, her palms sweating.

Darkness had fallen on the drive here from the Maitlands', but it was still warm. Phoenix rested in a lowland valley, but the air here seemed thinner, drier than in the mountains they'd left behind—had it only been that morning?

Shane stopped at the last door on the porch and fumbled with the key in the lock. Behind him, a giant yellow neon sombrero tipped forward and back in a gesture that seemed more drunken than welcoming. La Casa de Amigos—The House of Friends—the green blinking letters shaped like saguaro cacti proclaimed.

Gigi wondered if anyone really called this place *home* for more than a few hours at a time. From what she'd seen on the way here, the motel wasn't in the best of neighborhoods. The parking lot was nearly empty, and the few vehicles scattered around were mostly older models, many in serious need of repair.

The building was laid out to look more like a rancho bunkhouse than a motel. Along the slat-wood porch, rough-hewn pine benches sat recessed into little alcoves along the wall of the single-story stucco facade. A small light fixture shaped to look like an antique lantern hung beside each numbered door.

The door to room 126 swung open.

In the parking lot, a rusted old sports car pulled crookedly into a space. A man and woman both got out the driver's door, brown bottles in their hands.

The dog shot out from behind the Honda toward the couple. He looked to be about six months old, part Great Dane—that would be where he got his coloring, a pattern called Harlequin—and part something undefinable. The pup sniffed the people's shoes and the man kicked at him. The dog skittered off, stopping to bark once.

"Oh, Shane," Gigi said, tears coming to her eyes at the dog's plight as she realized what the pup was doing. "He's checking everyone that comes in."

"Looking for his family." Shane's eyes weren't teary, but she thought she saw something there. Something deep and wrenching.

He nudged the small of her back. "We have to get inside. Out of sight."

Shane leaned through the doorway, flicked on the light, then stepped back to let her pass through. The room across the threshold didn't look as bad as Gigi had expected. The double bed was neatly made with a pale-yellow spread. The carpet was sandstone in color, and looked fairly new.

"Doesn't look so bad," she said half-aloud.

"What were you expecting, La Cucaracha?"

"No. Cockroaches I can handle, if I have to. I was more afraid of finding a bed that vibrated and mirrors on the ceiling."

Hesitantly she stepped inside. When the faint aroma of pine cleaner greeted her instead of the stale odors of cigarettes and sex, she sighed in relief. Maybe this place wasn't as disreputable as she'd thought.

The outside light blinked off behind her, and she turned in time to see Shane finish unscrewing the bulb on the porch lantern. "We'll be able to see outside better without it," he explained without her asking.

As if to prove the point he pulled back the corner of the curtains and scanned the area outside the window. When he turned back, he dropped the car keys on the small table beneath the window, slid out of his jacket and hung it across the back of the chair pushed against the table. "You want the shower first?" he asked without preamble.

What she really wanted was those keys. The Jeep was gone now, and with it the killer's chances of finding them. No one could track them to this hotel. Once she was gone, Shane could call Bill or call a cab or call the devil for all she cared. She'd be long gone.

But she didn't dare hope he'd be so careless as to leave the car keys in her reach if she offered to let him clean up first. No, he was smarter than that. Getting away from him would take time, and patience.

Neither were Gigi's strong suits, but she forced herself to nod and back toward the small cubbyhole she assumed was the bathroom, carrying her bag with her.

Soon the pounding of hot water on her tired body had her thinking less about escape and more about sliding between cool, clean sheets and closing her eyes, just for a little while. Even if she could escape from Shane tonight, she wouldn't get far. The steamy water had liquified her muscles.

She shut off the water and pulled herself out of the shower before she fell asleep upright. Wearing a fresh pink T-shirt and bicycle shorts, she zipped her survival bag closed and stepped into the main room. A wisp of steam curled over her shoulder and disappeared into the stillness.

Shane sat by the window in the little chair that looked about as comfortable as a torture rack. Exhaustion pulled at his eyelids as his heavy stare fell on her. Her fingers curled reflexively around the handle of her bag.

She cursed her reaction. Why did she have to feel every look from him like a caress?

"Your turn," she said, trying not to sound affected.

He nodded and pushed himself out of the chair. A step away, he leaned back and snagged the keys in his fingers. On his way across the room, he stopped in front of her. His gaze ran from her wet curls over her fresh pink T-shirt, flowered bicycle shorts and clean, white socks, then latched on to the nylon backpack pressed to her chest.

Her skin tingled as if she'd been tickled with a feather.

His eyes narrowed. "Just what do you have in that bag?"

"Just a few personal things. Overnight stuff."

He reached out and pushed up on the bottom of the bag, taking some of its weight in his hand. "Feels like a lot of stuff for overnight."

She smiled falsely. "You know women. We aren't happy if we don't have half a pharmacy with us."

"Uh-huh." He reached for the strap of the bag. She jumped back, tightening her hold. "What's in the bag, Gigi?"

"Nothing of your concern."

"Everything is my concern tonight."

He reached again for the bag. She tried to back up, but her shoulders hit the wall. He pulled on the nylon; she resisted.

"Don't!"

"What have you got?"

"Nothing. It's mine—"

He tugged hard and the bag jerked from her grasp. As easy as that he inflicted his will on her, and her weariness gave way to a wave of rage.

"Give it back!" She shouldered into him and made a grab for the bag. He easily held it out of reach.

Pulling at the zipper, he turned the bag upside down, dumping its contents onto the bed.

When he raised his gaze, his eyes were beyond tired. They were worn. Aged. "Well, well. At least we don't have to worry about having enough cash to tip the maid."

He picked up one of the packets of bills and fanned its edge with his thumb, then threw it back on the bed with the others. ''There must be ten-thousand dollars here.''

''Twelve,'' she replied irritably.

He picked up the manila envelope from the top of the pile and pulled out the papers she'd bought with the rest of her cash. ''Driver's license, Social Security card, birth certificate.'' He dug deeper, then raised his eyebrows as he pulled his hand out. ''Passport. Very thorough. Tell me, who is Arena Vega? Another retired veterinarian friend?''

Heat rose in her cheeks. ''It's a made-up name. If this identity didn't work, that's my backup. I was going to leave the country. If I survived.''

He looked at the papers more closely. ''These are good forgeries. They must have cost you a pretty penny.''

''Lots of pretty pennies.''

He threw the envelope on the bed next to the money and picked up the dirty clothes she'd stuffed back in the bag. She cringed as the handgun slipped from the folds of her T-shirt. His jaw hardened as he turned the gun over in his hands. ''Nice. Taurus M80 revolver. Brazilian made. It's a good gun for you—not too heavy, not too bulky. I suppose if sneaking out on me didn't work you were just going to shoot me?''

Her cheeks flamed. ''I have no intention of shooting you.''

''Good, because I have no intention of letting you.'' He shoved the pistol in the waistband of his jeans and stuffed everything else back into her bag.

She sat frozen. He shuffled to the bathroom and stopped outside the door. Her spine stiffened under his dark study.

''Take off your clothes,'' he ordered.

''What?''

''You heard me.''

''You've lost your mind.'' Her heart raced in her chest. ''I'll scratch your eyes out before I let you—''

''Relax. You're not going to have to scratch anything. I'm

tired and I'm dirty and I'm sore and all I want is a couple of minutes in the shower without having to worry about you running off on me. I figure even you aren't desperate enough to wander down the highway naked this time of night. So either you get under those covers and take your clothes off yourself, or I'll come over there and help you. You choose."

For an instant she considered fighting—rushing for the door or throwing a lamp—not because she really wanted to fight, but because it rankled her to meekly submit to caveman tactics. Tired or not, though, she got the feeling he was spoiling for a fight after finding that gun, and she would not be manipulated. She picked her own battles.

Besides, he really did look tired.

Glaring at him, she slid underneath the covers and wriggled out of her shorts and shirt, throwing each article in his direction as she removed it.

His face cast in shadows thrown from the bathroom bulb, he stood statuesque as one by one her clothes hit his bare chest and slid to the floor.

When she'd finished and her bra and underwear rested at his feet, puddled scraps of satin and lace, he arched one eyebrow. "If I didn't know better, I'd say you were teasing me."

She angled her chin up dramatically. "If I didn't know better, I'd say you were enjoying it."

The flutter of a butterfly's wings would have roared like an airplane propeller in the quiet of the room. After an extended silence, one corner of his mouth twitched upward in what she hoped was humor. "I just might be."

Shane retrieved her clothes and stuffed them in the bag with her other meager belongings. He stopped with one hand on the bathroom door frame and turned her way, the playfulness vanished from his features.

"Be careful," he warned. "Because if your teasing ever becomes a serious invitation, I won't turn you down."

* * *

Shane cut off the water after ninety seconds. Two minutes was too long with Gigi alone in the room. Besides, thanks to her lascivious undergarments, he'd had to shower in much cooler water than he'd planned. Who'd have thought the no-frills veterinarian had a taste for black lace?

He wondered what other tastes she preferred that he might not know about. Just imagining almost made him have to turn the cold water back on.

With a groan, he pushed the shower door open and reached for a towel. The woman was going to drive him crazy.

He listened a moment to the quiet on the other side of the door. Quiet worried him. He supposed she could have fallen asleep already—he knew she was exhausted even if she wouldn't admit it.

Then again, maybe she wasn't asleep.

He flicked the towel around his hips and charged into the room, immediately swearing at the sight of the empty—and coverless—bed.

Damn her stubborn soul!

In two steps he was back in the bathroom and out again with his gun. "Gigi?" he half whispered, yanking the door open.

Darkness cloaked the night, hiding her secrets. Shane willed his eyes to adjust faster and stepped onto the porch, his gun raised.

"Dammit Gigi, answer me!"

The silence set his nerve endings alight. He felt the rush of adrenaline and the acceleration of his heartbeat that came with danger, and fear.

Where was she? He had no doubt Gigi had left the room of her own free will, but she could have run into anything once she got out here.

He never should have left her.

Hitching the towel higher on his hip, he moved into the parking lot. Pebbles dug into the soles of his feet. Little shards of glass and who knew what else dug deeper. Ignoring everything but the night and its sounds, listening for anything out of place, he worked his way through the vehicles, stopping to check between and inside each one as he crept along. When he reached the Honda and found nothing, defeat weighed on his shoulders like an ox's yoke.

He scanned the porch, the lot, the street beyond one more time. "Gigi?"

In the dark alcove outside their room, Gigi closed her eyes against the slump of his shoulders, the way his arm, gun defiantly outstretched only moments ago, dropped uselessly to his side. But closing her eyes couldn't block out the agonized break in his voice as he called her name. His worry for her was as unwelcome as it was undeserved.

She'd expected Shane to come flying out in a hot rush of rage, not a coolly calculated maneuver to protect her from some nonexistent danger. She'd only meant to show him she couldn't be kowtowed by hard-handed tactics or plied by soft sexual innuendo. She'd never meant to scare him.

The butter-colored bedspread rustled as she gathered it around her on the pine bench and stood. Shane wheeled around at the sound, his gun raised again in an instant.

"Shane?" she called softly. She stepped out of the shadows.

He crossed the parking lot and hopped over the porch rail, nearly losing his towel in the process. Then he stood before her, his chest rising and falling too fast. His pale eyes sparkled in the starlight, drinking her in greedily.

"You're all right?" he finally asked. She nodded. Gradually his breathing slowed. He dragged a hand through his wet hair. "What are you doing out here?"

The answer was as simple as the question, and yet Gigi couldn't get the words out. At a time when her life seemed dictated by other peoples' actions, she just needed to feel in control of something. Of anything. Of whether she lay naked in a bed waiting for a man to protect her, or wrapped a bedcover around herself like armor and faced the night on her own. But she couldn't tell him that.

She sat on the bench again, preferring the shadows to the moonlight. "I needed some air."

"Air?" In a single word, he managed to express both his frustration and his perplexity.

She nodded again. He looked into the night a moment, tugged the towel higher on his hips, then dropped to the bench next to her. "I guess I could use some air myself."

He still hadn't shown her the anger she deserved. In a way she wished he would yell and get it over with. It would be easier to swallow than his quiet concern.

He shifted back on the bench. The heat of his thigh warmed hers where he brushed against her. She glanced down and felt a smile tug at her lips.

"What?" he asked, tilting his head to look at her.

Her smile grew another inch. She tugged lightly—very lightly—at the corner of the towel. It draped barely halfway down his powerful thigh. On the underside, she'd bet it covered significantly less.

"You're going to get splinters," she warned. The laugh she'd been suppressing bubbled up.

He shifted gingerly. "Mm. I would have dressed more appropriately, but someone else had already taken all the good linens." He tugged playfully at her bedspread toga until she stopped him with her hand over his.

"Why are you doing this?" She nibbled her lower lip.

"Because you needed some air."

"I mean all of it. Putting yourself in danger." She lowered her eyes. "Putting up with me."

He waited until she had raised her gaze again to answer. "Because I'm a lawman."

"And you think I'm a fugitive?"

"No, I think you're in trouble."

"Ah, yes. You're DEA. You live for trouble."

He sighed. "Not really. Not anymore."

"Then, why…?"

"Because enforcing the law isn't just what I do. It's who I am."

A car passed on the highway out front. Shane watched until its red taillights faded in the distance.

"You shouldn't be doing this alone," Gigi said. "Even your friend Bill said so."

"Ah, so you were eavesdropping on me and Bill."

"Of course," she retorted, then gave him a wry look. "I had to know if you were talking about me."

"All you have to do is say the word, and I'll call for backup." Before she could consider the possibility, or the implications, he continued. "But you have to know that this is not DEA-related. Without Margo's backing, I'll be pulled off the case and you'll be left with whomever they assign from the marshals' office." She swallowed hard, not wanting any of that, but not wanting the alternative, either. "I know it's tough for you to sit around and wait for Margo when all your instincts are telling you to run, but it's the safest thing to do. You can trust Margo, and you can trust me. We'll keep you safe."

"Or die trying."

Some of the tension eased from his face as he stared at her, thoughtful. "Is that what this is really about? You're worried about me?" He cupped the back of her head in his palm, threaded his fingers through her curls. "I'm happy that you care enough to be concerned, but you don't have to worry. I'm good at what I do. I can keep us both safe."

Gigi forced back the tears rising in her throat. She'd heard those words before. When she'd been in protective custody, they assigned a young marshal to the safe house. His name was Tom. He had two kids, a girl and boy four and six years old. He showed her pictures. When the shooting started, he locked her in the cellar. But there were lots more shots, and some yelling. She'd gotten scared and climbed out a little window over the crawl space and ran. She looked back as she ran across the yard and saw Tom limp out onto the porch. He saw her, and waved for her to keep going. Then she heard another shot, and he fell. And she ran. She ran into the woods and didn't look back again.

Clasping the towel to his hip, Shane shoved himself to his feet. "Come back inside with me, Gigi." His voice was rougher than it had been. When she hesitated, he extended his free hand back to her. "Don't worry, I'm not going to die for you."

She touched her fingers to his tentatively, and he grabbed hold and squeezed. She wanted to tell him not to make promises he couldn't keep, but before she could, he spoke again.

"At least not tonight," he said.

Chapter 5

The early morning sun inching over the horizon warmed Gigi's back as she balanced two coffee cups in one hand and twisted the key in the doorknob with the other. At the click of the lock, she pushed her way into the room hip first, unconcerned about the squeak of door hinges as she passed.

If her rattling around the room, running the water faucet, and clearing her throat several times—loudly—earlier hadn't woken him, a few squeaky hinges weren't likely to disturb his rest. He snoozed happily through it all, lying the wrong direction on the bed, his feet at the head, his head at the foot, as he'd fallen asleep.

He'd stood over her last night, a sexy, lazy grin warming her cheeks, while she crawled into bed, and waited patiently while she fixed the bedcovers, unwrapping the bedspread from around herself and trying to straighten it over the mattress without dropping the sheet clutched against her chest.

Then once she'd settled, he started to crawl in with her.

''Don't even think about it!'' she warned, then slapped his hand away from the covers and clicked off the lamp.

But he hadn't disappeared in the darkness, as she'd hoped. At least not all of him. The white towel slung around his hips shone in the radiant moonlight filtering into the room. Above it, his straight white teeth glowed just as brightly.

He was smiling.

Teeth and towel floated to the foot of the bed. And then the towel disappeared.

His smile got wider.

"I won't think about it if you won't," he said, and crawled between the top sheet and the bedspread, his head at the footboard.

She thought about it. She thought about it a lot.

But that was hours ago. He hadn't moved since then. She was hoping the scent of caffeine would rouse him.

Swinging around the edge of the door and shoving it closed with her foot, she turned to find him sitting on the edge of the bed in his blue jeans, bare-footed and bare-chested. Her first impression was that he looked incredibly good with the light streaming through the doorway behind her, casting a warm glow to his golden hair and burnished chest.

Her second impression was that he was really mad.

His elbows rested casually on his thighs and his thumbs twirled between his knees with deceptive calm, but the tension in his shoulders and neck gave him away. His muscles bunched and released like a caterpillar inching its way along a sidewalk, each length of sinew delineating itself from the others in the rippling play of skin over moving mass.

Uh-oh.

"You fibbed," she said brightly, hoping to avoid the storm she felt brewing.

He scoured his hand across the back of his neck. "About what?"

"About sleeping lightly." Kicking the door shut behind

her, she extended one of the cups of coffee to him. "You sleep like a log."

"So you took that as an invitation to leave?" The gruffness in his voice didn't stop him from accepting the offered coffee.

"You also snore. I couldn't stand the noise."

He took a sip, winced, and blew on the steaming cup. "I don't snore."

"Okay, you don't snore. I just needed my morning caffeine fix. But I brought some back for you. Doesn't that count for anything?"

"I'm surprised you came back at all," he groused.

She was beginning to think that Shane was not a morning person. "Mm, I can tell you were worried by the way you came charging after me."

He took a long draft of coffee, then set the cup on the night table. "You took the key."

Her brow furrowed. "So?"

"I didn't figure you'd bother to take the key if you weren't planning on coming back."

A warmth not unlike that she'd felt outside with the sun on her back crept over her. "You trusted me?"

"I was going to give you thirty more seconds, and then I'd have been on your a—" The corners of his mouth lifted in a ghost of a smile. "Heels."

He got up and went to the window. "Everything quiet out there?"

"I didn't see any hit men, if that's what you mean."

She fluffed the pillows and straightened the covers, but couldn't bring herself to sit on the bed with him so close. Instead she leaned against the dresser. Try as she might not to notice, she couldn't help but admire the breadth of his smooth back, marred as it was by a bullet's trail, as he stood staring out the window.

She offered to apply a new coat of antiseptic cream and a

fresh bandage. By the time she'd finished, his mood didn't seem as black. It seemed as good a time as any to bring up the question that had been weighing on her. "What do we do now?"

"We wait," he said without turning around.

"Your friend isn't going to be back for a while. We can't just sit here."

"Sure we can." Reaching for his coffee with one hand, he jammed the fingers of his other hand in the back pocket of his jeans.

"Look, I tried. I came to Phoenix and went to your friend's house. But I can't stay in one place and just wait. Not with *him* on my tail." She got her backpack from the chair and tossed it on the bed.

Shane turned around, one hand still in his pocket, as she was folding yesterday's blouse into the bag. "No one knows we're here, and this place is quiet. It's safe."

"*Safe* isn't a word I believe in any longer." Wheeling around to get her personal items from the bathroom, she walked into his chest. He swung his cup out of the way, but not in time. Coffee splashed over him.

Instinctively she swiped the liquid off his skin with her hand, afraid she'd burned him, but found the coffee had already cooled to lukewarm.

It was his skin that was hot.

"You don't have to believe in the word," he said. "Just believe in me."

Oh, how seductive that suggestion was—more enticing than his granite sculpted body, more alluring than the husky timbre of his voice, more tempting than the roguish shadow of new beard growth shadowing his jaw.

But she wouldn't depend on anyone but herself ever again. She wasn't sure she knew how. Flushed and flustered, she backed away. "We don't have enough food."

"When we finish what Bill gave us, we'll go to the store,

pick up some munchies and eat here as often as we can. If we get desperate, we'll hit the drive-throughs.''

She swallowed hard. ''I could wash the two outfits I have every other day, but you need some clothes.''

He chuckled sardonically. ''And here I thought you liked having me run around half-naked.''

''Hardly.''

This was supposed to be a serious conversation. He shouldn't be able to make her laugh. So why were her lips quivering just because he'd straightened his back and puffed up his chest almost imperceptibly?

Her breath hitched. She couldn't stop her gaze from falling to territory it had no business exploring. When she recovered and lifted her look, a slow grin spread across his face.

Despite her best efforts to contain it, a matching smile broke across her face.

''Careful,'' he said, chucking her lightly under the chin and then wiping his thumb across her lower lip as if he could erase her smile, ''if you start looking at me like that, I might just take it as a challenge.''

And I might just accept, she thought.

By afternoon, neither of them had much to laugh about. Tedium had set in.

That was the danger in witness protection, Shane had learned over the years. With each hour that dragged by, the body's ability to maintain a state of readiness diminished. TV numbed the mind even as inactivity numbed the body. Production of adrenaline and endorphins essential to alertness dropped. Boredom became carelessness. Carelessness got people killed.

Flicking the TV remote control to mute, Shane sat up on the bed and stretched. He needed to move. He needed to think.

He needed to kiss that pout off of Gigi's face.

That ought to get her adrenaline flowing. And probably his endorphins—nature's painkiller—as well, since she was likely to slug him.

She sat at the tiny table by the window with one leg curled under her on the chair, leaning over the puzzle book they'd picked up earlier, along with a deck of cards, munchies, and a change of clothes for him. She twirled a pencil absently between her fingers and she was frowning slightly, obviously deep in thought. One day, he hoped she'd devote that kind of undivided attention to studying him.

Without looking up, she asked, "What's a five-letter word for courageous?"

He lifted his eyebrows, grinned. *"Shane?"*

She rolled her eyes.

He sighed. "How about *brave?*" he asked, pulling his gun off the table as he stood.

Gigi rolled the pencil eraser across her chin. He tucked his weapon in the back of his jeans and pulled the hem of his newly purchased T-shirt over it.

"It ends with *y,* I think."

He shrugged, unable to come up with anything. She tipped the pencil against her lips and nibbled endearingly on the tip. Fascinated, Shane stopped and watched. A slow burn started in his groin and spread outward until he had to stifle a groan. Tearing his eyes away, he headed for the door.

She looked up, all innocence. "Where are you going?"

"To check the grounds. I'll check a couple of times a day while we're here, just to see who's about or if anything looks out of place."

"You're leaving me alone?"

He didn't know whether to be relieved or feel guilty at the tiny tremor in her voice. Not long ago, she couldn't get rid of him fast enough. Now she didn't want to see him go. And he didn't want to leave.

"Just for a few minutes," he said, then he reached for her

backpack and pulled out the handgun and box of shells she'd brought. He loaded the gun quickly and pressed it in her palm.

"What's this for?" She looked at the rubber-gripped Taurus as if it might bite her.

"I'll leave the room key here," he said by way of an answer. "When I knock, make sure it's me and make sure I'm alone before you open the door."

From the look on her face, he could see she still hadn't caught on. "In case someone gets the drop on me and makes me bring them back here."

"You wouldn't lead anyone back here."

"I might if they threatened to blow my head off if I didn't." He paused to let that sink in. "In that case, it's your job to shoot them before they shoot me."

He reached for the doorknob.

"Wait! I—I can't do that." She stood up, holding the pistol carefully, as if it might go off if she jostled it. "I don't really know...how to use it," she confessed.

"You don't know how to fire a gun?"

She shook her head, worrying her lower lip between her teeth. "I'm not sure I could shoot a human being, anyway. I don't think you want to die finding out."

He snatched the weapon from her hands. "For God's sake, then, what are you doing carrying the thing?"

"It came with the fake IDs—one price for everything." She shrugged. "The getaway package special."

Incredulous, he removed the bullets and tossed the useless weapon on the bed. "Great. Just great."

Even as he grumbled, though, something swelled in his chest. There was something alluring about a woman with a killer on her tail who had never learned to use her gun because she didn't think she could shoot another human being. That combination of naiveté and optimism was rare. He supposed that was because people with an outlook like that didn't survive long, these days.

Reaching for the doorknob again, he softened his tone. "At least make sure I'm alone before you open the door."

"Wait!"

He turned.

She twisted her hands in front of her. "Will you teach me?"

"If you're not willing to shoot someone, what good would it do?"

"I could shoot someone, maybe," she admitted softly, sincerely, "if someone else's life depended on it."

He flattened the smile that threatened to shine across his face. "Someone like me?"

She snatched the pistol off the bed, quickly looking away. "I said maybe."

Stepping up behind her, he wedged one foot between hers and spread her legs to shoulder width, then cupped her elbows and brought them level, her arms outstretched before her. His hands were big enough to wrap around hers, adjusting their position and grip on the gun.

"There," he said, a sudden gruffness in his voice that had little to do with anger at Gigi and a lot to do with regret that this woman ever felt she had to learn to use a gun. And sadness that she was doing it for him—because she was afraid she might be called on to protect him.

"A two-handed grip is best. Keep your back straight, shoulders relaxed, arms level."

The sudden realization that as much as he liked touching her, smelling her, he'd rather be doing it for any reason other than teaching her proper posture for taking a life assailed him.

"Shane? What do I do now?"

He winced at the looming loss of innocence. "Ease the trigger back."

When she pulled, the barrel of the gun tipped up forty degrees. "Good." He forced a smile to his lips. "You just killed the light fixture."

She frowned. "What did I do wrong?"

"Nothing. It takes a while to get used to the feel of the gun and the weight of the trigger, that's all."

"But I don't have a while. I need to know how to do it now."

"Then try again." He straightened her elbows. "Now squeeze," he said. "Gently."

Her body jerked as she fingered the trigger.

"You've got to relax," he said. "You're way too tense."

She tried again, but did no better. Her face was drawn, her cheeks pale.

"What are you thinking about when you fire?"

Her eyes grew round. Her lips quivered. "I—I can't help it." She lowered the gun, desperation swimming in her liquid eyes. "I see Uncle Ben, when he gets shot."

Shane's gut twisted. He took a step back. "*Uncle* Ben? One of the men you saw murdered was your uncle?"

"No. Not really. Just a friend of the family. But he liked for me to call him Uncle."

He exhaled a long breath. An uncle, but not by blood. Still, it must have been devastating to watch someone she cared for die. No wonder she didn't like guns.

Dammit, what was he doing teaching her to shoot? She was a veterinarian. She mended little animals and wayward DEA agents. She was a healer, not a killer. Suddenly he didn't ever want to see a gun in her hands again.

"That's enough for today," he said.

She grabbed his elbow. "No!"

He turned, curious. She'd set her jaw in a stubborn jut. "I have to learn to do this."

"Not today, you don't."

He took a step away.

"If you won't help me then I'll figure it out on my own."
She lifted the weapon and pulled the trigger again, as roughly
as before.

He should leave. Walk away from her while he still could.

As if distance mattered. No matter how far away from her
he got, she'd be with him, in his mind. He'd look at the wispy
clouds and be reminded of the fine tendril curls at the edges
of her face. A bird would call its mate and he'd imagine her
singing his name. She'd bored her way into his body somewhere south of his brain, and he couldn't get her out.

He paused, unsure what to do next. He'd like to think, in
typical male hormonal fashion, that she'd never need to defend herself, or him. That he'd always be there to protect her.
But realistically, he knew better.

Eight years in the DEA had taught him that in the end,
survival came down to one thing: kill or be killed.

Gigi deserved a chance to live.

Steeling himself against the unpleasantness, he stepped up
close behind Gigi. So close that he felt her heart thunder
against his chest and the tightening of her buttocks against
his groin.

"Do you really want to learn?" he asked with his hand
wrapped loosely around her middle, holding her to him.

"Yes."

"Then relax."

He felt her shoulders loosen, no more.

"Relax," he soothed, splaying his hand across her middle
and urging her to rest against him.

Gradually her body molded to his. "Close your eyes."

"Is this a new technique?" she asked nervously. "Marks-
manship for the blind?"

"Do you want to learn how to do this or not?"

She complied and he molded his hands around hers on the
gun, feeling the steel warm to her touch.

He settled her more firmly against him until the back of

her thighs rested against the front of his and his hips cradled her bottom. Closing his own eyes against the exploding sensations set off by the friction between them, he circled his arms around her chest and hunched his chin over her shoulder.

"Now promise me one thing," he said.

"What?"

"You won't ever pick up this gun unless it's to defend yourself."

"What do you mean? Why?"

"Don't ever do it for me," he said, covering his embarrassing swell of sentimentality with impatience. "I can take care of myself, I don't want you to try to protect me."

"What's wrong," she joked nervously, turning her head so that her cheek bumped his chin. "Afraid I'll miss and hit you instead?"

"No. I'm afraid you won't miss and you'll have to live with killing someone. Now promise."

Her pause lasted less than a heartbeat. "No."

He let go of her hands, and the gun. "Dammit, Gigi. I don't want you to kill because of me."

"And I don't want you to die because of me. Can you promise me that you won't?"

He couldn't make that promise, because he would die for her. He would step in front of another bullet or a speeding car or a madman with an ax, whatever it took to keep her safe.

But that was his job. He was trained for it. Sworn to it.

In a way, he guessed she was, too. Sworn to preserving life. Even his.

"Don't worry," she whispered. "I don't plan to kill for you." She found his hands and guided them back to hers, onto the gun. "At least not tonight."

Shane's breath shuddered in his chest, hearing her use the same words he'd used last night against him.

He stretched his arms along the length of hers. The outside swell of her breasts brushed his biceps, soft and warm. He focused on the feel of the gun. The target.

"Clear your mind. Think about something benign. A long stretch of fence. Nothing but desert all around. Feel the quiet, the calm. Picture the beer bottle on one of the fence posts."

Her shoulders dropped as her muscles softened.

"Good. Now breathe in." He inhaled with her. The scent of plain soap and springtime in the mountains nearly broke his concentration. "Hold it," he urged, referring to the air in her lungs. "And…squeeze."

She curled her finger back smoothly.

He felt her smile flood her whole body. "Better. Again."

They repeated the process three times. "Now open your eyes." He pointed at the mirror across the room. "Use your reflection as the target."

She focused on her "target" and breathed in. Her lungs filled, pressing her more deeply into him. Her finger curled inward.

He looked over her shoulder and her blue eyes shone back at him from the mirror, serious and compelling. Her closeness suddenly hit him like the concussion from a real gunshot. It blasted him back a step.

This game was headed into dangerous territory.

"You've just about got it," he said. He pulled a penny from his pocket and set it on top of the square barrel, centered over the sighting channel.

She looked at him curiously.

"Keep practicing," he said. "Until you can fire five times in a row without the penny falling off."

With that, he wheeled and walked away. On his way out the door he glanced over his shoulder and paused. "Gutsy," he said.

"What?"

"Five-letter word for courageous." He nodded toward the forgotten crossword puzzle. "Ends in *y*."

She nodded, and he closed the door behind him. He walked away, followed by the steady *click, click, click* of someone pulling the trigger of an unloaded gun.

It was Wednesday night, and the prospect of spending another night in the same bed as Gigi without touching her was enough to give Shane the sweats. They'd settled into a comfortable companionship the past couple of days. Too comfortable. Keeping his distance was getting harder and harder.

But she still didn't trust him. She refused to talk about New York or the murder or her life before it had been turned upside down. Every time he turned the conversation toward anything she found remotely threatening, she shut down.

He could find out what he needed to know, if he chose. Run her description and the few facts he had through NCIC and the New York police databases.

But if he made those phone calls, he could tip off the original leak. And besides, he'd promised Gigi he wouldn't. He never would have made that promise if he'd known he'd be strung out this long waiting for Margo to get back.

But he had made it, and he wouldn't break it.

Unfortunately, that meant putting his libido on hold. No matter how attractive he found her. No matter how appealing her wit, her intelligence, her ever present energy, he couldn't get any closer to her without knowing who she really was. He didn't dare.

So he'd retreated outside. Again.

He sat on the landscape timber embankment behind La Casa's pool shed with a fine sheen of sweat pasting his shirt to his back and tried to figure out how to get through one more day.

One more night.

Something knocked against the wood on the other side of

the pool shed and Shane's hand automatically rounded his back. His gun was in his hand before he caught a flash of black-and-white spots and heard the muffled whine.

Drawing in a breath to restart his heart, he shoved the pistol back into his jeans.

It was just the dog, the mutt someone had abandoned here.

The pitiful creature was living under the pool shed. Shane had seen him the first time he'd come out to check the grounds. The dog wouldn't come out from under the building, but crawled to the edge, so that his crusty nose and dirty paws stuck out. He stared at him warily from there, not retreating, but not coming any closer, as if he'd not quite judged him friend or foe yet.

That first day, Shane had sat quietly and talked to the dog. Since then, he'd made it a point to bring along a treat on his rounds—some scrap of junk food he'd purposely leave unfinished.

In the beginning, he'd dropped the food near the edge of the shed and kept walking. Later, he'd set the food a few feet out and stopped to rest, watching for the poor thing to creep out of its hiding place, grab the morsel and run.

By the second day, the dog—Shane called him Oliver, after Oliver Twist, begging for his gruel—ventured within a few inches of Shane's foot to take his treat.

Slowly, Shane pulled the pièce de résistance from his pocket—a quarter of a greasy cheeseburger he'd saved from the lunch he'd picked up at a joint down the road.

"C'mon Oliver," he called softly. "Good stuff tonight."

He heard the thumping again, and recognized it as the dog's tail whacking the underside of the building. Gradually the dog's black-and-white-and-brown—the brown was mostly dirt, and maybe a little dried blood—coat appeared. The mutt slunk toward Shane, his belly close to the ground and his tail tucked.

Shane tore the burger into pieces and offered him a bite.

Within inches of Shane's hand the dog stopped and sniffed. He let loose a frustrated whine, dropping his nose to the ground. His eyes were dull and pleading.

"Not this time. You want it, you have to come and get it."

The dog stretched his neck forward, pulled back, stretched forward again, snatched the burger, jumped back and swallowed the bite whole.

Shane grinned in victory. "Gotcha!"

They repeated the process three times. When the burger was gone, Shane wiped his hands on his jeans, then patted the dog's fuzzy head. "I bet you'd tell me your name if you were able," he said, thinking about Gigi. "Wouldn't you?"

The dog looked on, hopeful.

"Sorry fella, no more treats. I've got another lost soul's trust to earn. And I don't think she's going to fall for the hamburger trick."

Shane strode back to the hotel room, whistling, then stopped short outside the door to their room, instantly on alert. The curtains at the front window were pulled back. He hadn't left them like that—the opening gave anyone who passed a clear view into the room. Changing his angle a few degrees, he could see Gigi in the middle of the room, her revolver extended in front of her, her brow furrowed in concentration.

The warm night air suddenly chilled.

He reached for his own weapon, moving closer to the door, balanced on the balls of his feet. Ready.

He checked Gigi's position again to be sure he wouldn't hit her by mistake if it came to a firefight.

Then he stopped, lowering his gun as the muscles of his arms suddenly turned to rubber.

Her eyes were closed.

Fascinated, he watched her through the window like some Peeping Tom. Her chest rose in an even breath, stretching the knit of her ribbed tank top. Shane couldn't hear any sounds, but her lips formed an unmistakable shape as she pulled the trigger over and over. "Bam. Bam. Bam," she was saying to herself.

The penny sat rock steady on the barrel of the gun.

She was practicing.

Shane's mouth went dry. He hated seeing a gun in her hands, but damn. The woman had verve! When she decided to do something, she tackled the task with the tenacity of a beaver with his sights on a hundred-year-old sequoia.

And she had good hands, as he'd known she would. She guided the trigger back flawlessly again and again, the barrel of the pistol never wavering. His pulse pushed blood to his sex with every stroke.

He wanted her. He wanted that concentration on him. Then he wanted to break that single-minded focus, driving her mad until she couldn't think of anything but the sensations he created within her. For her.

But before he took her body, he wanted her mind. He wanted her trust.

Unclenching his fists, he took a cleansing breath and wiped the carnal images from his mind. Raising a knuckle, he rapped on the door. "Everything's okay. Let me in."

A second later the door swung open. Gigi stood aside, her face slightly flushed and her eyes gleaming with excitement.

She closed the door behind him and threw the dead bolt. "Watch," she said.

She raised her pistol and carefully placed the penny on the barrel. Then she faced her own image in the mirror. After she'd fired five perfect, imaginary shots, she flicked the barrel of the pistol up, and caught the penny in midair in her fist.

She turned to him, her eyes shining. "I think I've got the hang of it."

He closed his hand over the barrel of the gun, set it aside on the night table, and then, forcing a liquidity he didn't feel into his limbs, stretched out on the bed, propping his hands behind his head. "So I see."

"I want to try it for real. With bullets."

"I doubt the motel manager would appreciate that."

She laughed. "Someday maybe we can get to a range."

He lifted a shoulder noncommittally. "Maybe." He picked up the cards from the table by the bed. "In the meantime, how about practicing a different kind of dexterity? Care for a game of chance?"

She eyed him suspiciously, excitement still pink on her cheeks. "I don't think I want to play games with you, Shane Hightower."

"That's too bad," he said, letting a hint of dark desire slip through in his voice, "because I can think of lots of games I want to play with you."

He had her hooked; he could see it glinting in her eyes. "What's the matter? Afraid I'll take advantage of you?"

She angled her chin, gave him that aloof look of hers. "I'm not the type that's easily taken advantage of," she said.

"All the better." He dealt the cards out in two piles, one in front of himself and one at the other end of the bed. "I do like a good challenge."

She lowered herself gingerly to the bed and picked up her set of cards. "What are we playing, gin rummy?"

"Poker."

She glanced at the cache of cash tucked under the edge of the bed. "Planning to make off with my money?"

"I don't want your money."

"Then what are the stakes?"

He fanned out the cards in his hand and studied them seriously, then looked up at her. "What do you say we play for something a little more…revealing?" He purposely misled her by raking a hot gaze over her body.

She flushed, taking the bait. "I haven't played strip poker

since I was seventeen,'' she said. ''And I certainly don't intend to play it now.''

''Who said anything about stripping?'' he asked innocently.

''Then what did you have in mind?''

''Ante is one honest answer to any question asked.''

She considered a moment. ''And what do I get if I win?''

''The same, of course.''

''Humph. Hardly fair.''

''Oh, come on,'' he said smoothly. ''Don't tell me you're not the least bit curious about me.''

''So what if I am?''

''Play a hand. You win, anything you want to know is fair game.''

She spread her cards and glanced down. ''Anything?''

''Anything.''

''One rule. Nothing about the case. Deal?''

''Deal.''

''You're going to regret this.''

Her eyes blazed with merriment. Just seeing that expression made anything he had to give up worthwhile. ''Not a chance.''

He was already making up the questions in his head. Categorizing, ordering and scripting, like he would any interrogation.

Now all he had to do was win.

Chapter 6

Shane sized up Gigi over the top of his cards. She was nibbling her lower lip again—a good sign, he hoped.

She tapped the back of her cards with one fingertip. "Why were you outside so long tonight?"

"You want to ask a question, you have to win a hand." He ignored the face she made at him. "Let's see what you've got."

"Pair of eights." She slapped her cards down.

Smiling—but not so broadly as to be misconstrued as gloating—he turned his hand over so she could see. "Pair of kings."

Gigi looked like a prisoner—albeit a nonrepentant one— headed for the gallows. "Can't I take a dare instead?"

"We're not playing Truth or Dare." He looked up sharply. "Just truth."

"So, what's your question?"

He took his time, thinking it over. A thousand things he'd like to know about her flitted through his mind. Like what kind of music she liked and whether she knew how to dance country-and-western. If she ate Thai food—he'd noticed a take-out place a few blocks away and thought he might pick some up tomorrow, instead of burgers, to cheer her up.

And then there were the things he shouldn't even want to know about, but did. Like whether her skin was the same milky gold all over, or if she had tan lines.

In the end he settled for something safe. He didn't want to scare her off after just one hand.

"Why did you become a veterinarian?" he asked.

She relaxed visibly. "Because animals are more civilized than people."

"In general, or just a few particular members of the species?"

"Uh-uh." She gathered up the cards. "That's two questions. You want another answer, you've got to win another hand."

So, she'd picked up the gauntlet. Things could get interesting from here.

Shane won the next hand easily.

"Out with it," Gigi groaned.

He grinned. Sooner or later he'd work his way around to what he really wanted to know—who she really was and exactly what had happened in New York—but for now, he just wanted to have some fun with her. "Are you really a blond, or is it a disguise?"

"A gentleman wouldn't ask."

"What gave you the idea I was a gentleman?"

Her lips pursed and she scooped up the cards. "I'm a natural blond. And you're going to pay for that."

He smiled, liking this game more and more. "Not unless you win a hand."

"We'll see," she said sweetly.

A few minutes later, he won another round and started his attack by disguising a serious question behind the fun they were having. "When you left New York, did you leave a man behind? Someone special?"

"Yes." She lowered her gaze, busied her hands straightening the deck. When she looked up at him again, he wished he hadn't asked. "He was tall, athletic in his day. His hair was a sophisticated gray."

"He was older?"

For some reason, the thought of Gigi with an older man disturbed him. She needed someone young to match her vigor.

Her eyes took on a far-off look. "Yeah. So old that I worry he might not be around by the time I can get back. Even if he is, he probably won't be able to...perform...the way he used to."

Shane gagged on the soda he'd been drinking. She couldn't possibly mean what he thought she meant. Could she?

She sighed melodramatically and looked up at him surreptitiously, as if checking his reaction. "Such a shame. I did so enjoy our early morning...rides."

"A horse. You're talking about a horse." Shane narrowed his eyes. "At least I hope you're talking about a horse."

A bubble of laughter burst from Gigi. "Of course I'm talking about a horse—my jumper, Skywalker. What did you think I was talking about?"

"I thought you were flirting with me again."

"Now why would I do that?"

"To distract me from the next hand, so you can win and have your turn to ask a question."

She grinned. "Did it work?"

He cleared his throat, dealing the cards. "Yes," he admitted. "Seriously," he said, needing more than the jokes she'd given him. "Isn't there anyone you regret leaving behind? Family?"

Her gaze fell. She picked at a piece of lint on the bedspread. "My father..." Then she snapped up the cards and shuffled. "My turn."

He wondered what that meant, what she wanted to say about her father, but if he wanted to ask, he had to win another hand. He picked up the hand she dealt and prepared for some serious gambling.

"I'll see your one question and raise you two," Gigi said.

He'd torn the matches out of a La Casa matchbox, and they were using them as poker chips. She tossed her matches into the pot.

He studied her determined mien. She was bluffing. She had to be. Wasn't she?

If she was bluffing, she was good at it. But then she would have to be, to have lived under an assumed identity for nearly three years.

"Call," he said. He threw his matches into the hefty pot. Whoever won this hand was going to learn a lot about the other. "What've you got?"

"What's the line they say in all the old movies? Read 'em and weep?" She spread a full house—aces high, no less— on the bed in front of her crossed legs.

He tossed his cards facedown, surprisingly anxious about what questions she would ask. There were some things about him she was better off not knowing.

Her first question turned out to be easy enough. She wanted to know his favorite movie star. They debated the relative merits of Michelle Pfeiffer and Julia Roberts.

Her next questions were as lighthearted. By the time she held her last "chip" in her hand, he almost forgot to be nervous.

Until her eyes turned pensive. The headlights of a car on the highway shone through the curtains for a moment, then moved on. The noise from the highway had tapered off some-time while they'd played. It was late.

"Why are you thinking about quitting the DEA?"

The rush of self-recrimination that always accompanied any serious thought about his work flooded his system. This time he suspected the heat in his blood had as much to do with his foolishness for underestimating this woman, whoever she was, as with his mixed feelings about the DEA.

He should have known better than to play games with her. She was nobody's fool. This was supposed to be about getting information out of her, but now she'd turned his tactic to her own advantage. Instead of finding out what she'd been hiding, he was going to have to expose things about himself better left buried.

But he'd made the bet; he wouldn't welsh. "A lot of reasons. I guess...I'm just not sure I'm good enough anymore." He used to be good enough. He used to be one of the best. He was well-suited for the job. DEA agents were nomads, the fewer roots they had, the more they could concentrate on the job, wherever it took them. Shane was perfect. He didn't have any roots—any family ties—at all. He could play any role, be anybody, because he didn't know who he really was.

"But you said it's what you do. It's who you are."

"Maybe it's not who I want to be."

"Why not?"

"It's a tough job." He sounded irritable, even to himself. "I'm tired of trying to save the whole world."

Especially when so much of it didn't seem to want to be saved. Or maybe he'd been jaded by one bad experience. Either way, it was time to get out. An agent with doubts, about himself or his mission, was a danger to himself and his team. And Shane had lots of doubts.

"Tired people take vacations, they don't quit."

"You don't give up, do you?"

"No. And I didn't think you did, either."

"Don't you ever get tired of it, Gigi? Living somebody else's life?"

"I'm not living somebody else's life, I'm just using somebody else's name."

He wished it was that easy for him. "I've worked so many undercover assignments, been so many different people, that sometimes I worry I might forget who I really am. I have a hard time distinguishing between Shane Hightower, human being, and Shane Hightower, DEA Agent."

"Maybe that's because they're the same person."

"No. It can't be that way. If you can't separate the two, you can't do the job. You make mistakes."

"Everybody makes mistakes."

"Not the kind that get good men killed." He scrubbed his hands over his face, knowing she wasn't going to let him off with half an answer. "The assignment in Utah was my first one after over eighteen months of leave. It was…sort of a test. To see if I could still do the job."

"You made the arrest."

"Yeah." He made a derisive sound. "And nearly got myself and a couple of civilians killed doing it."

"That wasn't your fault."

He smiled wryly. "It never is."

Gigi fiddled with the covers on the bed while he paced the room. "Why had you been on leave?"

His mouth tightened like a vice. He wasn't sure he could open it to answer. Wasn't sure why he wanted to try. He never talked about this. Never.

"A raid on a drug warehouse had gone bad. I was hurt—"

Her expression darkened. "Seriously enough to keep you out of work for eighteen months? My God—"

"No," he assured her. "Not that seriously."

"Then what?"

"I just needed some time after…to get my head together."

He waited for her to laugh in derision or scowl in recrimination. Instead, she turned her face up to him with such an expression of care and empathy that it hurt to look at her.

He wasn't used to being the object of that kind of concern. "Two years ago," he continued, the story he never told flowing out, unstoppable as a flooding river, "an informant—Lucia Espinoza—came to me with information about a major drug op on the West Coast. She said she wanted out of the life. I believed her. She set me up undercover in the organization, and I worked there four months, making sure I could catch all the major players with their hands dirty."

"What happened?"

"It turned out one of those players was her brother. When it came time for the bust, she couldn't betray him."

"So she betrayed you instead?"

He nodded. "A good agent was killed in the raid. Two more were hurt, including me. Although I got the least of it. I was lucky."

"You couldn't have known."

"But I did know. I knew Carlos was her brother, and I kept pushing anyway. I—" He spun around, his hand raking the hair back from his forehead. He clenched it into a fist when he saw that his fingers were trembling. "Damn."

Seconds stretched on like days in silence.

Finally Shane picked up his gun from the table and methodically checked the clip, occupying his mind with anything but the memories—the guilt and the hurt. "I'm going to check outside."

"You just checked a little while ago."

"Well I'm checking again."

"Were you in love with her?"

Not only was she nobody's fool, she was too intuitive for her own good.

He pulled the door open. Outside, the night was quiet, the darkness undaunted by the sliver moon—as pale and thin as his heart—hung in the black sky. His grip tightened on the doorknob. He should answer her question before he left. She deserved to know what kind of man he really was.

"No. I wasn't in love with her," he said. "I was just sleeping with her. But it still shot my judgment all to hell."

Life was never simple. Nor was Shane Hightower, or so Gigi figured. It was getting harder and harder to think of him as just a cop who had gotten in the way of her plans. It was getting harder and harder to think of him as a cop at all, and that was dangerous.

She guessed she'd fallen for those trust-me-baby blues after all.

She thought of him alone out there, alone in the dark, patrolling the hotel grounds, keeping her safe, and she knew she had to go after him. She'd opened the wound that had driven him outside. She was too much of a healer at heart not to try to mend it.

She found him near the pool house.

He looked up at the sound of her footsteps and she saw him slide his gun back into the waist of his jeans. At least he wasn't so distracted that he'd let his guard down.

He was sitting on a short landscaping wall. His hand dangled down beside his leg, resting on a black-and-white lump she couldn't quite make out in the dark.

The lump moved, and Gigi heard a low whine, then the unmistakable thump of a tail on the ground.

She covered her mouth with her hand, her heart expanding as she recognized the stray dog that had been running in the parking lot the day they'd checked in. Any vestiges of doubt she'd had about Shane Hightower's trustworthiness vanished.

"You shouldn't be out here," Shane said as she drew close.

She lowered her hand, trying not to give away the depth of emotion raised in her by seeing Shane's hand absently scratching behind the mutt's ear, as if he didn't even realize how much comfort he was providing.

"I was worried about you being alone," she said. "I didn't know you were meeting a friend."

He pulled his hand away from the dog's ear, and the animal snuggled close to the side of his leg. "Darned dog's seen me out here so much he's started following me. I can't get rid of him."

"Uh-huh." She sat next to Shane on the landscape timbers, careful not to frighten his friend. "And here I thought all the food you were stashing in your pockets before you came out here was for you to snack on."

Shane looked away, clearly embarrassed. "I don't like to see anything go hungry." He looked down at the dog, reached out and patted his head. "Even if it is ugly as a two-headed goat."

She leaned over and slowly moved her hand toward the dog. "You're not ugly, are you fella?" When he didn't balk at her touch, she traced her fingers along his back, hips, and legs, feeling for injuries.

"Is he okay?" Shane asked.

"I think so. Besides being a little malnourished." She sat up. "Maybe we should think about getting him something to eat besides crackers and peanut butter cookies."

Shane shrugged. "I guess I can pick up some dog food next time I'm out."

"Good. Because I don't like to see anything—or anyone—hungry, either." She looked at Shane pointedly and softened her tone. "Or in pain."

"I thought you said he was okay."

"He is. I'm not so sure you are."

She sensed, more than saw, Shane stiffen. The dog at his feet must have felt it, too, because he whined and squirmed closer.

Gigi scanned the field of stars above, thinking how many wishes there were to be made in the world tonight. She wished for a few less secrets. "I don't think you were honest with me in there. Or maybe you're not being honest with yourself.''

"How's that?''

"You must have cared something for that woman, or her betrayal wouldn't hurt so much.''

"I cared all right. I cared about putting her brother out of business, even if I had to use her to do it. Sound like love to you?''

"It sounds like you had a job to do. An important one.''

"I made love to her and then I turned her against her own brother—or tried to, anyway. I don't know why I thought she'd choose me over her blood family, just because we'd enjoyed a few hours in the sack. Ego, I guess.'' He shook his head. "I should have known better.''

"You threw her a lifeline; she was the one who couldn't hang on.'' She might as well have been talking to a statue, for all the impact her words seemed to be having. "But if pretending you didn't care about her makes it easier to accept what she did, then go right ahead. Don't let me interrupt your delusions.''

She twisted to stand, but his hand shot out and stopped her before she made it up. His touch unbalanced her, and she plopped down, nearly in his lap.

The look he gave her sent a quiver of something—anticipation, apprehension, or maybe pure appetite—arrowing down through her. His lips were a mere whisper from hers.

And then even that small distance was gone.

His mouth was warm and giving—as opposite from the granite impression she'd had of him a moment ago as black was to white. Yin to Yang. Male to Female.

His teeth nibbled at her lower lip and then he suckled the tender spot, coaxing a moan from her throat. Her lips parted under his gentle assault and his tongue invaded. One of his hands cupped the back of her head. The other curled around her waist, cradling her closer.

She felt as if she was being drawn into him, inside him. She closed her eyes and saw the shrouded secrets of his soul. Felt his hurt.

Felt his need.

His burgeoning erection pressed into her hip, awakening an arousal of her own, a curling fist of pure want, winding around her femininity.

She should stop him while she still could—while *they* still could—but his hand felt so good, skimming up her rib cage to cup her breast. She arched against his palm, her nipple rising, tightening, aching under his touch.

She couldn't stop. Didn't want to stop.

But he did, apparently. The clear air of a warm Phoenix night touched her where his hands had been only seconds ago. She opened her eyes to see him standing beside the pool. Over his shoulder a cluster of stars glittered like the lights of a far-off town down a lonely highway.

He offered no soft words—either of apology or in invitation to continue in the privacy of their room what they'd started here by the pool.

Finally he reached for the hem of his shirt and pulled it over his head.

"What are you doing?" Gigi pulled her knees to her chest and locked her arms around her legs.

"Going for a swim." He extended his hand while he toed off one shoe and then the other. "Care to join me?"

"I don't have a suit."

"Neither do I."

"The water is probably freezing."

"This is Phoenix. Nothing ever freezes."

He kneeled beside her, a glimmer of danger in his eyes and more than a little seduction in his voice. "Besides, we could both use a little cooling off, don't you think?"

The water wasn't freezing, but it was chilly enough to make her gasp and suck in her breath as she hopped into the shoulder-deep pool. Her T-shirt billowed above her waist and she tugged it down. She caught Shane staring as her over-sensitized nipples puckered further, tight points clearly distended against the wet shirt molded to her breasts.

She crouched lower in the water until the surface lapped around her collarbones. "What now?"

Hands resting lightly on her waist, he turned her until she faced away from him. "Have you ever played Marco Polo?"

"More games, Hightower?"

"Have you got something better to do?"

She swirled her arms in the water, buoying her weight. If he wanted to pretend nothing had happened between them, she'd go along. For now. "It's like blind man's bluff, right?"

"Right. You close your eyes and count to five while I move away. Then you call out, 'Marco.'"

"And you have to answer, 'Polo.'"

"You follow the sound of my voice and try to catch me. If you touch me, you win. Then I'm it."

The thought of touching him—in the water or out—sounded pretty appealing. Maybe he wasn't denying what had happened after all. Maybe he just needed her to make the next move.

To feel pursued.

The thought made her heart thump. "Okay," she agreed. She closed her eyes and started counting. "One. Two."

Water rippled to her left. She hadn't heard him move; he was good. This wouldn't be easy. That was okay. She liked competition. And a challenge.

"Three. Fourfive," she finished quickly, lunging to her left at the same time.

Her fingers found nothing but water.

He was really good.

"Marco," she called.

"Polo."

His deep, quiet voice, so much more resonant with her eyes closed, caused a vibration deep inside her.

"Marco."

"Polo."

She ducked under the water and swam a few feet ahead. When she broke the surface she immediately called the signal and targeted his response as behind her. She wheeled and half ran, half swam in that direction. She'd played this game as a child. The trick was to gradually herd your opponent into a corner, where he couldn't get out without passing nearby, then feel for the movement of water and lunge.

She moved tentatively toward the direction of his voice. Somehow, childhood games had never prepared her to stalk Shane Hightower.

She stopped, listening and feeling the currents of the water. "Marco," she called out.

He didn't answer. He must have been underwater.

She waited a few seconds and called the signal again. Still no answer.

The temperature of the water seemed to drop. Chill bumps rose on her arms and thighs. Seconds passed while she waited for the soft splash that would tell her he'd resurfaced, but that sound never came.

"Marco." Her lips trembled on the word, and she told herself it was from the cold.

Only the cicadas answered her.

"Shane?" This wasn't funny anymore. He couldn't have been underwater that long.

Suddenly she was painfully aware that they should never have been playing games at all. Someone was trying to kill her. He could be here. He could already have killed—

Panic laced her blood with pure adrenaline. She opened her eyes and lunged for the side of the pool, already half out of the water before she saw him.

Shane squatted on the concrete a few feet away. Water ran

down the center of his chest, matting the fine spread of light-colored hair and dripping next to his feet. Oliver was stretched out next to him, resting his head on his paws.

Confusion stopped her cold. He didn't seem to be hurt, or in danger.

"You're not in the water," she said, still trying to sort out what was happening.

"No, I'm not."

He rose and walked to the edge, where she still hung in the water.

"But that's cheating."

He squatted back down. Nearly on eye level, just inches away, his gaze burned a path past her confusion and she knew. Knew he'd done this—scared her—on purpose.

But there was one thing she didn't know. She met his stony gaze with a rock-solid stare of her own. "Why didn't you answer when I called?"

"Maybe because I wanted you to know what it's been like for me the past few days, groping around blindly after you. After the truth."

His words hung between them until finally she began to understand. While she'd pried open the door to his past and trampled over his perceived failures and regrets like a stampeding buffalo over a field of daisies, she'd given him nothing of herself in return. She'd left the pool. Held herself out of reach.

He must have seen understanding sink in. "I don't even know your real name," he said roughly.

The need to reestablish a connection with him, to regain his trust, warred with trepidation. She was cautious with the truth for good reason. Her life depended on it.

But so did his. He'd put his blind faith in her, and she hadn't answered his call. Hadn't given him a fair chance to win. Like the woman who'd betrayed him two years ago, he'd thrown her a lifeline, and she was letting it slip through her grasp.

Slowly she lifted her hand from the edge of the pool and held it toward him, a silent request. After only a moment's hesitation, he took it, but his eyes were shuttered.

When she stood on the pool deck beside him, he turned to walk away. Pulling in a deep, calming breath, she pulled him back. Nothing was slipping through her grasp. Not tonight.

"My name now is Gigi McCowan," she told him. He slanted his head away, his mouth thin, disappointed. She pulled him back. She would give him the truth, but she also wanted him to know it wasn't as simple as a name. "But once upon a time I used to be Julia Ferrar."

His gaze was dark, impenetrable. "I don't understand."

"When I left New York, I changed more than my name. I became a different person. For once I stood up and did what I needed to do, what I thought was right, not what I thought my father would want me to do or what everyone expected. Starting over was hard, but it made me strong."

He shook his head. "I have a feeling you've always been strong, no matter what your name was."

"Maybe. But I'm happy with who I am now."

"You can't hide out forever."

"That's what you're here for, right? To find out who killed those men in New York and send him to jail. I don't want to live looking over my shoulder anymore, wondering if someone is behind me with a gun, but I don't ever want to go back to being Julia Ferrar." Her voice cracked. "I'm not sure I even like her."

Shane folded her gently into his arms and rocked her. She buried her face in the side of his neck. He smelled clean and strong.

When her breath had steadied, he blew out a breath of his own. "I know what it's like to have doubts about who you are."

From what he'd told her about his past, she could see why. But it was hard to imagine Shane less than supremely confident about anything.

"So what do we do now?" she asked.

He pulled his head back until he could look at her. "Now we go inside and you tell me all about New York."

"And then?"

"Then I'm going to fix it so that you can be whoever the hell you want to be." He cupped her jaw with his sturdy fingers and lifted her face until her gaze met his. "In the meantime, I guess it won't hurt for you to be Gigi McCowan for a few more days. It'll keep me from tripping up every time I have to say your name, anyway."

His smile warmed her from the inside out. She felt her own lips curve in answer. A few more days, that was probably all they had left together.

So why did she feel like he'd just promised her forever?

Chapter 7

Gigi had grown accustomed to waking quickly. Three years of waiting for a killer to find her had trained her to gauge her safety—or lack of it—in that first wakeful heartbeat. This morning was no different, except that this morning, her senses told her she wasn't alone.

A soft snore snuffled up from the foot of the bed. Gigi smiled in her slumber, thinking for a moment it was Shane. Despite his protests that he wasn't a gentleman, he'd very nobly slept between the bedspread and the top sheet, with his head at the foot of the bed, each of the last three nights. He hadn't snored before, but she supposed it wasn't unusual for someone to be an occasional snorer. She didn't mind. The sound was reassuring, in a way. Peaceful.

Until she realized the muffled sawing couldn't be coming from Shane. He wasn't at the foot of the bed.

Something must have interfered with her security sensors this morning, because she'd been awake a minute or more before she realized she was caught in the circle of a pair of strong, warm arms. Or that an even stronger, warmer body pressed against the length of her back. How could she not have felt the soft sough of breath tickling behind her ear?

She recognized Shane from nothing more than the breadth of his palm where it rested on her hip. But who the heck was snoring?

Her eyes blinked open wide and focused on the far end of the bed. Oliver lay curled in a circle next to Shane, his mottled black-and-white head pillowed by a bulge that was probably Shane's foot. The dog's muzzle twitched as he snuffled again, and his paw scratched impatiently at the bedcovers. Chasing rabbits in his dreams, Gigi thought.

She let her eyes drift shut, looking for a few rabbits of her own. The early morning sun filtering in through the nappy curtains over the window turned the room a soft golden shade. The warmth seeping into her body from Shane's all night long had eased her muscles like a warm oil massage. She felt languid. Content.

And for the first time in three years, she allowed herself to relax. Really relax. She basked in the luxury of hovering in that almost-sleep state, dreaming of blue skies and bluer eyes.

She couldn't recall exactly how Shane had come to be snuggled up behind her with nothing but her thin T-shirt separating skin from skin, but she didn't trouble herself over it long. It felt too good.

Vaguely she remembered tossing restlessly during the night, her sleep disturbed by the memories she'd dredged up talking to Shane. Out by the pool, with a quarter moon backdrop and under a ceiling of stars, she'd told him everything. How surprised she'd been to see Uncle Ben, her father's business partner and best friend, with another man she didn't know, but found out later was an assistant D.A., in the horse barn so late at night. How she'd seen Ben give the assistant D.A. a book. The shots and the bloody mess of death.

The police arrived quickly. She was still in shock, she thought. Another man showed up almost as soon as the uniformed officers. A tall man, with perfect skin and an expensive haircut.

The man had identified himself as the chief District Attorney Paul Branson and taken her away. Distraught over the death of his colleague, he'd warned that this was a sensitive case, and told her not to talk to anyone but him about what she'd seen and heard.

She'd waited in his car, watching out the window as the garish lights from the police cars flashed over Ben's body like something from a house of horrors.

Branson had taken her to a house he called safe and locked her away with strangers.

She told Shane how scared she'd been when the newspaper headlines announced that the prosecution had an eyewitness to the murders. The information had been leaked to the press by the insider in order to scare her into silence, the D.A. told her later. Branson had also told her that he had a suspect, but not enough evidence to make an arrest. He didn't know how long she could be in hiding. Indefinitely, maybe.

Finally she replayed the full story of the attack at the safe house for Shane, ending with how she'd abandoned everything she'd known—family, friends, job—cleaned out her bank accounts and "borrowed" the identity of an old veterinary school mentor, Dr. Gigi McCowan, and became a new person.

He'd listened patiently, interjecting a quiet question now and again, showing his understanding with a squeeze of her hand or solemn nod.

Then she'd waited for his judgment. For his condemnation that she'd run from her duty. His proclamation that she should have stayed and seen the killer brought to justice at any price, no matter how long it took. No matter what it cost.

But his judgment never came. Instead, he wrapped his

arms around her and rocked her until she had to bite her lip to keep from crying at the sweetness of it. He'd threaded his fingers through her hair, which the desert breeze had dried into wispy curls. "You're a hell of a fighter. You know that?"

He held her a long time. Eventually her eyelids had grown heavy and her muscles took on a fluid tone, and he'd taken her inside and laid her on the bed. She wondered for a moment if he meant to make love to her. For a moment, she wished he would.

But her limbs were lethargic. She felt drained, physically and emotionally. She tried to tell him, to explain.

He shushed her with a finger over her lips, smiling, then pulled the covers up to her chin and kissed her good-night on the forehead, like a parent tucking in a beloved child.

The first hours of sleep passed peacefully. Later she woke to the sound of her own whimpering, swallowed by the darkness, and an engulfing sense of loneliness that left her as hollow as when she'd been eight years old and woken up alone, frightened and missing her mother.

But the creak of the bedsprings soon reminded her that she wasn't eight years old, and she wasn't alone. Ensconced in the warmth of Shane's arms, she had slept undisturbed until dawn. But now that the sun was up, she was ready to get on with the day. Today they would talk to Margo Maitland, and take the first step toward bringing her three-year nightmare to an end.

Gently she extricated herself from Shane's grasp and eased out of bed.

"So, was it good for you?"

"What?" She stopped midstride on her way to the bathroom and wheeled to face him. His hair fell carelessly over his eyes. He looked sleepy, sexy, and oh so seductive.

"Never mind. I can see that it was."

"What are you talking about?"

"Your night's rest." He quirked one eyebrow in question. "What did you think I was talking about?"

"I thought maybe you were delirious."

"Deliriously happy to see the shadows gone from under your eyes."

His lopsided grin wormed its way straight to her heart. Not quite sure how to take this lighthearted Shane, she dug at the rough carpet with her toes and then hedged toward the bathroom. The brooding, loner agent had been easier to understand.

"I'm sorry I woke you," she finally said to fill the silent space between them.

"I've been awake half an hour."

His admission only flustered her more. There was something frighteningly vulnerable about knowing he'd held her so intimately, watching her sleep, for half an hour.

She dealt with her perceived weakness the only way she knew how—head-on. "In that case," she said, tilting her chin regally, "I hope it was good for you."

His grin widened into a rogue's smile. "It might have been, if you'd wiggled your bottom against me just a few more times."

"Wiggle—?" Flames licked across her face. She whirled, then slowed her step just enough not to appear to be running—she hoped—and sought sanctuary in the tiny bathroom. The cool tile under her feet slowly seeped the steam from her veins.

She should have known better than to try to beat Shane at his own innuendo. He was a master. And when he turned his full skills on her, she seemed to lose all ability to think coherently, much less fire off a quick-witted retort.

Her composure gradually returning, she stepped into the shower and adjusted the water. Other men had teased her, flirted with her, outright tried to seduce her, but none of them had the stinging effect of one rapier remark from Shane. He seemed to know just what to say to get a reaction out of her.

Unless it wasn't his words she was reacting to, but the man himself. He was appealing, no doubt about that—an outer layer of boyish charm not quite concealing a bad-boy attitude, both guarding a wounded soul visible only in rare glimpses, when his trust-me-baby blue eyes turned solemn, haunted.

Three days cooped up with him would make any woman fantasize about throwing him to the ground and finding out for herself if *all* of his body was as impressive as what she'd seen so far.

Her imagination conjured lots of ways, with him, to release three days' worth of pent-up energy. Maybe the waiting wouldn't be so bad if she was limp from exhaustion. Used beyond thinking, beyond caring.

Too bad she'd come to that conclusion on the day the waiting was to end. Then again, maybe it was for the best. She had a feeling that if she and Shane ever did get together, nothing would ever be the same again.

Smiling wryly, she twisted off the water faucet, stepped out of the shower, dried herself and slipped the thigh-length T-shirt she'd slept in back over her head. Determined to get herself back on even footing with Shane, she opened the bathroom door and breezed toward the dresser to pull out some clothes for the day.

Halfway across the room, she stopped. Shane sat on the foot of the bed in his briefs, his cell phone in his hand. His tanned face had paled to the color of parchment.

"Shane, what is it?"

When he raised his gaze to hers, his eyes were as vacant as an Arizona ghost town. "It's Bill Maitland," he deadpanned. "The police answered the phone at his house. He's been shot."

* * *

Shane dodged a moving van changing lanes and tried not to let himself think about what would happen if he got to the hospital too late. The officer, who'd answered the Maitland's phone and relayed the news when Shane had called, hadn't been certain of the extent of Bill's injuries. The officer only knew that it was bad. He could already be gone... No. Shane refused to acknowledge that possibility. He'd make it in time, and once he got there, everything would be all right. It had to be all right; he couldn't live with anything less.

A glance at Gigi told him that guilt weighed as heavily on her as it did on him. Her shattered expression almost cracked open the defensive wall he'd built around himself wide enough for him to reach out to her, to comfort her as he had last night. But when he tried, he found no comfort within himself to give. He struggled to dredge up a single kind word, and came up only with a gruff, "Don't."

She turned to him. "Don't what?"

"Blame yourself."

She turned to look back out the side window, as if the passing warehouses and train yards held some special interest. After a moment, she said, "I don't blame myself. I blame you."

A knife in his heart wouldn't have hurt as much, but she'd only said what he'd been thinking. "Well, we finally agree on something."

He should never have involved the Maitlands in this. Someone must have connected them to him. Bill wouldn't have told them anything, no matter what they'd done to him. He never should have gone to the Maitlands' house.

God, what had he been thinking?

He glanced at Gigi. Despite her words to the contrary, he saw the guilt in her expression. And the pain.

"Is there any chance this has nothing to do with us?" she asked. "That it's about Margo's case?"

He wished he could have said yes, but it would have been a lie. "If Margo thought there was even the slightest chance something she was working on would put her family in danger, she'd have ordered protection at the house. And she wouldn't have let the kids within a hundred miles of there."

Gigi turned back to the window, and his heart ached for her. Ached for them both.

"I told you this would happen," she said. "That they'd find me and someone would get hurt."

She turned to him and the glacial facade she'd put on broke, shifted in her tear-shimmered eyes. "You should have listened to me."

Shane flexed numb fingers on the steering wheel. "Yeah, I should have listened."

The next breath she inhaled was as ragged as a war-torn flag, riddled with holes, frayed and burned around the edges. Still, she drew her shoulders up—his proud little soldier. "Then listen now. I won't be responsible for any more deaths. When we get to the hospital, I'm leaving."

"Like hell," Shane growled. He whipped the Honda onto the shoulder of the highway. A chorus of horns sounded from behind them as cars swerved around. Turbulence from an eighteen-wheeler passing too close rocked the sedan.

Shane braced one hand on the headrest behind her, the other on the dashboard in front of her, then leaned across the seat toward Gigi. "You're not running out on this—on me—now. You're right. What happened to Bill is my fault. I've managed to hurt the only people I ever thought of as family. It's damn well not going to be for nothing. I'm going to nail the freaking cretin responsible for this, and I need you to do it."

"How, Shane? You don't even know who you're looking for. You don't even know where to start."

"No, but you do. No way is some bad guy going to all this trouble to get rid of you if you don't have anything on him. Something you saw or heard that night is important—even if you don't know it. We just have to figure out what.''

She shook her head, her brow crumpling in confusion. ''But how?''

''By going over the details. Every sight, every sound, every smell you can remember from that night. But that's going to take time, and right now I don't have time. I have to get to the hospital. I have to see Bill, and I have to know you won't bolt the first time I turn my back to you.''

Indecision warred in her expression—fear and compassion, guilt and tenacity. A diesel tanker rumbled by leaving the air acrid with exhaust. Determined calm settled on Gigi's face in its wake. ''I won't bolt—yet. But so help me, Shane. You'd better know what you're doing.''

He should have felt relief—he'd gotten what he wanted. She'd capitulated. Instead he just felt empty.

''Don't worry. I know exactly what I'm doing.''

He should. He'd had plenty of practice in revenge. It seemed like only yesterday that he'd brought his last quest for vengeance to an end. But not before it had consumed eighteen months of his life. Now he was starting another crusade. This time he wouldn't fool himself into mistaking revenge for redemption. He wouldn't hope that once he'd had his reprisal against Bill's attacker he would feel whole again; he'd just hope there was enough left of his soul to feel at all.

Ten minutes later, his defensive walls firmly back in place, he slammed the car door in the parking lot of Phoenix's University Hospital. ''Have you got the Taurus?'' he asked.

''In my purse,'' Gigi called, climbing out the other side of the car. She looked back. ''What about Oliver?''

Shane whistled the dog out of the car and hustled toward the hospital in long strides, listening for Gigi's hurried step behind him to be sure she was close.

Near the base of the white marble steps that led inside the building, a hedgerow cast a line of shade on a small grassy area. Shane commanded, "Down," and Oliver obeyed. But as he stepped away, the dog let out a frantic whine. One look at the dog told him he thought he was being abandoned again.

Impatient to get inside and see about Bill, Shane hesitated only a second. It would have to be enough. His hand lingered on the cur's scratchy-coated head. "I'll be back for you boy. I promise," he said none too smoothly, then walked away, Gigi on his heels.

At the end of a narrow hall smelling of floor wax and suffering, a tall, thin man with close-cropped light-brown hair and wire-rimmed glasses slumped against a wall, his hands in his pockets. Shane recognized him even before the man raised his head. "Ronnie? How is he?"

Bill Maitland's son raised a devastated gaze to Shane's. Dreading the answer, and Ronnie's reaction to his presence, Shane hung back, out of striking distance.

Ronnie had been seventeen and obviously resentful the first time Bill had brought Shane home for dinner. Not that he blamed the kid—he'd intruded on the time and attention of Ronnie's parents. By the time Shane was spending whole weekends at the Maitlands', coming to blows was inevitable. One Saturday, when Bill and Margo went on an impromptu excursion to the movies, Ronnie popped Shane in the jaw hard enough to rock him back on his heels. Shane barely pulled his own punch in time.

He could have pounded Ronnie Maitland, but he didn't. He was supposed to be older, wiser. Ronnie was eighteen then, but just out of high school. Shane was a sophomore in college. Age and size had not proved to be the biggest reasons he'd held his temper in check, though.

Shane had looked at Ronnie and in that instant seen the defiant chin he'd inherited from his mother and the deep-pocketed eyes he'd inherited from his father. Ronnie was Bill and Margo's son, their blood, not him. Shane would never usurp his place in their lives. He had no business trying.

Since that time, he'd carefully maintained just that little bit of distance from the Maitlands, no matter how they'd tried to draw him into their family goings-on. He held himself apart from them so he would remember who was blood, and who was not.

This morning, it wasn't Shane's deference to Ronnie's position as family that kept Shane across the hall from him as he talked. It was guilt so burdensome it bordered on shame.

"He's in surgery," Ronnie answered. "They had to wait until they got him stabilized before they could even try to take the bullet out. I don't know much else."

"Were you there when it happened? Did you see who shot him?"

"No. He was alone. I came by to pick him up—we were all going to the movies, him and Rhonda and the kids and me—" Ronnie's voice cracked.

"Where is your family now?" Shane asked impatiently. He felt Ronnie's pain as well as he felt his own, but he had to make sure no more Maitlands died today. Check that. He had to make sure no Maitlands at all died today. Bill wasn't dead. Not yet.

Ronnie raised his head, his gaze unsteady. "Why?"

"You need to get some uniformed officers on them."

"Already done. Mom ordered it by phone from the airplane. She's on her way back." His voice didn't crack then. It was solid. Deadly hard. "What's going on here, Hightower? What do you know about this?"

Shane drew up his back, taking a deep breath. He couldn't tell Ron everything, but he wasn't a man to shy from his responsibility. "Someone was looking for me, I think. Bill had been trying to help me get in touch with your Mom."

"Dammit, Shane!" Ronnie exploded, glaring momentarily at Gigi again, "You involved my father in one of your—"

At that moment, a man wearing pea-green medical scrubs and a complexion that didn't look much healthier pushed open a door and padded toward them with little sterile paper covers over his shoes muffling the sound of his footsteps. "Mr. Maitland," he asked, looking from Shane to Ronnie.

Ronnie stepped forward. Shane deferred, but didn't back off. He couldn't step away without hearing what the doctor had to say. His heart pounded and his throat went dry in the second it took the doctor to speak.

"Your father came through the surgery without complications, Mr. Maitland. We repaired the damage from the bullet, but we're concerned about the degree of internal bleeding. He's stable for now. The next twenty-four hours should tell us more."

Shane backed away silently. His throat was still parched and his stomach boiled like an evil cauldron. Bill was stable—but he wasn't out of the woods. That was all he needed to know. These few minutes while Ronnie got the details from the doctor would likely be Shane's only chance to see Bill, and he wasn't going to miss it.

A uniformed guard leaned on the counter around the nurse's duty station. Shane swore.

Gigi took a deep breath. "You stay out of sight. I'll distract them."

"No. You stay with me."

"No one knows we're here. It's safe. But I can only give you a minute."

He knew he shouldn't do it. He had to look out for Gigi.

But he also had to see Bill. He nodded tersely. "Just one minute."

As he stepped into the doorway, Gigi moved down the hall, spinning in circles and looking lost. "Oh, my. This doesn't look like the right ward."

The guard at the desk straightened.

Gigi stroked his arm. "Maybe you could help me. I seem to be lost."

Shane grinned. It was the guard who was lost. She had

him hooked. A minute later, he and the duty nurse both were pointing and waving and giving directions. Shane slipped around the corner.

Inside Bill's room, Shane stared in horror at the withered figure lying still on the bed. He'd expected the tubes dripping lord-knew-what into his system and the hissing ventilator and beeping monitors, but he hadn't expected—couldn't conceive of—Bill's deathly stillness and quiet.

Bill Maitland had an infectious passion for life. Bill had a way of making everything around him bigger, brighter, clearer—a trait he shared with his wife of thirty-one years, Margo. In that way, they were both like older versions of Gigi.

At least he had been until today. The alabaster-skinned man on the bed with a tube in his nose and another in his throat bore little resemblance to the friend Shane knew.

Seeing him like that, there was only one thing to do. In a gesture as foreign to him as picking out a Mother's Day card, he reached out and took Bill's hand. He rested his fingers on the man's palm. Shocked at the cool, dried-leather feel of his skin, Shane wrapped the man's fingers around his own. In a voice as rough as broken glass, he told Bill to hang on. He wasn't ready to let go. Not yet. Maybe not ever.

Looking at his friend, lying so limp, Shane wrestled with a sense of shame as powerful as any he'd felt. And he'd felt a lot in his life.

He'd been foolish—selfish—to think of Bill as family. He didn't deserve a family. He had come into life alone and that was how he would leave it. The best he could hope for was to not leave too much wreckage in his wake as he passed through it.

A flood of emotion filled his passages until he had to open his mouth to draw in a noisy breath.

He felt as raw as an exposed nerve. Outside in the hallway

he heard Gigi chattering nervously with the nurse and the guard. She was getting louder, warning him, he thought.

"I have to go, Bill." He hoped his friend could hear him, would know he had come. "I'm sorry."

He squeezed his friend's hand one last time, then let it fall back on the bed, the sight haunting him as he slipped out of the room.

Three steps down the hall he stopped, wincing and wishing he'd turned the other direction down the passageway. A man built like a linebacker—but showing the effects of some forty-five years of gravity on what had once been an impressive bulk—strode purposely down the hall, shrugging off a brown suit coat and loosening his tie as he walked.

Shane stopped, holding Gigi back by extending his arm out beside him. "Hugh Fitzsimmons," he said.

"Your boss?"

He never answered. Fitz bore down on them before he had a chance. "Well, well, that was easy. I thought you were going to make me chase you all over the state before I caught up with you."

Shane ignored the barb. "Hey, Fitz. How are the kids?"

Fitzsimmons tugged at his tie, the knot already hanging three buttons down his shirtfront. "They're teenagers, how do you think they are? They're driving me crazy. And don't make nice. You're hip deep in trouble with me, Hightower."

"What are you doing here, Fitz?" Shane asked wearily.

"Bill Maitland gets shot a few days after you go missing from Utah in a blaze of gunfire and you don't think I know you have something to do with it? I figured you'd show up here. I just didn't know it would be so quick." He shot a glance at Gigi. "This the veterinarian who's missing from up there, too? There's a whole town pretty upset about the two of you taking off without a word. Some big-shot corporate type from L.A. named Randall has been calling my office every day, wanting to know what's going on."

So Eric was looking for him. Looking for Gigi, most likely. Mariah would be worried.

Shane decided to avoid the issues of Utah and Gigi altogether, if he could. "What do you know about what happened to Bill?"

"I know he took two in the gut, close range."

Shane blanched at Fitz's lack of tact.

"What do you know about it?" Fitz finished.

He glanced sideways at Gigi, saw the worry on her face, the tension in her shoulders. He'd promised only to talk to Margo. But dammit, Fitz was going to demand an explanation. His boss was like a bulldog when he got his teeth in a juicy bone like this. But he'd given his word...

Shane squared his shoulders. "Nothing."

Fitz's face darkened. "Bull."

Shane hesitated, feeling the noose tighten. "I'll fill you in later." He tugged on Gigi's elbow, urging her to make a quick escape with him.

Fitz stopped them both with a booming voice. "You'll fill me in now, agent, or this pitiful performance you call a career is going to be over before you know it."

Slowly Shane turned, feeling like the clock had just struck midnight even though it was just midday. His time was up.

He finally had to decide once and for all between Shane Hightower the DEA agent and Shane Hightower the man. The choice was easier than he'd expected. Because enforcing the law wasn't about badges or careers. It was about helping people and standing up for what was right.

With Gigi, he had a chance to do just that. To keep his promise. To make one last stand.

Without a moment's regret, he reached to his back pocket and drew out the leather wallet that had held his badge for the past eight years. Dropping it at Fitz's feet was easier than he expected. Gigi and Fitz looked down in disbelief. Shane held his gaze level. "This pitiful performance is over now."

Fitz's face squished up so that the bridge of his nose wrinkled. "Then I believe you owe me more than a badge."

Anger rose like a hot air balloon in Shane's chest. He knew what Fitz wanted. And he knew it was a lousy time to give it up. Unfortunately, he also knew he had no choice. His weapon was DEA issue.

He pulled the pistol out roughly, checked the load and the safety and shoved it at Fitz. His boss's hands remained at his sides.

"You sure you want to do this?" Fitz asked in a voice softer than it should have been. As if he didn't want to hear the answer he knew would be coming.

Shane physically lifted Fitz's hand and slapped the gun into his palm. "I've been sure for nearly two years. I just haven't had the guts to do anything about it."

As he walked away, it seemed like two decades, two lifetimes. His step was unusually light, as if he'd sloughed more than just the weight of his badge and his gun. He'd sloughed a responsibility he could no longer bear.

Gigi stepped in front of him as they waited for the elevator, looking shell-shocked. "Are you all right?"

"Do you still have the revolver in your bag?"

She nodded.

"Then I'm fine."

She looked about ready to rebel—he knew that wasn't answer enough to satisfy her—when a man stepped out of a doorway behind them. Shane automatically reached for the gun that wasn't there anymore in the moment before he recognized Ronnie.

Ronnie looked from Shane to Gigi. "You're leaving?"

"Yeah."

"You saw him already?"

Shane felt a prick of guilt at sneaking in to see Bill before Bill's own son had visited him. But what was a pinprick to the open wounds his other faults had left. "Yeah."

Surprisingly, Ronnie's eyes held no anger. Or at least if they did, it couldn't be seen through the sheen of weariness on Ronnie's eyes. "Good." He swallowed hard. "Dad would want you to stop in before you left."

Shane could only nod, a sheen of his own rising behind his eyes. He took a step past Ron, but Ron stopped him with a hand on his arm.

"Tell me what she needs to know to help you," he said firmly.

"What?" Shane asked.

"Mom will be here soon. Tell me what to tell her."

Ronnie was offering to help, after what Shane had done? Shane shook his head. "No. She'll have enough on her mind."

"She'll need something to keep her busy while she waits, or she'll go crazy." Ron smiled weakly. "Besides, Mom'll have both our butts if you walk out of here like this. So tell me."

Troubled, Shane looked to Gigi. He saw her mind turn the possibilities. Finally, she nodded.

"Tell Margo—*if* she is able—to look into a double homicide in New York some three years ago. A prominent businessman and an assistant district attorney. I need to know who was on the suspect list."

Ronnie nodded brusquely, as if glad to have something to do besides wait.

Shane started to leave, then stopped. "And Ron, tell her to be careful. There may be someone on the inside in this."

"You be careful, too." He looked back and forth from Gigi to Shane. "Both of you."

He put out his hand. Shane held his own back only a second, then reached out and clasped the hand of his one-time rival for Bill and Margo's attention in his own. Ronnie looked at him, his eyes hurting, but warm and intelligent. Caring and not at all grudging.

Sometime in the last ten or eleven years Ronnie had grown up, and Shane hadn't noticed.

The elevator doors chimed open. Shane and Gigi stepped inside. Shane held the doors back with one hand when they started to shut. "When he wakes up, tell him I love him."

"He already knows. But I'll remind him."

Shane let the door close.

Outside, he stopped long enough to collect Oliver, who leaped all over them both in joy. He also pulled the pistol out of Gigi's bag and stuffed it in the back of his jeans.

Halfway across the parking lot, he hissed and jerked her back. Two men were leaning over Bill's Honda, peering in the windows. He leaned around the minivan shielding them from the men's sight and pointed them out to Gigi. "Recognize either of those guys?"

"No."

He pulled out the gun he'd just taken from her.

"What are you doing?" she asked, her voice high and tight.

"Going to get some answers."

She grabbed his sleeve before he crept around the front bumper of the van. "Are you crazy? There are two of them."

"And one of me. Odds are in my favor." The old feelings were back. Confidence. Immortality. All the things that made a good DEA agent. Too bad he wasn't one anymore.

"What are you going to do with them if you catch them?" she reasoned desperately. "Beat the truth out of them in a hospital parking lot?"

"Who says I was going to give them a chance to talk?" he asked irritably, cocking the gun. The men who maybe shot Bill were twenty feet away, and she was talking common sense. He didn't want to hear it.

"You're not going to kill them."

"Why not?"

"Because I know you."

He sighed. "What do you want to do, let them go? They're the best lead we've had."

She looked anxiously at the men and then at the hospital. "There were all kinds of cops in there. Call them."

"And leave Bill unprotected. Not a chance."

"What about me? Are you going to leave me unprotected?"

Those were probably the only words that could have stopped him. And they did. Dead in his tracks. He lowered the gun.

Angrily, he pulled out Bill's cell phone and stabbed in a number from memory.

"Fitzsimmons."

"It's me."

"Change your mind already?"

"No. But if you're interested in finding out who shot Bill Maitland, you might start by asking the men crawling all over his car in the south parking lot."

He hung up and pulled Gigi away from the minivan, careful to keep them both out of sight of the men prowling the parking lot.

"What now?" she asked when they were a hundred yards away.

He pointed across the lot. "See that red Jeep Grand Cherokee over there?"

"Mm-hm."

"That's our ride."

When they reached it, he bent over and fished around under the bumper. "Fitz has a teenage daughter who is always locking the keys in the car. She's done it so many times he had to get one of those magnetic boxes to hide a spare in."

He found his prize and pulled it out, then unlocked the door for Gigi. When he'd settled in the driver's seat across from her, she asked, "We're stealing your boss's car?"

"Ex-boss. And not only that, we're stealing his house, too."

Chapter 8

"You're sure this is a good idea?" Gigi asked, clutching Shane's hand as they walked up to the porch.

"I just quit my job. You think they're going to look for me at my boss's house? Even he doesn't know we're here."

Fitz's house turned out to be a vacation cabin on Lake Pleasant, outside Phoenix. His daughter must have been as bad with house keys as she was with car keys, because Shane walked straight to a fake rock in the middle of a cactus garden, bent over, and came up with a door key.

Inside, he pulled a second set from a rack in the hall and gave them to Gigi. "Hang on to those. I want to keep the place locked up while we're here."

Gigi took the keys without question and walked around the house, checking out the large master bedroom and bath on the ground floor. In the kitchen she found enough canned goods to hold them a few days, and spotted a compact washer-and-dryer set in the mudroom by the back door.

At least they wouldn't have to hand-wash their clothes any longer.

The living room was both spacious and cozy, with a stone fireplace—although she couldn't imagine why, in Arizona—and a nook full of colorful throw pillows nestled in a bay window.

If she didn't look outside, she might have thought she was back in the mountains. But she did look out. The view was pretty in its own way, even if it wasn't as heavenly as the scene out the massive glass wall of Shane's Utah home.

Here, the land was level instead of jagged, but it gave a welcoming impression, and opened up more of the sky. It was quieter, without so many birds to fill the silence with song, but quiet was good for thinking, and she and Shane had a lot of thinking to do about what had happened and what to do next. A trail marked by a few sentry pines led the short distance to Lake Pleasant. The water's surface glittered like a sleek sheath of blue-and-silver-sequined satin rippling in a kind breeze.

Shane sat on a boulder by the waterfront with Oliver lying by his side. Physically he was only thirty yards from the cabin, but emotionally she had a feeling he was in another world. A world where he felt responsible for Bill Maitland's shooting.

She hadn't helped any, easing her own guilt by turning her anger on him earlier, blaming him. Surely he knew she hadn't meant it. That she'd only lashed out from fear and frustration.

Still, the damage was done. He'd pulled away from her. It hurt, watching him sort through his pain alone after their closeness this morning, but she let him be, sensing his need for solitude.

She busied herself putting together a meal from what she could find in the cupboards and sitting in that cozy bay window seat, waiting for him. Willing him to come inside. To come to her.

By dusk, she couldn't stand it a minute longer. She scuffed her feet as she walked up behind him, making him aware of

her presence long before she rested on the rock beside him.
"I scrounged up some soup and some potted meat from the
supplies inside," she told him, searching for safe ground to
start a conversation, "I can heat it up whenever you'd like."

"Thanks." He didn't even turn his head.

"Shane...I'm sorry."

"For what?"

"For saying that I blamed you for what happened to Bill."

He shrugged. "Why shouldn't you blame me? I do."

The sun touched the horizon and set the lake on fire.

"None of this is your fault. You were only trying to
help—"

He stood abruptly and she had to clench her hand to keep
from reaching out to him.

"We should go in." He shoved his fingers in the front
pockets of his jeans, hunching his shoulders and looking at
the ground. "It's going to be dark soon."

They walked inside and she cooked a meal, which he
hardly touched. When she volunteered to do a load of laundry, he gave up his dirty shirt, throwing the clean replace-
ment she'd found for him in a closet over the back of the
couch.

"How about a little radio?" She reached for the dial of a
boom box on a table in the dining room.

"No. I need to hear what's happening outside."

Squashing her annoyance at his curt tone, she let her hand
fall to her side. He was right. With the road outside being
gravel, they'd hear if a car approached, if the house was
quiet. Shane had closed the blinds and insisted on lighting
only a couple of small candles instead of turning on a lamp.
He didn't want them to make easy targets through the window. The candles bathed the room in dim, watery light. The
smell of tallow weighed down the air.

She couldn't bear to be in this house with him—how long?

A day? Two? Maybe more?—with nothing but darkness and tense silence to fill the gulf between them.

"Bill is going to be all right," she suggested. "I know it."

His head snapped up, his eyes glinting like steel in the semidarkness. "Is that your medical opinion, Dr. Ferrar? Treat a lot of gunshot wounds in horses, do you?"

"No, but I've treated you for them twice now."

His eyes still gleamed defiantly, but his chest deflated enough to let her know she'd at least partially hit her mark.

"A couple of scratches is hardly the same thing as two rounds in center mass," he muttered.

"No, it's not. But I've talked to a lot of patients' families after surgery. I know how a doctor words things when he's preparing them for the worst, and that isn't how that doctor was talking to Ron Maitland."

Shane's scowl buckled. An ember of hope burned in his soulless eyes. He looked at her with such longing, such need to believe what she was saying that her heart cried for him. She wished he would put his head on her shoulder and cry for his friend. It would have been easier to take than that yearning stare.

But she knew that would never happen. Her proud protector buried his pain deep inside him. He'd never let anyone bear a part of his burden.

The moment stretched; time ran as slowly as molten wax down the side of a fat candle. Shane had combed the long length of his hair back. She reached up and brushed it down over his eyes.

His lips parted, as if he needed more breath, and impulsively she let her hand fall to his back, ran it up and down the length of his spine, over the taut muscles of his shoulders in a soothing stroke.

He leaned into her touch for a hint of a moment, his eyelids drifting shut. Then his chest heaved and he pushed away from her. Disappointment weighed heavy on her limbs, and she dropped her numb hand to her thigh.

Shane shuffled across the room with his back to her, looking upward. "I want you to sleep up in the loft tonight."

She followed his gaze to a ladder against the far wall and a little room she hadn't noticed before, tucked between the rafters of the cabin's vaulted ceiling. She hadn't noticed the loft earlier. "Why?"

"You'll be out of harm's way if someone kicks in the door. They won't be expecting you to be up there."

A sick feeling washed through her stomach. "And where will you be?"

"Down here. In the big bedroom."

In the big bedroom. In the big bed. Alone. And she'd be alone in the loft. She would have laughed, if it hadn't been so sad. She'd slept by herself all her life. Now, after four nights with him, she couldn't bear the thought of sleeping without him.

Swallowing her pride and mustering up all the confidence that a woman who'd been rejected all her life, starting with her own father, could muster, she stepped up close behind Shane. Even without touching him she could feel the warmth—and the hurt—radiating from him.

She circled him from behind with her arms, brushed her hands through the bristly hair of his chest. "What if I said I want *you* in the loft tonight?"

He jerked away as if he'd been stung. "Don't."

"Don't what? Don't touch you? Don't try to make you feel better? Don't try to make this night a little easier for you?"

He stalked the room like a lion circling his pride, occasionally throwing a glance her way. "Yes."

The fine thread of her control snapped. She was humiliated. And afraid. "It's all right for the big, bad DEA agent to protect and console the poor witless female, but when he's hurting, heaven forbid he should accept a little comfort in return.''

''Is that what you think I want from you, Gigi? *Comfort?*'' He stopped pacing in front of her and leaned forward. Just a fraction, but it was enough. The room seemed to shrink. His presence overshadowed everything—time and place. A male in all his glory, conquering all that stood in his path, lording over all he left in his wake.

Her breath hitched, but she refused to back down. She reached out and flattened her palm against his bare chest. Her confidence grew with each beat of his pounding heart. He could pretend disinterest. He could pretend to be unaffected.

She knew better.

''What do you want from me, Shane? Tell me.''

An explosive blast of air hissed from his lungs. He took a quick step back, raking the hair off his forehead and pulling at the roots. ''Dammit, Gigi. You can't touch me like that, look at me like that and expect to slip into bed later all safe and prim and proper. I'm not that noble, and I'm not that strong. Not tonight.''

''Maybe you should let me be the strong one tonight,'' she said quietly.

''I'm trying to protect you.''

''I know that. What I don't know is what you're trying to protect me *from.*''

In a flash the room turned. Or maybe she turned, but not of her own free will. The rough stone of the fireplace pressed against her back. Shane pressed against her front.

Even if there had been a fire in the hearth, it wouldn't have been warmer than the heat radiating from his body. He pressed a kiss against the tender flesh of her neck beneath her ear. He suckled on the column of her throat. He grazed his whiskers along the valley between her breasts, abrading her even through the cotton of her T-shirt.

When his leg wedged hers apart, she opened herself oblig-

ingly. Before she'd recovered from the multitude of sensations created by his thigh gyrating against hers, his hand
found her breast and molded her to his touch. His mouth
found hers and their tongues danced, mated.

Her heart pounded as raucously as his had been beating
when she'd touched him a few moments ago. Her head was
spinning, her world contained in the bubble of pleasure surrounding her.

Desperate for a gulp of air, she pulled her mouth away.

"That." He cupped the back of her head, steadying her at
the waist as he eased himself away from her.

"What?" she asked dizzily.

"What you're feeling right now," he said, still not making
sense. "And this." He grasped her hand and pressed it over
the juncture of his legs. "That feeling that you can't get
enough air. That you're drowning. That your heart is going
to explode. That nothing else matters or ever will matter.
That's what I'm protecting you from."

"I don't understand." She hadn't moved her hand, didn't
want to, though the heat of him burned her fingertips where
he pulsed against her.

He threaded his fingers through the curls at her temple.
"Since the day we met, we've been like two trains steaming
headlong toward each other on the same track. When we
collide, lady, there's not going to be anything *comforting*
about it. It's going to be a helluva wreck. Are you ready for
that?"

Her chest rose and fell rapidly against his, but she couldn't
get enough air. She felt lightheaded. Dizzy.

Aroused.

Shane stared at her, his blue eyes mesmerizing her.

Breathlessly, she pulled together two words. "Choo-
choo."

Shane's conscious mind spun in a vain attempt to catch
up with the unconscious demands of his body. Things had

happened fast—too fast. One second he'd been arguing with Gigi. The next he had her pressed up against a wall again, lifting her until she fit him just right, supporting her thighs as she wrapped her legs around his hips and pulled him closer.

Their mouths fused. Hot, wet and hungry, he tasted her. Her flavor was as unique as the rest of her. Tart, like a lemon drop.

She skimmed her hand over his chest and pinched his nipple and the shock blasted straight to his groin. Not that he needed any further stimulation. He was already painfully hard. The soft cotton of his briefs chafed like sandpaper. Focusing on anything beyond getting out of the confining undergarments and into the smooth, wet heat of her was beyond him.

He cupped her behind and lifted her away from the wall. "Upstairs," he managed to gasp, and stumbled toward the ladder.

Dear God, a ladder. How was he going to climb and carry her and not break both their necks?

Halfway across the room, he forgot about the ladder. If Gigi rocked against him one more time, squeezing him with her legs and arching her hips, he wasn't going to last long enough to get there anyway. He stopped behind the sofa, resting her on the back while he reached over to the table and snuffed out the candles with his fingers.

Gasping, Gigi snatched his hand, examining his fingertips for burns. He didn't have any—he'd been putting candles and matches out that way since he was a kid. But he liked the way she studied each fingertip in turn, then drew it into her mouth and soothed it with her moistness just in case.

Her suckling nearly put him over the edge. He picked her up again and headed toward the ladder.

She looked at him curiously, and he answered her unspoken question. "I still want you in the loft tonight."

"Because its safer?"

"No," he said, the truth spilling unbidden off his tongue. "Because it has a skylight."

The exquisite curiosity in her expression captured him. Pulled the beat from his heart. He'd slept up there once when he and Fitz had spent a weekend here resting up after a tough case. He'd never forgotten how beautiful the tapestry of light in the sky had been that night, or the healing peace he'd found staring up at it. He'd hoped Gigi would find the same solace, sleeping in the loft.

Now, he realized, he wanted more than for her to see the beauty of the night. He had his own selfish reasons for wanting her in the loft. "I want to see the stars in your eyes when I make love to you," he admitted.

Her whole demeanor softened, like he'd just pulled a dozen roses from behind his back.

The ladder didn't prove too difficult. Gigi climbed on her own with Shane just one rung behind her, his arm wound protectively around her waist as her behind wiggled provocatively against his chest. By the time he crawled over the top rung and flung himself onto the futon mattress on the loft floor, any pretense of civility was beyond his reach. He was feeling primitive. Savage.

A blood lust made him pull her down on top of him and strip her T-shirt in one explosive burst of movement. Rolling her beneath him, he claimed her breast with his mouth. He tasted her soft flesh and pulled at the hardened tip with his teeth, reveling in the sharp little sounds of pleasure she made and the arch of her back as she rose to meet him.

He fumbled with the drawstring of her shorts a moment and then had them off, hardly noticing the grating rip of fabric as she shoved the garment insistently out of his way. And then his fingers were parting her, inside her, stunned but not surprised at her heat and wetness. She was as ready as he was, maybe more.

She was close to climax. He could have her there in seconds with just the right touch, just the right urging.

Never one to let someone else call all the shots, Gigi pushed his wrist away, then unbuttoned his jeans, unzipped his fly and took matters into her own hands.

Shane pulled back a groan as she squeezed him gently. This was what he liked about Gigi—not what she was doing to him physically, although that wasn't half-bad, either—but her initiative. Her independence. Her zest for living and her zeal for experiencing everything that life had to offer.

How many other women would have saved themselves the way Gigi had? How many would have turned their backs on the cops and the system that had failed them and taken their safety—their very survival—on themselves? And of those few that might have, how many would have made it, as she had?

Not many, he suspected.

Finally letting his groan slip as she worked her magic fingers along his length, Shane rolled to his back, carrying her with him so that she straddled him, and let her explore.

She splayed her palms across his chest, massaged his pectorals, scraped her nails lightly down his rib cage, all the while her hips hovering just over his, swaying out of reach then swooping daringly low, caressing lightly. He closed his eyes, wrapped in a blanket of sensation—the feel of her moistness against him, the sound of her short, choppy breaths, the heady smell of arousal.

When she went quiet and still, he opened his eyes. Gigi looked down on him serenely, as if she was listening to something inside herself, savoring a favorite piece of music.

"What are you doing?"

In answer, she reached behind herself and pulled his knees up so that his thighs made a backrest for her. She leaned against him, poising herself over him and started to slide slowly, excruciatingly slowly, down.

He tried to stop her with his hands on her hips. He opened his mouth to explain that it was too soon. That he wanted to pleasure her in other ways before they joined in this final, irrevocable act.

But she never gave him the chance.

"Shh." She placed her fingertips over his mouth like a kiss. "Maybe I want to see the stars reflected in *your* eyes while I make love to you."

And she did make love to him. He let her control the rhythm and the flow, raising and lowering her body over him until his fingers cramped from clenching the twisted cover of the futon. Until the starlight she'd wanted to see in his eyes glistened off his sweat-sheened body as well. Until his lungs burned and his groin was on fire.

He'd heard other men banter indiscreetly in the locker room about "taking" a woman. The phrase had always left a sour taste in his mouth—as if their partners were inanimate and uninvolved.

He much preferred Gigi's style of lovemaking. A woman couldn't get much more involved in the event than she was at that moment, bobbing up and down on his sex. A sensual haze clouded her crystalline gaze. She looked lost in the act. Lost in him. He couldn't imagine anything more humbling. Or more arousing.

He let her control the pace as long as he could stand it, then when the need for release drove all semblance of sanity from his mind, he gripped her hips and held her down as he thrust upward, hammering himself into her with as much force as he could muster.

She groaned and leaned back against his thighs again, angling her hips to embed him deeper and pulling his knees under her arms for support. Her head tipped back, exposing the creamy, gulping column of her throat to the moonlight. Her milky breasts bobbed with the power of his strokes.

He was on the brink, couldn't hold on much longer, but he didn't want to cross that barrier without her. Hardly able to find breath for the words and not slowing his jackhammering hips a beat, he reached out for her hand and pulled her down to his chest. "Come here, baby. We're almost there. Come with me."

"I can't," she nearly sobbed.

"Sure you can." His voice sounded strangled, almost incoherent even to himself. "We'll do it together."

He slipped a hand between their bodies and between her legs. "Ready?"

Not waiting for an answer, he found the center of her sensuality among her swollen folds and pressed hard with his thumb and forefinger. Her back arched and she let out a long, strangled cry as her body shuddered immediately around his. He let go with a guttural moan of his own and followed her into oblivion.

Sweet, sweet oblivion.

Some minutes later—he couldn't be sure how many— Shane realized he was engulfed in darkness. A black that was blacker than any night. And then he opened his eyes.

Gigi's chin rested on his shoulder and over her, a star-sequined heaven shone down on them. Apparently recovering at about the same rate as him, she turned her head toward the skylight a moment, then lowered her head back to his chest.

"Wherever I end up living next," she said dreamily, "I'm going to have to get one of those."

He couldn't have agreed more. In fact, he would cut the hole in the roof for her, if he had to. Not that he planned to wait for her to get settled somewhere else to see the stars reflected in her eyes.

Gently he turned them so that she was beneath him.

"Again?" she asked breathlessly.

He pasted a kiss on the end of her nose, watching her eyes glitter. "There's a lot of starlight left yet tonight, sweetheart. And I plan to make use of every minute of it."

The next morning, entwined in each other's arms, they watched the sky turn from velvet gray to aqua, too exhausted and limp to move. The sheets were twisted into tangled ropes around them. Their clothes were nowhere to be seen.

Gigi turned her head and sighed contentedly against his neck. "I should get up and get us something to eat."

"Maybe I should get up."

She stabbed a finger in his gut. "You've been up quite enough for one night, don't you think?"

He rolled on top of her playfully. "Oh, I don't know. I think you could still get a rise out of me, if you tried."

She tensed a little beneath him. The pitch of her laugh scaled too high, as if it were forced.

"Are you sore?" Fanning her hair out on the pillow behind her, he searched her eyes for the truth and found what he needed to know. "I'm sorry. I should have gone easier."

"Nah." She reached out and stroked the two days' beard growth on his jaw. "You just should have shaved."

He shucked into his jeans while she pulled her T-shirt over her head, then he followed her down the ladder.

"It looks beautiful outside," she called without looking back as she hurried across the living room. "I'm going to clean up and then maybe get some air. Why don't you fix us something to eat?"

"That wouldn't be a good idea."

She looked back. "Why not? Can't you cook?"

"I can cook just fine. But it wouldn't be a good idea for you to get some air."

"Why not? We were outside yesterday."

He raked his hand through his hair, realizing too late that

he should have told her last night what he'd seen—why he'd stayed sitting out on that rock out front so long. "Yeah, I meant to talk to you about that."

"About what?"

He pulled in a deep breath and prepared to be blasted. "We're being watched."

Shock and incredulity settled on her face. "Watched?" she said. "By whom?"

"A few of my *buddies* from the agency, I think."

"You think?" she chided. Incredulity was fast giving way to anger.

"One of them looked like Bald Billy Mac—an agent I worked with a couple of years ago."

"But why would your buddies be watching us? And how did they find us?"

"I figure Fitz set them on us. Maybe he had us followed from the hospital—although I sure didn't catch a tail and I don't remember Bald Billy being that good. More likely he traced us using the car. Fitz never mentioned having one of those antitheft vehicle locator systems, so I didn't think to check."

He glanced up at her and shrugged. "Sorry."

Gigi's spine looked stiff as a flagpole. "You've known this since last night," she said as if she'd just realized there was no other time he could have seen the men spying on them, "and you didn't think to tell me?"

He gave her a dry look. "I got distracted, if you recall."

"They could have been watching us!"

"Relax, we kept the light low in here, remember? And no way could they see into the loft, even if they had night vision equipment, which I doubt. There aren't any windows up there except the one in the ceiling."

"You still should have told me."

"When would have been the best time for that, do you think? When I was on top or when you were?"

Her face flamed. He instantly was sorry he'd embarrassed her. Last night wasn't something he ever wanted her to regret.

"Gigi..."

She stomped into the bedroom without giving him a chance to apologize. Seconds later, the bathroom door slammed shut hard enough to shake dust off the roof. He waited to hear the click of the lock on the bathroom door, took a deep breath, then grinned. He suspected her huff was as much morning-after jitters as real anger. She hadn't looked him in the eye all morning.

Not that he blamed her. He wasn't entirely comfortable with last night, either. Not because he regretted it, or because of some puritanical sense of guilt about what they'd done, but because of the sheer intensity of it. He'd lost control—no—freely and willfully given up control. Surrendered himself to her, body and mind. It was like she'd climbed inside his body, the way she knew exactly what he wanted, how he needed to be touched, without him asking. And he'd known the same about her, somehow. He'd just *known*.

They hadn't just had sex last night; they'd made a connection. A connection so strong that to break it would be like amputating a limb. He might never be whole without her.

And that scared him.

His only consolation was that he thought he saw the same fear in her eyes. Because they couldn't stay together forever, and they both knew it. As close as they were physically, emotionally they still hadn't closed the gap between them.

She was still his mystery woman. Though she'd told him the story of the murder she'd witnessed and her escape from New York, she still had secrets. He'd bet on it.

And he was still who he was—a man without ties. Unrooted. Like a boat that had broken its mooring he drifted from port to port, but called none home.

What kind of future could they have?

Shaking himself out of his reverie before it became a foul mood and spoiled the contentment—however temporary—he'd found with her, he pushed his worries aside.

If they didn't have much time together, he didn't want to spend however many few hours or days they had left separated from her by a locked bathroom door.

Fortunately, he'd excelled in the DEA course on lock picking. He'd give her two minutes, in hopes that the hot water would pound some of the unruliness out of her.

Then he was going in.

Chapter 9

Gigi didn't believe for a minute that the flimsy lock on the bathroom door would keep Shane out, and she was right. She hadn't even rinsed all the shampoo out of her hair before the door swung open.

"It's just me," he said quietly, as if she would be afraid.

She wasn't afraid. She knew Shane would never have allowed anyone to sneak in on her.

She waited for him to say more, but the room was quiet. On the other side of the filmy shower curtain, a blurry silhouette rustled through drawers and in cabinets. Busying himself somehow, he started whistling. After a few bars, she recognized the theme from an old aftershave commercial.

He was shaving! Of all the arrogant, macho, sexist— If he thought just because he'd shaved that she was going to let him…again…

Before she'd worked up a really good, indignant outrage, she heard the rustle of denim hitting the floor. Despite the steam floating around her in the shower, making every breath heavy and moist, her throat went dry. Her body tingled—in memory of last night, or in anticipation, she wasn't sure. Didn't want to know.

The shower curtain pulled back and Shane, in all his smooth-shaven, naked glory stepped into the shower with her. Feeling unbearably exposed, she turned her back, chiding herself for the wave of embarrassment that seared her veins. Ducking her head under the spray, she turned her head left, then right.

His hands found her scalp, massaging, and despite her best efforts to remain aloof, within a few moments she melted into his touch.

"I really meant to tell you about Bald Billy," his voice whispered next to her ear.

She frowned, struggling for detachment, anything to stop the meticulous stripping away of her defenses by his magic fingers. "Why do you call him Bald Billy?"

A deep chuckle rumbled up through his chest, vibrated into her back where he pressed against her, slick and soapy. "Billy got caught in an explosion when he busted a meth lab about five years back. He wasn't seriously injured, but he was definitely singed. He lost his eyebrows, temporarily. They grew back, but the name stuck."

His expression grew serious again. He cupped her face in his hands. "No way they're here to do anything except watch. Fitz wouldn't have sent someone I'd recognize and posted them out in the open where I'd see them unless he *wanted* me to know they were there. I think it's his way of telling me he wants to help. Otherwise, he'd have me sitting in the cooler for grand theft auto right now."

"But you quit the DEA. Why would he want to help?" She ducked her head under the water.

"Maybe because I saved his life once."

When she pulled her head from beneath the shower stream, she found herself looking up at troubled blue eyes through a roguish layer of very uncoplike long hair that tried to hide them. She left the hair falling over his forehead this time. After all, he wasn't a cop any longer.

"It was a long time ago," he explained—actually avoided giving an explanation—before she could ask. Whatever had happened between him and his boss, he clearly didn't think it was important at the moment. "But Fitz has always cut me a lot of slack because of it—more than I deserve. I would have told you if we were in any kind of danger. I swear it."

"I believe you."

Relief eased some of the tension from his face and unfanned the crow's feet at the corners of his eyes.

"By the way," he said, brightening considerably. "I called the hospital while I was waiting for you to cool off." He looked like a kid with a juicy secret for about half a second, then blurted it out. "Bill's condition has been upgraded to 'Good.'"

Gigi hugged him. "That's wonderful!"

"Yeah," he agreed, hugging her back, then asking with just a hint of caution, "Does this mean we're officially past our morning-after awkwardness?"

She winced. "Was I that obvious?"

He picked up the soap and put it in her hand, guiding both to his chest. "No. But I figured you weren't the type to hop in and out of a man's bed without a second thought. And even if you were, last night was…different. Kind of…awesome."

His look challenged her to deny it. She didn't.

"Very awesome," she agreed, circling the soap over his copper, flat nipple. "Overwhelming."

"Breathtaking," he groaned as she moved to the other side of his broad chest.

"Staggering." She rubbed against him, her nipples leaping to attention as they brushed the wet, wiry hair of his chest.

His hot gaze ran the length of her body, making her shiver. "Stunning," he said.

He pulled her close, his even hotter, slick body fit to hers. His hands coursed the length of her back.

"Mmm, inspiring," she murmured. She felt his smile as his mouth passed over the tender spot on the side of her neck, nibbling. She also felt a hard spear of flesh tangling in the curls between her legs. Looking down, she admired the full steely length of him. Her eyes widened. "Monumental."

He curled his tongue around the shell of her ear. "I happen to know a surefire cure for morning-after jitters."

"Really? What would that be?"

"Put it off until afternoon," he said.

The gleam in his eyes gave her a pretty good idea how they were supposed to spend the time until then for this great cure to work.

She raised her knee along the outside of his thigh, stroking her foot along his muscular calf. "If we're going to procrastinate, let's do it right. If we put our minds to it, I'm sure we could forget all about jitters for at least, oh, say a week."

He laughed, grazing his knuckles up the sensitive inside of her thigh, surprising her, and she couldn't keep from wincing.

His grin leveled immediately. "You really are sore."

He wet a washcloth hanging on the spigot, then pressed it gently between her legs. She moaned and bit his shoulder.

"Easy, baby." He resoaked the cloth and laid it against her again, working his hand gently against her abused muscles and tenderized flesh. His hands were as meticulous today as they had been urgent last night. "I'm sorry I hurt you."

After a few more repetitions she leaned against him.

Her body should have been relaxing. Instead it flexed like tensile steel. Her breathing had picked up a rapid pace. Her fingers curled into a fist and thumped on his collarbone demanding...something.

The way he had been touching her—an asexual touch meant to soothe, not arouse—had nevertheless incited her to fever pitch. "I thought you were going to cure me of my morning-after blues," she complained.

Shane stopped his ministrations and gentled his finger under her chin, tipping her head up. She didn't even try to hide her wanting. Her need.

He smiled at her patronizingly, charmingly. "Don't worry. I'll take care of you."

Impatient, she reached down to encourage him to hurry. He pushed her hand away.

"No. Not like that," he told her. He reached out and shut off the water, then grabbed a towel and wrapped it around her like a mother buttoning a child's winter coat before sending him out into the snow.

After carrying her to the king-size bed in the back of the cabin and securing the blinds on the window, he did take care of her. Very good, very thorough care.

The kind of care that left her shuddering and weak, lying in a puddle of her own sweat and twisted sheets within minutes.

The kind of care that made her very glad he'd shaved.

The Arizona sun bore down a little harder each day. Spring in the desert was giving way to hard-boiled summer, and even the deceptively cool blue sky and the crystal glitter of Lake Pleasant couldn't keep up the illusion of comfort against the fiery fingers of the sun reaching out to blister the land.

Wiping his forehead on the sleeve of the golf shirt he'd picked out of Fitz's closet, Shane squatted and looked Oliver in the eye. "This is it. Show me what you've got, big guy."

He waved the orange Frisbee he'd found in the laundry room in front of the dog's nose, then stood and flung the disc across the yard. Oliver ran after it, his eyes on the sky.

The young dog hadn't recovered completely, physically, but he'd put on some weight. He no longer walked all curled in on himself, his back hunched, head sagging and tail tucked tight between his legs. Best of all, he'd learned to play, running and jumping and barking like the pup that he was as Shane taught him a few simple games.

Frisbee proved to be his favorite. The bright disk hit the grass, and Oliver dutifully carried it back to Shane, panting and shaking his head for Shane to throw it again. This time Shane tossed the toy lightly, careful not to send it too far. Oliver loved games, but he tired easily. Shane didn't want to overtax the dog's healing system.

This time Oliver caught the disk in the air. Gigi clapped and whistled from her place on the porch. She'd been the one to encourage Shane to take Oliver out for some exercise, and she liked to watch. He hadn't wanted her outside, but she'd seemed so disappointed at having to observe through a window that he had compromised, and agreed she could watch from the porch. Besides, that way, he could keep an eye on her.

And he did like keeping his eyes on her.

Three days of making love should have dulled his craving for her. Instead it had only put a desperate edge on it.

Even now, watching her watch him from the porch, his mind conjured powerful, arousing images. Moving pictures of him carrying her inside, laying her in the middle of that big bed downstairs and doing every unmentionable act to her that he knew how to do—plus a few he didn't, but had always wanted to learn.

Even as he thought it, he knew that wouldn't be enough. He wanted her again and again and again. He couldn't get enough of her.

Maybe because he knew they were running out of time.

They were living in a bubble—a fragile sphere of fiction detached from the cold facts of murder, hit men and crooked cops. Sooner or later, their bubble had to burst. When it did, it was over. *They* were over.

The hell of it was, he wasn't sure he wanted it to end.

Unfortunately it didn't look like he had a choice, since Margo Maitland's Jaguar had just turned into the drive.

Margo, a short woman with a personality as wiry and irrepressible as her curly gray hair, got out of her car and wrapped her reedy arms around him and squeezed tight enough to break ribs. He gave her a brief hug and then pushed back, searching for the words and knowing that nothing he could say could right what had happened.

"Margo, I'm so sorry."

Her warm, brown eyes latched on to him. "Did you shoot my husband?" she asked sharply as he opened the front door.

"No."

"Did you purposely set him up so that someone else would shoot him?"

"No, but—"

She dismissed him pointedly and turned to Gigi. "Then stop apologizing and introduce me to your friend."

When Margo Maitland ended a discussion, even Shane didn't dare argue. What good were apologies anyway? They were just words. Words couldn't make up for almost losing her husband. He'd find some other way make amends, through actions not words. However long it took, he'd find some way to make sure she never regretted the day Bill Maitland brought him home for Thanksgiving dinner.

"Margo, this is…" He looked to Gigi, not sure how to introduce her. A slight tilt of her head told him it was his choice. "…Julia Ferrar. But you can call her Gigi."

Gigi-Julia's smile said she approved of his choice.

"Gigi, meet Margo Maitland," he finished.

The women exchanged greetings as he ushered them inside.

Shane led Margo to the den while Gigi went to pour them

some iced tea. "Do you have anything on the shooter?" he asked, his mind still on Bill.

"Nothing concrete."

"But he was looking for me."

"I think so."

Shane dragged his hand through his hair. "How did he know about you, about Bill?"

"Like you told Ronnie, someone on the inside is involved in this."

"Someone with access to a hell of a lot of information."

"Maybe." Margo shrugged. "Or maybe they just did the legwork. It's no secret in Phoenix that we're friends."

Gigi came into the den carrying a tray of tumblers and a pitcher of tea. Margo gave Shane a strange look. "We're getting ahead of ourselves. Why don't we all sit down and take it from the beginning."

Shane lowered himself to the couch and Gigi sat next to him. Margo sat in a tufted chair, its floral print faded by the Arizona sun lambasting it through the windows.

"What have you found out, Margo?" he asked, impatience getting the better of him.

"Just the basics of the murders in New York." Margo set her tea on the coffee table. "But I'd like to hear Gigi tell her story before I draw any conclusions about what I've learned."

The style was vintage Margo Maitland—no-nonsense, down-to-business analysis of the facts—but something in her tone of voice gave Shane pause. She'd sounded a little *too* objective. As if she were having to work at it.

He watched her carefully as Gigi related her story again— how she'd seen her father's partner and a man she later learned to be an assistant D.A. in the stable; the car rushing by; the shots; being whisked away and warned not to talk to anyone. As he watched, Shane was more and more sure that Margo knew more than she admitted. She was a master interrogator, but so was he. And he had the added advantage of knowing her well. He read her reaction every time one of Gigi's answers triggered a moment of suspicion or a hint of disbelief.

"You said your father's partner gave the A.D.A. a book. What kind of book?" Margo asked.

"A notebook."

"Did you see what was in it?"

"Yes. I-I picked it up after I checked Uncle Ben's and the man's...after I verified they were dead."

"What was in it?"

"Just dates and columns of numbers. Except for the first page that had a Ferrar Industries logo on it."

"Your father's company."

"Yes."

"Where Ben Carlisle worked?"

Gigi shifted uncomfortably. "Yes."

Margo took a sip of tea and leaned back. "You remember the details of that night quite clearly, don't you?" she said coolly. "Even after all this time."

Shane's jaw tightened. He knew what Margo was implying—that Gigi had rehearsed her recount of that night. Suspects sometimes memorized their stories, including vivid detail to add realism, to keep from slipping up or giving a tenacious investigator a reason to doubt their lies. But Gigi wasn't a suspect, was she?

"I should," Gigi answered just as coolly, her face such a mask of purposeful dispassion that Shane had to wonder if she, too, hadn't guessed what Margo had been implying. "I've seen them in my dreams almost every night for three years."

One point for Ferrar. Good for her.

But Margo wasn't finished yet. "Did you ever ask the D.A. what the numbers in the book meant?"

"He said he couldn't crack it."

"It was encoded?" Shane intervened.

Gigi answered, "I don't know. He just said he couldn't make sense of it." She lowered her head, then looked up at him through a forest of tawny lashes. "I thought it might have been evidence of some sort of gambling operation," she said.

"Why would you think that?" Margo asked.

"Uncle Ben liked the horse races. He was a regular around the track. He liked to gamble—sometimes legally, sometimes not. I thought he might have gotten in over his head."

"And decided to turn in his bookie so he wouldn't have to pay his debts."

She shrugged. "It's possible."

"Did you tell Paul Branson your theory?"

"Yes."

Margo took a long drink of tea. The seconds ticked away interminably. Margo was headed somewhere with this line of questioning, and he didn't think he was going to like where she ended up.

"Ben Carlisle and your father had worked together a long time, hadn't they?" Margo asked.

"Thirty years," Gigi confirmed. "Since the beginning of Ferrar Industries."

"He was chief financial officer of your father's company?"

"Yes."

"I suppose he would handle a lot of numbers in that capacity."

"Yes."

"And your father would be familiar with his system—his code—for recording data?"

Shane's chest froze midbreath. Margo's question had hit him like a punch in the gut. He'd been expecting bad. He got worse.

Confusion rippled across Gigi's face in the form of a frown. "I suppose."

"Do you suppose your father could have deciphered the numbers in the book?"

"I don't know."

"Did the D.A. go to him for help?"

"I—I don't think so."

"Didn't you ever wonder why?"

"It never occurred to me."

"Didn't it?" Margo asked sharply.

"Margo!" Shane barked. Both women snapped their heads around toward him. The room fell so quiet that Shane could hear the pounding of his own heart. "What are you getting at, Margo?" he asked with more calm than he felt.

She leaned forward and set her empty tumbler on the table, meticulously folding a napkin beneath the condensation-coated glass. "Nothing. I told you, I haven't drawn my conclusions yet."

"But you have your suspicions."

"Suspicions aren't the same as proof," she said darkly, then brightened and straightened her back, blatantly changing the subject. "My, I believe I could use another cool drink." She looked pointedly at her empty glass.

Gigi's bewildered gaze glanced from him to Margo, then she ducked her head and reached for the tray she'd brought the drinks in on. Shane felt torn, his loyalty drawn and quartered between his old friend and his new lover.

He stopped Gigi, clasping her forearm. "No," he said, his gaze fixed firmly on Margo. "You don't have to send her away so we can talk."

A silent warning flashed in Margo's eyes, stirring his thick anxiety. She wanted to talk to him privately. But he couldn't do that to Gigi.

"We'll hear whatever you have to say together," he said.

"Shane..." The emotion that replaced the warning in her eyes set alarms clanging in Shane's blood.

Sympathy.

What could she have to say that would hurt him so badly she'd regret having to be the one to tell him?

"Spill it, Margo," he said.

Margo squared her shoulders. "The D.A. never went to her father for help."

"Why not?"

"Because one of his own cryptographers broke enough of the code to know that it was a record of money laundering, not gambling. Millions of dollars over several years." She looked from Shane to Gigi and took a deep breath before continuing. "The money was being filtered through Ferrar Industries."

Gigi gasped and Shane waited in silence, his blood chilling. He suspected the worst was yet to come, and he was right.

"The records implicated John Ferrar in the crime, although the D.A. could never make enough sense of the numbers to bring it to court," Margo finished.

"No!" Gigi cried.

Facts toppled one after the other in Shane's mind like a row of dominoes. Ben Carlisle was killed trying to turn over evidence of a money-laundering scheme to the district attorney's office. If John Ferrar was behind the money laundering, then that made him the chief suspect in the murder case as well—a murder case that had never gone to trial because the only witness—his daughter—had run away.

Or had she?

"There must be some mistake," Gigi pleaded.

His breath too short, Shane looked up at Margo. God, he hoped Gigi was right. That there had been some mistake.

"That doesn't prove Gigi knew anything about it." He wasn't sure if he was trying to convince Margo, or himself.

Again he saw the sorrow flood her eyes and he prepared for another blow. She turned her gaze to Gigi.

"Did you see Ben Carlisle that day, before you saw him at the stables?"

The very way that she asked told Shane that Margo already knew the answer.

Gigi's gaze darted around like an animal looking for escape. "I—he was at my father's. I used to have dinner there the first Sunday of every month, and he was just leaving when I arrived."

"Did you talk to him?"

"No."

"Why not? You said he was like an uncle to you."

Margo's hard interrogation twisted like a knife in Shane's gut, but this time he didn't interrupt her.

"He was in a hurry."

"Why was he in a hurry?"

"I don't—" She swallowed hard. The pulse point at the base of her neck danced frantically. She looked at Margo. "How do you know all this?"

"The police interviewed your father's household staff. I read the transcripts."

"Then you already know why he was in a hurry," Gigi chided.

"But Shane doesn't," Margo answered quietly. "Why don't you tell him?"

Gigi turned to him, and the bleeding wound inside him dried up. He turned to stone. She was finally going to tell him her secrets, and irrationally, he wished she wouldn't.

"They were arguing," she said, her eyes bright with suffering.

"Did you hear what they were saying?" Margo asked.

"No. When I walked in the house I just heard angry shouting. Then Uncle Ben stomped out. He didn't even stop to say hello or goodbye. He just left." Her bright eyes flared defiantly. "It doesn't mean anything. They'd argued before, about business."

"What time was that, Gigi?" Margo prodded.

"A little after five."

"Phone records show that at 5:22, Ben Carlisle made a call from his cell phone. The call went to the New York County District Attorney's office. By nine-thirty, he was dead."

Shane let his eyelids fall shut.

"Did you tell Branson about the fight between Mr. Carlisle and your father?" he heard Margo say.

"He didn't ask," Gigi answered.

"And you didn't volunteer."

Gigi kept her silence.

Shane couldn't have forced words through his thickened throat, even if he had something to say. Even if by some chance Gigi hadn't known about the money laundering, she'd known that her father and his murdered partner had had a blowout just hours before that partner was killed. She had to know that would put her father under suspicion, yet she neglected to mention that little fact to the D.A. or to him. And he'd bet there was more she was holding back.

He smiled tightly to himself. Just like in bed—he knew when she didn't give herself up completely.

He was a fool. Twice a fool, because he should have known better. This wasn't the fist time a woman had lied to him to protect her family.

But it would damn well be the last.

Every nerve in his body screamed at him to jump up. He was too close to her. He was suffocating. One thing he'd learned working undercover, though, was how to control his impulses. At least most of them. Where the hell had his iron control been when he'd decided to make love to her?

He tamped down his emotions, schooled calm onto his face, and forced himself to stay on the couch, his hands still, no matter how badly he wanted to do something, break something. He wouldn't give her the satisfaction of seeing him lose it.

No, he'd lose it later. In private.

"What do you want to do, Margo?" He purposely cut Gigi out of the discussion.

"I spoke to the D.A. in charge of the case. He wants to talk to her ASAP."

"Fine by me," he said, cutting his gaze to the floor. "The sooner she goes back to New York the better."

He tried not to look at Gigi, but he couldn't help but see the bewilderment on her face as his gaze skimmed by her.

"Shane?" The quaver in Gigi's voice drilled straight through to his heart, but he'd get over that in time.

Shane couldn't stand the pressure any longer. The air seemed to push at him from all sides. He had to get out of there. Out of the room. Out of the house. Out of the damn desert. Maybe he'd go back to the mountains, where it was green, and cool....

He stood. "I guess you don't need me any longer. I'm sure Fitz's boys are still outside. They'll keep an eye on her until you can get rid of her." He headed for the door.

Margo followed him out. "Shane." She stopped him in the hallway with her no-nonsense voice. Struggling to hold back the rising red tide inside him, he turned.

Margo touched his arm lightly. "You okay?"

"Sure." He shuffled from one foot to the other. "Why wouldn't I be?"

Margo's expression was enough to tell him she wasn't buying it, but she let it go. "She told the truth about one thing, at least. Someone on the inside is leaking information about this case to the wrong people. Paul Branson is concerned about it, too. He's asked me to arrange protective custody for her here to limit the involvement of any of the New York offices. I'm going to put her at Shelton House."

"Shelton House?" Shane couldn't quite keep the surprise, or the worry, out of his voice. "That place is the DOJ's equivalent to Fort Knox. Do you really think that's necessary?"

"Remember the two men you had Fitz pick up in the hospital parking lot?"

"Yeah. They might have been the ones who shot Bill."

"One of them was the chief of security for Ferrar Industries. The other was a P.I. who admitted he was on John Ferrar's payroll."

Shane rolled his head back on his neck. "*Daddy's* looking for her."

"The question is, what will he do when he finds her?"

Shane shook his head. At this point, he couldn't even begin to guess.

"There's more," Margo continued. At this point, he didn't know how much more he could take. That didn't stop Margo. "According to his office in New York, Mr. Ferrar was called out of town unexpectedly three days ago." She looked grim, and Shane knew she was thinking that was the day Bill had been shot. "The secretary wouldn't say. But we think he's here, in Phoenix."

"Have you checked airline records? Hotels?"

"We're working on it now." Margo touched his arm. "Shane, I want you to go to Shelton House, too."

He stiffened. "No way."

"Someone wants her very bad—maybe her father, maybe not. But whoever it is, he's already proven that he doesn't care who he has to hurt to get her."

"I can take care of myself."

"I know you can," Margo said gently. "But I know you. You're too close to this to just walk away."

Damn, she really did know him well. One look at him and he might as well have put on a slide show for her, demonstrating how he and Gigi had entertained themselves the last few days.

"I'd worry about you, if I thought you were out there working this thing on your own." She gave his forearm a gentle squeeze. "And I've got enough to worry about right now, don't you think?"

The sudden image of Bill, lying still and pale against stark white sheets flashed through his mind. Using his guilt over Bill's injury against him was a dirty trick. "That's not playing fair, Margo," he grumbled.

"All's fair in love, my boy. If a little trickery is what it takes to keep you safe, then I'm not above it."

He knew what he was getting into. His already stretched control would have to give a lot further. Every minute in captivity with Gigi would feel like an aeon in hell. But he would do it, because Margo had asked him. Besides, it might be a good idea to stick close to Gigi, no matter how much it hurt. The last time he'd gotten between a woman and her family, a good agent had died. He needed to make sure that didn't happen again.

He nodded curtly. "I'm not sure why you're even bothering with me, after all that's happened. But I'll go. For now."

"Good. While you're there, think about this—we don't have all the facts in this case yet."

He jerked his head to one side negatively. "Don't make excuses for me, Margo. We both know she's guilty, and I'm an idiot for ever believing in her. But then, I've always been an easy mark for conniving women, haven't I?"

Margo rocked back on her heels, a disapproving frown creasing her forehead. "It's way too early for you to be handing down judgments, Shane. On yourself—" She looked past him toward the den. He angled his head enough to see Gigi standing in the open doorway, looking ravaged. Damn. How long had she been listening? "—or anyone else."

Margo walked away, leaving him to face Gigi alone.

He turned in time to see a fresh, fat tear slip off her thick eyelashes. She yanked the back of her hand across her face, swiping it away as if she loathed showing him that one small weakness.

As if that were important, compared to the other weaknesses he knew of her, like the way she liked to be kissed on the soles of her feet. The way she liked to be touched, exactly, between her legs. The way her left breast was more sensitive than the right.

God, even hating her as he did, he wanted to make her weak again, right then, right there. He bit his tongue to stop the surge of blood to his groin.

She spread her legs shoulder width—a fighting stance. "Since you've already tried and convicted me—" she said, angling her chin up in an admirable display of false bravado. God help him, her moxie only made him want her more. "Maybe you wouldn't mind telling me exactly what I'm supposed to be guilty *of.*"

He'd been wrong earlier, he realized then, about the bubble he and Gigi had been living in bursting. It hadn't burst. It had exploded in a nuclear-force blast.

And at the moment, he wasn't sure either of them would survive the fallout.

Chapter 10

Gigi drew on a reserve of strength that had dwindled during the past few years of living in constant fear. She leaned against the door frame in a pose she hoped looked casual when in reality, the solid wall was the only thing keeping her on her feet. Her knees wanted to fold under the maelstrom in Shane's eyes.

"Well, are you going to run down my crimes, or just send me to the gallows guessing?" She shoved off the wall and strode down the hallway on rubber legs.

His eyes were darker, more dangerous than she'd ever seen them. Feral and hungry.

"How about murder? Is that a good enough crime for you?"

Gigi stopped, stunned. "I didn't kill anyone!"

"Then why did you leave New York?"

"I told you—I ran for my life."

He advanced, looming over her until she could smell his borrowed aftershave. Feel the warm wave of his tea-sweetened breath. "Did you, Gigi? Or did *Daddy* send you away so you couldn't testify against him?"

Her heart twisted. "I don't understand."

"Come on. You're a bright girl. Surely you can figure it out."

Desperately she reached for his logic. "You think my father raided the safe house in New York and sent me to Utah to keep me from talking?"

His satisfied scowl told her he did. "A federal marshal was killed in that raid. If we can prove you knew about it or participated in any way, that makes you as guilty as your father. You know what the penalty is for killing a federal agent?"

"I didn't—" Arguing about what had or hadn't happened in New York seemed useless. He'd made up his mind. "Someone tried to kill me in Utah, too. You saw it!"

"I'm the one who got shot, not you. Maybe *Daddy* was looking out for you again. Didn't like you cozying up with a lawman."

"If I knew my father was behind this all along, why would I have gone with you?"

"I didn't give you much choice, did I?" Though he covered it quickly, she heard his breath catch. "You know, I can understand why you lied to me, strung me along until Daddy could catch up and spring you loose again. But what I can't figure out is why you slept with me. What did you hope to gain?"

She flinched. "What makes you think it was about *gaining* anything?"

"Everything is about getting something, sweetheart. Even if it's only a few days of good sex before you have to go on the run again."

A few days of good sex. That was how he defined what they'd had. In a way, she guessed he was right. They'd never made any commitment to each other. Never talked about staying together after all this was over.

Now they never would.

"Or maybe it was more than sex?" he said, his eyes narrowing. "Maybe you figured if you stuck with me, you could find out exactly how much the D.A. in New York knew about what you and dear old Dad were up to." A twisted smile coiled on his face. "As long as you were pumping me, why not pump for information, too?"

Gigi bit her tongue to hold her anger back. He could make what they'd shared sound like some triple-X video if he wanted to. She knew better.

"So that's it? Four—no, *three* hours ago—you made love to me like I've never been made love to before. And now you've decided it was all some trick, and you're just going to turn your back on me?"

His nostrils flared and his pupils dilated. He slapped his palm on the wall over her shoulder and leaned closer over her.

"No," he said, seething. "I'm not ever turning my back on you again. At least not without patting you down for weapons first."

She hissed in a breath, shocked at the venom in his words, his tone. Her palm cracked against his cheek. The echo resounded in her ears as she drew her stinging hand back to cover her own lips, which she'd pursed in disbelief.

She'd never hit another human being in her life, not counting soft punches in the mock battles of her jujitsu class. The feeling of delivering a real blow was at once empowering and humiliating. Only he could have made her react out of sheer instinct like that.

"You really are a bastard, you know that?"

Oliver trotted down the hall and sat beside Shane, looking from him to Gigi and whining pitifully.

The corners of Shane's mouth curled in a sickly, dangerous

smile. He put his hand on Oliver's head and quieted the dog. "I'd rather be an honest mutt than a lying blue blood any day."

"I was talking about your behavior, not your parentage, and you know it."

"It doesn't matter." He shrugged with practiced indifference, but the sharp, white crevasses at the corners of his eyes gave away his true concern. "You're right either way."

Gigi blanched. Shane, she realized, had little tolerance for imperfection. In himself, or anyone else. "Then what does that make me?" she asked quietly.

A whore, she supposed, if he really believed she'd traded herself for information.

"Don't worry," he said ruefully. "You're not the first woman to use sex to get what she wants from a man. Hell, you're not even the first woman to do it to me."

With a sick certainty, she understood why he'd been so quick to judge her. "You think I'm just like her, don't you? Like Lucia—betraying you to protect my family."

She expected to see hurt, fear and frustration swirling close to the surface when she looked deep into the blue pools that were his eyes. Instead, she saw only calm. Dead calm. A lifelessness like she'd never seen in him before.

"In a way I don't blame either one of you," he said. "Family loyalty is an admirable trait." His wan smile reappeared briefly. "Not quite as admirable in crime families as it is in good families, but still commendable."

She would have told him what she really felt toward her father—and it wasn't loyalty—but he wouldn't listen. He was too distant. Too hurt.

"I can't go back to New York," she said desperately. "They'll kill me."

"So what will you do, run again?"

His dispassion exploded her temper. This was her life they were talking about! She struck again, intending to hurt, but this time with words, not a physical blow. "What will *you* do? Crawl in a hole and lick your wounds again?"

"Is that what you think I did while I was on leave?" His head tipped back and he let out a raucous laugh, then leveled a serious stare on her. "Honey, I don't run away from my problems. I hunt them down."

Understanding spread through her like a fever.

"I spent my eighteen months of leave turning over every rock and examining every bug until I found Lucia and her brother. They won't be selling drugs—or murdering federal agents—ever again."

"You—you killed them?" Angry as she was at him, a part of her still withered to think he could take a life in revenge. Even the life of a drug dealer.

"No, I managed to stay within the limits of the law. Just barely," he added dryly. "Although I guess you could say I'm responsible for ending their lives. Lucia's brother is on death row—I didn't have to kill him. The state of Arizona will do it for me. As for Lucia, she's doing life without parole in maximum security. And I don't guess that's really much of a life at all, is it?"

My God, what it must be like to see someone you loved go to prison for life. To be the one who put her there. She could only imagine what that had done to him.

He had protested that he hadn't loved Lucia. Just like he'd claimed her time with him at Lake Pleasant was just a few days of good sex.

She knew better.

She touched his jaw, a feathery, uncertain stroke. "I'm sorry. That must have been very difficult—"

He swatted her hand away. Pressed closer, her sympathy seeming to incense him. "Don't even think about running, Gigi. Inside Shelton House, Margo will make sure you're protected, even from me. Outside of it, you take your chances."

A spark was back in his eyes. Had she woken a sign of life, somehow?

"Maybe I like to gamble," she said, hoping to fan the flames. She'd learned to play the odds pretty well from her Uncle Ben. And she was willing to bet Shane didn't have it in him to do her any real harm.

"Not for the stakes I have in mind." He leaned against her farther, just a fraction more weight than he had been plying against her, and she felt his arousal at her hip.

"You think I'd let you touch me again?"

He inhaled a deep breath, shifting his chest against her breasts. She didn't have to look down to know that her nipples had peaked in response. He smiled in satisfaction.

"Purely a physiological reaction," she explained.

"Mm-hm," he murmured, a grinding, sexy hum near her ear. "Our minds may hate each other, but our bodies are still very much in lust."

His step back seemed to require more effort than it should have. The sudden rush of conditioned air against her fevered skin made her shiver.

"If you leave Shelton House," he said. "I *will* find you. And then we'll both find out just how physiological a reaction can be."

This time, she believed him. When it came to his ability to get a reaction out of her, she wouldn't bet against Shane Hightower. All the odds were in his favor.

Shelton House wasn't bad for a prison, she decided later that night, ducking guards as she headed into the kitchen for a midnight snack. Margo's safe house turned out to be a century-old ranch surrounded by a vine-covered wall broken only by rusted wrought-iron gates. The house itself was a two-story stucco affair with a red-tiled roof and two huge, rambling wings that veered back from the main living area to surround a courtyard full of wild roses. Narrow hallways twisted and turned through the wings like a maze, opening to dozens of bedrooms and twice that many nooks and crannies perfect for sitting. And brooding, which was what she'd been doing until the rumbling in her stomach grew too loud to ignore.

She hadn't eaten much at dinner. Wonderful as Bald Billy's three-layer lasagna had smelled, her stomach had rebelled at the thought of a heavy meal. Maybe she could find some fruit or a bagel left over from breakfast.

At an intersection of passageways, she paused, picturing the house's floor plan and mapping out her route, not taking the most direct path. She preferred to wind around the old place, exploring and studying antiquated furnishings and artwork as she passed.

The place must have belonged to someone with money, she thought, pausing to look at a handmade vase signed on the bottom by the artist. Probably a drug dealer's house, she realized with a grimace, seized by the DOJ.

Two more left turns and the hardwood floor gave way to glazed tile. Gigi slowed her pace, her stomach fluttering until she wondered if her persnickety digestive system would tolerate even a bagel tonight. A light shone from the breakfast nook at the end of the kitchen, another through the half-open door to the walk-in pantry, but no one was in sight. She listened a moment for sounds of life, then let out a slow breath. She was worrying about nothing. No one was around. Shane was off hiding somewhere, as he had been since they'd arrived, and Billy and the other agent, Jeff something, were in the den, playing cards.

Slowly she turned the corner into the kitchen. She was perfectly safe—

She jumped so suddenly she slipped and almost fell on the polished tile. Her heart leaped to her throat and her hand automatically covered her mouth, as if to hold in the scream rising in her breast. It took her a full second to recover enough to speak. "Margo." Her heart thumped uncomfortably. "You startled me."

Margo closed the cabinet door she'd been leaning behind and stepped from the shadows into the circle of light in the breakfast area. "Sorry about that."

"It's okay. I guess I'm just a little jumpy tonight. Did you come here…alone?"

"Don't worry. I take precautions. No killers followed me down to the pantry." Margo sat down in the breakfast booth, unwrapping a block of cheese and slicing off a piece. "Or is it Shane you're worried about bumping into tonight?"

"I'm not sure which would be worse at this point." Gigi looked up quickly, a new possibility taking root in her thoughts. "He is still here, isn't he? He hasn't left?"

"Oh he's here all right." Margo looked toward the pantry. "He's just…laying low, I suspect."

"You mean he's avoiding me."

"Avoiding a confrontation, perhaps. Shane's always been a master of self-control. I don't think he likes it that his feelings run so close to the surface around you."

"You mean his anger."

"Cheese?" Margo offered her a slice of cheddar. Gigi shook her head and reached inside the refrigerator for a bagel.

"I don't think what you're seeing is anger."

"Then it's a pretty good imitation," Gigi retorted.

Margo smiled. "Granted, his reaction to you is quite…volatile. But I've known Shane a long time. I've seen him angry, and I've seen him hurt. But what I see in him now is more than either. It's deeper."

Gigi ran her thumbnail down an old scar in the butcher-block tabletop. How was it that she was the one someone was trying to kill, the one unjustly accused of more than one crime, and yet she felt guilty for making him miserable? "He won't even consider the possibility that he might be wrong about me.''

"Maybe he's afraid to. Strip away that surface layer of anger and he might have to face up to the emotions underneath.'' Margo took a bite of cheese and chewed, making time for Gigi to consider her comment.

Gigi looked up speculatively. "What emotions?"

"Why don't you ask him?"

"Do I look like a masochist? I have no desire for another run-in with him.''

Margo shot her a knowing look. "That's why you're wandering around a dark house all alone looking for him.''

"I'm not looking for him. I—'' Fire swept over Gigi's face as the truth hit her. Margo was right. She hadn't come to the kitchen because she was hungry. She had been looking for Shane. Hoping to bump into him in a darkened corridor where he couldn't read from her expression what he'd done to her, how he'd devastated her. And what would she do if she'd found him? Talk to him? Yell at him? Hit him again? Hang on to him and beg him not to let her go?

"It doesn't matter," Gigi said flatly. "He obviously doesn't want to be found.''

Mustering her tattered dignity, Gigi took her untouched bagel and dragged herself to the kitchen door, where she stopped and looked back. Margo was studying her, her head slightly tilted as if trying to solve some intricate puzzle. "What would you have told him, if you had found him?" she asked.

"I don't know." Gigi shrugged, embarrassed. "Maybe that I'm afraid, too.''

Margo went quiet, looking toward the end of the kitchen, near the pantry, like she was expecting something important to happen. When it didn't, she turned back to Gigi, her eyes dark with disappointment and compassion. "Don't you worry about finding him,'' she said, her voice oddly fierce. "If he has any sense—and I know he does, somewhere in that thick head of his—he'll quit hiding in the shadows and come to find you.''

Wishing she could believe that, Gigi trudged out the door.

Hearing her padded footsteps disappear down the hall, Shane stepped out of the pantry and slouched against the wall, the crackers Margo had sent him into the storage room to get still trapped in his clenched fist.

''What was that about?'' he asked.

''Just trying to get a little insight about her. Thought it might help us figure her out.''

''What's to figure out? She's lying to protect her father.''

''You watched her interview today with the New York D.A.''

He'd watched all right. He'd never studied a human being so closely in his whole life. He'd absorbed every flick of her eyelashes, lived for every shortened breath as a question took her by surprise, died for every nervous clasp of her hands as she gathered herself for an answer. Through the whole interview, he hadn't seen a single sign that she was lying. And that bothered him. He couldn't see it anymore. After eight years in the DEA, he could pick a liar out of a crowded bar without hearing a word the person said, just by watching body language. He could feel it.

But not with Gigi. Too many other feelings got in the way.

''Surely you must have some doubts,'' Margo said.

''I have plenty of doubts. Mostly about myself.''

''Maybe that's because you've gone too long without looking inside yourself—facing up to what's really bothering you.''

''And what would that be, Dr. Maitland?''

''I don't know. But I think she does. Maybe you should ask her.''

''You're meddling, Margo.'' His hand tightened around the crackers he still held.

"No, dear. I'm simply having a late-night snack." Her voice was patronizingly patient. But when she raised her eyes to him, he saw past her patience. She was furious.

Margo had never had much tolerance for cowardice.

"If I'd been meddling," she said tightly, "I would have sent her into the pantry for the crackers—" she pried the wadded column of cellophane from Shane's clenched hand and sighed "—before you crushed them to dust."

Dust motes tickled the inside of Shane's nose and irritated his eyes as he crawled through the attic toward the little octagon window nestled under the roof peak. It hadn't taken Gigi long to find the one chink in Shelton House's armor. The ornamental window was the only one in the house not nailed shut.

Gigi straddled the top of a dormer overlooking the courtyard. Her knees were drawn up to her chest and the moonlight glowed off her pale cheeks. He didn't remember her being so pale. Was it just a trick of the light, or had she really become so porcelain, so fragile, in the last two days?

"What do you want, Shane?" she said without turning her head, as if she had some sixth sense that told her he was near.

He levered his body through the small opening, holding the two bottles of beer he'd pilfered from the kitchen out in front of him. "It's warm out. I brought you something cool."

"How thoughtful of you," she said dryly.

"Mind if I join you?"

"Why? Did you think up a few more crimes to accuse me of? A few new ways to humiliate me?"

Shane paused, balancing on the dormer slope and leaning one palm against the house's crumbling stucco facade. "I guess I was pretty rough on you, huh?"

"Is that some sort of half-baked apology?"

"Would you accept it if it was?"

"No."

"I didn't think so."

"Then why are you here?"

"I couldn't stay away." That much was true. It would have been easy to claim that Margo had shamed him into it. But he would have come looking for her tonight in any case. Because, torture that it was to be with her, staying away was worse.

He took a swig of beer. "I want to know what you're afraid of."

"What?"

"You said you were afraid. I want to know what you're afraid of."

He steeled his heart against the reflection of the stars in her wide eyes as she turned her head. It reminded him too much of seeing the stars in her eyes another night.

"You heard?" she said.

He nodded. "So can I sit, or not?"

She sighed heavily. "Suit yourself. But I'm warning you. One wisecrack and you're going to be picking thorns out of your hide for a week."

He peered over the edge of the roof to the tangled rose garden two stories below. "I'll try to restrain myself."

He settled his back against the crumbling stucco and stretched his legs across the red tiles in front of him while Gigi ignored him, staring across the moon-swept desert. Below them, Bald Billy and Jeff walked toward the back gate. Gigi's back stiffened.

"Don't worry," he said. "Change of shift. They're working two days on, two days off. They're just meeting the new guys at the gate to make sure everything is kosher before they let them in."

She relaxed gradually. "So, were you hoping I'd confess all my sins to Margo while you listened in?"

"No, I was hoping you wouldn't confess all of mine."

Her head tipped back and the moonlight illuminated the fragile column of her throat. "I think Margo has already figured out that we weren't playing Parcheesi while we waited for her up at the lake house."

"I'm sure she has. But those aren't the sins I was talking about."

"What could I possibly tell her that would embarrass you more than a blow-by-blow, pardon the pun, account of our sex-capades?"

"The things I said to you after she showed up." Shane hadn't slept much since then. A pair of wounded blue eyes as he'd shamed her—shamed himself—haunted his dreams. It had gotten so he didn't even want to close his own eyes, for fear of seeing her tortured face. He took another long drink, then finished, "She would pin my ears to the side of my head for good if she'd heard. She doesn't put up with crudeness. Or intimidation tactics."

He picked at the beer label with his thumbnail, glancing at her sideways. The silence was deafening. "In case you didn't notice, that was a half-baked apology."

She unwound one arm from around her legs and snatched the second beer bottle from his hand. "Accepted," she said sharply, then took a long swig. When she lowered the bottle, she kept her chin angled to the stars and said, "I don't suppose this means you believe me."

"I'd like to. But the facts are stacked against you."

"And the facts are all you care about, right? Never mind what your gut is telling you. What your instincts say. What you *feel*. Or maybe that's the problem." She drank from her bottle. "You don't feel anything anymore."

He frowned, rubbing the condensation from the bottom of the bottle onto his jeans. "Trusting my *feelings* has gotten me in trouble before."

"Lucia," she said matter-of-factly. "She might be in prison, but she's never very far away from you, is she?"

Shane didn't answer; he didn't have to.

Gigi rolled her eyes. "Tell me Shane, was she in bed with us, too?"

"If I'd been thinking about her, we wouldn't have been in bed."

"I'm not her," Gigi insisted.

"But I'm still me." Shane stared down at his empty bottle, wishing he had another. Several more. Enough to get ripping drunk. Then he could blame his rolling stomach on something besides uncertainty. "And John Ferrar is still your father."

"No, he is not!" she blurted, then reared back as if she'd surprised even herself with her outburst.

Despite the warm Arizona night air, Shane's blood turned cold. He stood at the window, feeling off-kilter by a lot more than the slope of the roof he stood on. "What?"

"He hasn't been my father since I was eight years old."

"When your mother died?"

"After she died, he didn't want me anymore. I might as well have died, too. He shipped me off to boarding school before the sod had taken root on her grave. No matter how hard I tried to make him love me—no matter how many riding trophies I won or scholastic honors I earned—it was like I didn't exist for him. So you see, that loyalty you're so sure is driving me to let him get away with murder—it doesn't exist. I owe John Ferrar nothing—least of all, loyalty."

Shane hesitated, trying to sort out fact from wishful thinking. "You were at his house that night."

"After vet school, I tried to get to know him again. I insisted on a regular dinner date. So the first Sunday of every month, we would sit at opposite ends of a long table and eat in silence until he'd finally look up at me and ask me if I've done something different with my hair. I'd tell him I haven't changed it since I was sixteen, and then he'd find some excuse to retire into his study and work. I'd have a cup of coffee in the kitchen with Carmella, his cook, and then I'd leave. That's what family was like in the Ferrar house, Shane. It's not like the movies."

He tried to understand. He tried to put himself in her place—to have a father who didn't want her. He tried to imagine what she would feel. And he failed.

It was all so foreign to him. Something so far beyond his comprehension that struggling to make himself understand it only reminded him how incapable he was of ever understanding.

He'd never felt the bond of blood to blood.

She cared for the old man, whether she admitted it or not. He could still hear it in her voice, see it in her eyes. When she said his name, he looked at her and saw the eight-year-old girl she must have been, grieving over the loss of her mother and trying desperately to earn her father's love.

Maybe she was still trying to earn his love.

"You tried to make it right with him," he said coarsely. "You must feel something for him."

Sadness filled her eyes, as if she realized he'd struggled mightily and lost. "I do. I feel sorry for him. Almost as sorry as I'm beginning to feel for you."

Her words cleaved his heart with surgical precision. He'd had some tough breaks in life, but he'd never asked for anyone's pity. Didn't want it.

But if she was telling the truth…

If she hadn't known her father was a suspect when she left New York, if John Ferrar or others unknown were really trying to kill her, then he hoped to God that when they tried again, they got him instead. Because if Gigi was telling the truth, then what Shane had done, the way he had treated her, was worse than pitiable.

It was unforgivable.

"Don't waste your energy feeling sorry for me," he said,

turning his back on Gigi to duck through the window. "I don't deserve it."

In the hallway at the bottom of the attic stairs, he stopped. Oliver's high-pitched whine reached him through the floorboards. The dog was downstairs, and agitated.

The foldaway stairs behind him creaked. "Shh." He held his arm out to stop Gigi from passing by. Oliver's whines persisted, along with a scratching sound like he was clawing at a door or window.

"What is it?" Tension twanged in her voice.

"I don't know. But I don't think he's just asking to go outside."

They crept down the stairs and found the dog at a darkened service entrance. Shane restrained Oliver with a hand on his collar, and drew his gun. "Go back to your room."

She grabbed a handful of his shirt. "No way."

"Don't argue with me," he snarled.

"I'm safer with you."

There wasn't time to debate. Oliver growled, low and deep. Shane opened the door silently and slid into the darkness with Gigi attached to his back. Oliver followed soundlessly on their heels, as if he understood the need for stealth.

Skirting along the shrub bed next to the front portico, Shane checked the drive. No sign of Jeff, Billy or the relief agents. The hair on the back of his neck stood.

He held the gun in front of him, two-handed but lowered, raising it only as he swiveled around the corner of the house. Nothing. But Oliver caught a scent and trotted across the yard.

Reluctantly, Shane followed. He didn't like being in the open with Gigi exposed in the bright light of the moon. He hurried across the lawn and caught up to Oliver near the front gates. The dog jumped up on the wall, growled and let out a plaintive woof. Shane tracked the broken ivy stems up and over the wall. Someone had breached the grounds.

He turned to shuttle Gigi back to the house and get a search started when a fireball lit the night sky. A heartbeat later the sound—a deafening blast—reached him. Instinctively he threw himself toward Gigi, propelling them both to the ground just as the shock wave rolled over them. Heat and miniscule bits of brick and wood and glass pelted his back, stinging like a thousand tiny pinpricks. He curled himself around Gigi, covering her body with his and wrapping his arms around her head. Oliver cowered at his feet.

He was still trying to hold Gigi down when she shoved him back, sitting and staring at the inferno that used to be Shelton House with wide eyes. The whole north wing—the wing where she had taken a room—was engulfed in flames.

A tremor racked her body. "Oh, my God. Jeff? Billy?"

"They were still outside."

Her tremor escalated to a full-bodied shake. "Margo?"

He ran his hands over her shoulders as if warming her from a chill. "She left before I came upstairs. I watched her car drive out myself. She wasn't in there. Nobody was."

Gigi reached out to stroke the dog's head. This time her hand didn't shake. "Thanks to Oliver. If he hadn't warned us—"

She didn't finish her sentence. There was no need. They both knew they would have been killed if it hadn't been for one stray mutt.

Gigi struggled to her feet, visibly gathering her composure. Shane tried to wrap his arms around her, to pull her back into the shadows near the wall, but she pulled away from him. Flames reflected in her eyes and the sizzle of destruction filled the air. Acrid smoke burned the linings of his nostrils.

"So much for your theory about my father trying to get me away from you. That explosion was supposed to kill us both." She coughed, choked on the smoke swarming around them now, then raised her watery gaze to his. "So how does *that* fit into your sense of family values, huh?"

Chapter 11

"It's true, isn't it?" she asked. "My own father is trying to kill me."

Gigi stood in front of him shaking and shivering and biting her lip, and everything Shane knew or didn't know or thought he'd ever known about family or loyalty or right or wrong crumbled under the force of her quaking. Only two clear thoughts formed in his mind.

The first was that John Ferrar had better hope that when Shane caught up to him, they weren't alone, because a man who would kill his own daughter was a freak of nature and didn't deserve to live.

And the second was that he had to get his arms around Gigi, right now.

She resisted, first by holding her body rigid then by jerking her hands up and beating on his back. Her fists pummeled his shoulders. "Damn! Damn! Damn him! Damn you! Damn you both!"

He held her as close as he dared, afraid she might shatter if he held her too tight. Afraid she might shatter if he didn't.

She dampened his shoulder with warm, wet tears, grinding her cheek against his shirt, and breathed in ragged, heaving gulps.

"Shh, baby. Shh." He rocked her against him, murmuring in her ear, praying she would stop. He didn't care about her fists—she wasn't hitting with enough force to hurt him—but her tears were killing him.

Gradually her flaying fists slowed to a flutter. Her sobs evened out to long, cleansing breaths.

He let her ease away from him.

Gigi swiped the wetness off her cheeks. "I'm sorry." A final shudder shook her shoulders. "I didn't mean to fall apart like that."

"It's all right. It was kind of reassuring, actually." She gaped at him. He gave her arm one last squeeze, then let her go. "I was beginning to think nothing ever got to you." Oliver rubbed his nose against Shane's thigh, and Shane automatically dropped his hand to soothe the dog. "It was kind of…intimidating for us mere mortals. Right, Oliver?"

A hint of a smile broke across Gigi's mouth. She sniffed once more, loudly. "You should have known better. *You* got to me, didn't you?"

He answered her smile with a grin of his own. In the distance, a siren shrilled out its warning in the night.

He held out his hand. "Come on. Time for us to go."

She took his hand without hesitation, but used it to hold him in place instead of following him. "But the police are coming."

"Then we'd better hurry."

"They'll be looking for us."

"No, they won't." Moonlight highlighted the confusion scrolled in her features. "They'll think we were in there," he explained, nodding toward the burning house. "We're better off dead."

Understanding dawned. "Or at least letting them think we're dead."

"It'll take days for them to sort through the rubble and figure out we weren't inside when it blew."

She took a step forward, then stopped. "But Margo…?"

"I hate to do it to her. But this place should have been safe. She would have made sure of it if there was any way she could have. Whatever is going on, even she can't stop it."

The siren drew nearer. He tugged her forward again. "We have to go now, if we're going."

"But where?"

"Anywhere but here. It's just you and me from now on."

Shane boosted Gigi over the wall, then helped Oliver skitter over and finally used the vines to pull himself up and to the other side. They dodged emergency vehicles racing down the street, covering their escape in the shadows of the sparse trees and by ducking behind buildings along the way.

"Do you know where we are?" Gigi asked, trudging down an empty stretch of road.

"Sure. We'll hit civilization again in another mile or so."

True to his word, twenty minutes later they passed the outskirts of an industrial area and quickly cut through to a four-lane road. They walked by a few boxy houses, three liquor stores and a tattoo parlor before he felt Gigi close in beside him. A rusted, low-riding old boat of a car that might once have been a luxury vehicle cruised down the avenue, heavy rock music pulsing from its open windows. The car slowed as it passed by them, and Gigi pressed close to Shane's side.

Even Oliver moved in closer behind him.

Without turning his head, Shane put his hand over hers and pulled her fingers over the pistol—her pistol—in his waistband, hoping she'd be reassured.

The car moved on.

Ahead a young woman in pink spandex paced nervously under a street lamp, an unlit cigarette dangling from one hand. The cruiser slowed again, pulling up next to her.

Shane slowed his step, watching. The hooker leaned over the driver's window. A hand shot out and grabbed her wrist, dragging her upper body into the car. The woman struggled, kicking at the door and clawing at the driver's arm.

Muttering an oath, Shane told Gigi to stay put. He reached the car in four long strides, chopped the driver's arm once to make him let go of the girl, then shoved Gigi's gun into the man's neck. He didn't have time for a lengthy discussion tonight.

"Put the car in gear and drive. Don't stop. Don't look back. And don't come back. Ever."

The car's tires squealed against the pavement. Shane turned to the hooker behind him. God, she couldn't be seventeen. Yet her honey-colored eyes held decades of experience.

"Hey, big man," she said, her voice shaking. "That was my rent money you just chased off."

"Yeah? Well now maybe you'll live long enough to get evicted."

He saw her shudder, but she was tough. She covered it by stepping closer in a low, hip-swinging stride. "Well, since you saved my life and all, the least I could do is thank you properly."

He felt Gigi at his back. The hooker's eyes flicked from him to Gigi and back. "I'll be real nice to you. Give you something real special." She flicked her hand out and brushed a chipped fingernail down the center of his chest.

Shane fought not to recoil from her touch. Instead he reached into the front pocket of his jeans and pulled out the bills he found. "How much for all night?"

Gigi's fingers clenched on his shoulder.

"Sixty bucks," the girl said.

Shane's jaw ticked furiously. Hell of a price for dignity. "I've only got forty." He shoved the bills in the girl's hand.

She grabbed for the bills, but Shane pulled them back.

"One condition," he said.

"Yeah, there's always a condition, ain't there? What is it you like? Something kinky?"

He pressed his last two twenties in her palm. "Just get off the street tonight. Get a room someplace decent if you don't have a place to stay."

The hooker frowned. "Alone?"

"Yeah. Alone. Take the night off. And while you've got all that time to think, think about calling the National Runaway Switchboard. Just dial the operator and she'll connect you—it's toll free."

"What are you, some kind of social worker?"

"No. Just someone who believes kids ought to be home in their beds at night, not out prowling the streets."

Her mouth curled into a sneer and Shane thought she might argue, but something painful swirled in her overmade-up eyes. She closed her mouth and stuffed the money down the front of her dress. She whirled, calling over her shoulder, "Whatever you say, big guy. It's your nickel." The girl sauntered away, swinging her considerable—if immature—assets as she went.

Turning, he met Gigi's appraising look. "What?" he asked curtly.

Her usually sharp blue eyes were as soft as a clear sky. "You. Saving the lost souls of the world."

"Some of those lost souls hit a little close to home."

She cocked one eyebrow. "There but for the grace of God…?"

"Something like that."

"Did you ever run away from the youth home?"

"No. I knew when I had it good. Three hot meals a day, a roof over my head and an education. They couldn't have kicked me out of that place.'' He turned and started walking, his arm looped through hers. ''My mother was a runaway,'' he said without looking up.

''Is that how you ended up in the state's care?''

He nodded, still shuffling along. He'd never thought much about being abandoned as an infant. It was a fact of life for him. He'd never had a family.

Given a choice, he'd take his life over Gigi's. She'd had her father for eight years, and a mother, too. Long enough to realize what she'd lost.

''How come you weren't in a regular home?'' she asked tentatively.

''I was, a couple of times. The first foster couple I lived with would have adopted me, but the wife was diagnosed with cancer and well…they just had too much to deal with.''

''I'm sorry.''

He shrugged. ''I was just a baby. I don't even remember them.''

''After that?''

''I was in a couple more foster homes. The Thompson family was nice, up until they decided to get divorced. Mr. Eaton got transferred out of state. Eventually I got older. And nobody wants teenage boys. So I went back to the farm.''

''The farm?''

''The group home.'' He looked at her sheepishly. ''Kid farm.''

She stopped, that look on her face again. The one so full of compassion it awed him. ''Some tough guy you are. Your hide may be thick as old leather, but your heart is tender as a baby's bottom, isn't it?''

He winced. ''I'm not sure I appreciate that analogy. But I guess it's better than you thinking I don't feel anything at all.''

''I'm beginning to think you feel more than anyone suspects. Including yourself.''

He shuffled his feet on the cracked sidewalk. "Yeah, well, right now I feel like this is not the kind of neighborhood to be strolling around in at this time of night."

"You have an alternative?"

"I did," he admitted. "There are some cheap flophouses a few blocks down this road. But..."

She smiled. "But you gave your flophouse money to that girl."

"Yep. Some hero I am. She's probably out looking for another john already and we're stuck on the street. We don't have any money, we don't have any food—"

"We have each other."

She brushed her fingers across his arm and a wave of emotion surged inside him at her touch. They had each other. It was that simple for her. She believed in him and for that reason alone, he wouldn't let her down.

She smiled at him. He couldn't imagine why, but it was genuine. "So tell me, Shane Hightower, while you're out saving lost souls of the world, who saves you?"

"I guess that would be you." Her smile brightened. Carefully he lifted her hand from his arm and pulled her along the sidewalk.

"Where are we going?" she asked.

"The train yard."

Fifteen minutes later they'd sneaked through the fence around the rail station and found an open car. Shane hoisted himself up, checked out the empty hull, then helped Oliver and Gigi up.

Gigi leaned against him as he steadied her on her feet. Instead of letting her go, he pulled her against him and covered her mouth with his. She leaned against him, opening her lips to his querying tongue, kissing him back then retreating, enticing him closer.

Before he realized he'd moved, he had her backed against

the wall of the rail car. Her legs had parted and he was between her thighs, hard and aching and pulsing against her.

He backed away with a forcible effort. "Stay here," he
ordered, hopping out of the car. "I'll be right back."

"Where are you going?"

"To see if I can scrounge up anything useful."

He'd thought long and hard on the way from the street
where they'd left the hooker to the rail yard. Tried to identify
the powerful tide pulling at him, sucking him under as they
walked. He was drowning and still he wanted to go deeper.
He didn't know where the current would lead, or why. He
only knew he had to get there. It was hell to want something
so bad you'd die for it, without even knowing what "it"
was.

Lust was the only name he dared give it. He wanted Gigi.
Wanted her with a ferocity that boiled in his blood. Wanted
her with a bone-deep desire that wouldn't be satisfied by a
hasty coupling up against the dirty steel wall of a railroad
car. He wanted to take her somewhere with satin sheets and
down pillows. He wanted to lay her down and make slow,
languorous love in tempo with the surf pounding the beach
until she screamed with the gulls. Then, with a sea breeze
refreshing their bodies, he wanted her again. And again.

The only problem was—he didn't think he could wait that
long.

Gigi huddled against the side of the car while she waited.
Despite the warmth of the night air, she shivered. Her skin
was still tingling from his touch, her senses heightened.
Aroused.

He would be back, she told herself. He wouldn't leave her
here. He wouldn't leave her alone.

A deeper shudder rattled down her spine and out to her
limbs. Foolish as it was, she had to go after him.

She didn't want to be alone anymore.

By the time she found him, he'd almost made it back to the rail car where he'd left her. She nearly shed her skin she jumped so fast when she cornered the end of a caboose and ran into him.

"Gigi, what are you doing out here?" he whispered, turning her by her elbow and propelling her back the way she'd come.

"I—I was afraid—"

"Of what? There's no one here but us."

"I know, but I was scared...." They stopped outside the door of the rail car. Shane dropped the bundle he'd been carrying, some kind of large tarp. "What's that?" she asked, grateful for the opportunity to change the subject.

"As close as I could get to satin sheets," he said, smiling mysteriously. He picked up the sheaf of canvas and plopped it inside the car door, then helped her in and scooped up Oliver and tossed him in gently behind her.

"I found the tarp over some crates back at the warehouse. I figured it would be at least a little bit cleaner than the floor in here."

He jumped into the car and cradled her jaw in his hand. "I'm sorry I can't do better for you tonight."

His thoughtfulness touched a sensitive place inside her. She'd dragged him from his life. Cost him his job. Nearly gotten him killed. And he was worried about making her sleep on a dirty floor? "The tarp will be just fine," she said.

"It's just for one night. Tomorrow—" he tangled his fingers in the curls at her nape "—tomorrow I'll find something better. I promise."

The enormity of their situation weighed on her. They had no money. Nowhere to go. "Where?"

"How about Mexico?"

"Mexico? We can't just— We don't have any papers."

A low, serious chuckle rumbled up from his gut. "I

learned a few smuggling tricks in my days with DEA. I can get us across the border.''

''And what then?''

''Then we start over. Work our way south.''

''Just like Butch and Sundance.''

''Just like Butch and Sundance.''

She tried to tell him that she wasn't sure she wanted to start over again. She'd already tried that, and it hadn't been all she'd hoped. Because when all the material things in life were stripped away—home, job, even friends and family—you're still who you were to begin with. With all the problems you had before.

But Shane's hand trailed down her neck, lingered near her breast and toyed with the top button on her sleeveless blouse.

Gigi gathered her thoughts before her ability to speak deserted her completely. ''Does this mean you believe me now, about my father?''

His hands only paused a second. ''It means I don't care anymore. None of it matters—what you knew or didn't know. All that matters is someone is trying to kill you. And I have to keep you safe.''

That wasn't quite the answer—the commitment—she wanted, but he slid the first button through the hole, paused to cup her breast in his warm, flat palm, and she couldn't pull together enough words to argue.

He moved on to the next button. ''You never did tell me what you were afraid of outside.''

The second button popped open. Then the third.

''I was afraid you'd leave me.''

His hand went still and he looked up, his eyes full of surprise. Then his expression grew fierce. ''I'm not your father, Gigi. I won't abandon you when you need me.''

A sense of unreality surrounded her. She should have crumpled against him, but she held herself back. Her rigid body wouldn't give in. How had he known? How had he figured out that was what she had been afraid of all along?

She let herself fall against him.

He yanked on her shirt, sending the buttons still fastened skittering across the floor and hauling her against him. One hand closed over her breast, shoving the cup of her bra out of the way until flesh touched flesh. His other hand spanned her throat just beneath her jaw, forcing her head up and back.

"Open your eyes," he commanded, and she obeyed.

He hesitated just long enough to squeeze her breast and roll his thumb over her peaked nipple before he continued. "You want to know what I'm afraid of, Gigi?"

Fighting back the fog in her brain that his manipulative hand on her breast was causing, she nodded.

He lowered his head and kissed her, openmouthed, hot and wet. "You're so damn strong. I'm afraid you don't need anyone. Including me."

Without waiting for any answer, he bent over and put his mouth where his hand had been. He laved her pebbled aureole until she bucked against him, and then he brought his mouth back to hers.

"Tell me you need me," he said against her lips.

"I need you."

He pushed her shirt off her shoulders and it fell back, hanging around her hips like a skirt, its hem still tucked in the waist of her shorts. He twisted his body and paid homage to her other breast, kicking the tarp open at the same time. "Say it like you mean it."

"I need you," she cried louder. And she did. She who hadn't let herself need anyone since she'd been eight years old and the person she needed had let her down—she needed Shane Hightower.

She sagged against him. Their mouths met, slid apart, and fused again. Shane bent her to the floor and followed her down. She opened herself to his probing tongue, let him explore and then kissed him back, demanding her own entry. Her hands slipped between them to tug on the waistband of his jeans. "I need you *now*."

Her shirt and shorts disappeared on a curse. His shirt sailed to the floor next to them. He rolled off her long enough to slide his blue jeans over his hips. She pulled on one leg while he kicked with the other.

When all the barriers were gone at last, Shane poised over her on straining arms. He stopped with the head of his arousal pressing into her wet folds. "Gigi, there's one other thing we're lacking tonight besides food, money and a decent bed."

"What?" she asked breathlessly.

"I don't have any protection."

"That wasn't a problem before."

"It should have been. I wasn't thinking—"

"Shane, I don't care about protection." She needed him so badly that she wouldn't have cared if the rail car had been slowly filling with acid.

"I do."

"I don't mean I don't care. I mean—it's just—the timing isn't right." She pictured the calendar and did a quick mental calculation. "We don't have to worry."

"Lots of kids in that home I was in got their starts because someone didn't worry when they should have."

She touched his chest and felt his heart knocking against her hand. "It's not the right time. But even if it was, would it be such a bad thing? You'd finally have a family. We both would."

Shane reared back and stood. He turned his back and left her on the floor, chilled and stunned. Her arms crossed over her chest, she rubbed her arms. She followed him to the door.

"Or is that what you're really afraid of?" she asked quietly. "That one day you'll have to face up to the fact that there are people in this world who love and care about you, and you won't know what to do about it?''

He stretched an arm out and leaned against the door frame. Moonlight glistened from his sweat-slicked body. "I wouldn't be any good in a family. I don't know how."

"You'll figure it out."

He wheeled and pinned her against the wall. Her breath caught at the violence of the move, but he caught her in time to keep her head from slamming against steel, gentled his touch in time to keep his weight from forcing the last of the air from her lungs.

"And if I don't?" he said. "If it's something I don't have inside me, a gene I was born without, like some freak?"

His arousal throbbed against her, more urgent than ever. The nerve center between her legs pulsed sympathetically. "Then I'll just love you, and you don't have to love me back." She tried to keep the pleading from her voice. She didn't want to beg. But she needed him, and he'd promised...

"You said you wouldn't leave me when I needed you, Shane." Reaching between them, she wrapped her fingers around his erection and guided him to her. "I need you now. Please don't leave me."

He groaned, pushing her back against the wall, impaling her, and burying his face against her neck in one move. "I won't leave you," he promised. "I won't leave you ever."

Then lifted his head and kissed her. Not out of anger, like she'd half expected, but with exquisite tenderness. Like she was some rare and delicate creature. And when he began to move inside her, his thrusts were just as gentle, every move more caring than the last.

The sliver of pale light shining through the door slashed across his face and she caught the steady relaxation in his features, like the unwinding of a clock wound too tight.

He rocked his hips against her, lifted her, then settled her down again, touching her so deep she thought he might split her in two. Again and again they moved together and she reveled in the slide of skin against skin.

At last there was nothing between them. No more secrets. No more lies. Just naked bodies and the naked truth—they needed each other.

The world rolled on the jut of his body into hers. She cried out in short, choppy bursts of joy and pure sensation. He growled, a lustful howl of mating, and pushed her thighs farther apart. He worked his hand between them and pressed on the swollen gathering of her nerve endings.

Her world shattered and fell around her in pieces. The aftershock of the explosion threatened to carry her away from him, and she clutched at him frantically.

He tightened his arms around her and she felt his release rumble up through his body, gathering strength as it rippled beneath her hands and shook him in a climax as intense as her own.

Gigi wondered if she'd lost her mind, hoping that they would make a baby with what they'd done tonight. But how could she not dream of holding a baby with cornflower eyes while the baby's daddy held her?

Shane moved first. His hands loosened their hold on her thighs as he lowered her to her feet. Lucky for her, he didn't let her go right away. She doubted her legs would have supported her.

Once she had her balance, she raised her head to find him staring bemusedly down at her. He stroked her jawline with a fingertip. "You're really something, you know that?"

Not quite sure what to make of what he said, she glanced over his shoulder at the rumpled tarpaulin. "I guess we didn't need the tarp after all."

"Don't worry. We'll make use of it."

"We will?"

"Mm-hm. The sun won't be up for a couple of hours." He moved his stroking to the length of her back and she arched against his hand like a pampered cat. "And I'm not nearly done with you yet."

She remembered he'd said something similar the first time they'd made love, under the skylight. He'd made good on his promise then. No doubt he'd be just as true to his word tonight.

That was the thing about heroes, she mused as he lowered her to the floor. They never made a promise they couldn't keep.

A slice of sunshine jabbed Gigi in the eye, loosening her tentative hold on sleep. Her shoulder ached from pressing into the hard floor. One leg was asleep, circulation cut off by the weight of Shane's thigh, thrown casually over hers. But her head was comfortable, pillowed in the crook of his arm.

Except for that light. It burned through her eyelids, taunting her with the revelation that, ready or not, morning had arrived.

Not just any morning. The morning she and Shane started off in a new life. One they would make up as they passed through it, leaving everything old, everything familiar behind.

Gigi's stomach turned uneasily. It could have been hunger. It could have been muscles protesting last night's gymnastics. Her hand floated above the fluttering in her abdomen. Or could it be a child, taking root?

She chastised her foolishness. It wasn't the right time of the month for her to conceive. But she left her palm lying protectively over herself anyway.

The enormity of their situation crashed over her. She was about to take off for a foreign country with a man who wasn't her husband—had no real commitment to her—with no money, no passport, no name.

And she might be pregnant. Even if she wasn't, she could find herself carrying a baby at any time, given the way she and Shane couldn't keep their hands off each other and the fact that they didn't have the money to buy anything to prevent it.

What kind of medical care could she get in Mexico or somewhere farther south? How would she care for a child, if she had one?

The thought of giving a baby anything but the best—health, home, education—stripped her to the bone.

Then there was the one ravenous doubt that ate at her mind. One she didn't dare voice. What if Shane left her? She was well aware of his doubts about making a long-term commitment to her, much less a child. If it got to be too much for him, would he abandon her in a foreign country with no identity and no way to get home?

Despite the rising heat inside the rail car, Gigi shivered. Shane stirred behind her, yawned, and stretched.

Gigi turned to face him and met peaceful blue eyes. A skyscape more serene than she'd ever seen in him before.

"I can't do it," she told him. "I can't go to Mexico."

The calm in his eyes never wavered. "I know."

"You do?"

"Sure. I knew before I asked that you'd never go." He pushed a curl out of her eyes. "It's okay. I understand. You're not a quitter, Gigi."

"But you asked anyway." She shook her head, trying to catch up with his train of thought. A train that obviously wasn't on the same track she was.

He shrugged.

"Was it all a joke then? What would you have done if I'd said yes?"

He staked her in place with a stare. "Then we'd be crossing the border by now, and I'd be damn happy to be there. No joke about it." He eased back a step, breathing hard. "But you're not ready to give up on this yet, Gigi. I know you aren't. You're not ready to give up on him."

"Who?"

"Your father."

"Oh, please. Not with the family bit again."

"You're the one who said you couldn't go to Mexico."

She grabbed his hand and pressed his palm to her belly. "This is why I can't go to Mexico. We might have made a child a few hours ago, Shane. And even if we didn't last night, we will, sooner or later. Do you really want to raise him or her on the run in a foreign country?"

"What I really want," he said, obviously choosing his words carefully, "is to keep you alive."

"I've been alive for the past three years. I've even had some good times and made some friends I value. But being alive and having a life are two different things. I won't settle for just being alive anymore. I want my life back."

"Relax. I said I understood. But we're running out of options here."

"There has to be something else we can do."

"Sure," Shane said sarcastically. "We can give your father a call and ask him what the hell is going on."

Gigi's heart tripped. "You're right."

He scowled. "I am?"

"Yes. I need to talk to him, to hear his side of this."

"Good luck. Half the federal government would like to hear his side of this. If they can't find him, how do you think we will?"

"Margo said he's in Phoenix, right?"

"She said she thinks he's in Phoenix."

"Then like you said, we'll call him."

Shane's scowl deepened. "I don't think I like the sound of this."

"My father has one of those satellite pagers. It works anywhere in the U.S. It transmits text, as well as numbers. I can page him and ask him to meet us. If he is in Phoenix, he'll come, I know he will."

"While you're at it why don't you just paint a big red target on your back to make it easy for him to spot you."

She drew a calming breath. "We can set it up wherever we like and tell him to come alone. He'll come, I know he will."

"You still don't believe he's behind this, do you? You can't believe he'd try to kill you."

"I don't know. But I know I have to find out."

"Even if it kills you?" He reached out and touched her stomach. "And our maybe-baby?"

"You won't let that happen." She took his hand and squeezed. "I know you won't."

"You have a lot more faith in me than I do," he said.

But she knew by the torment in his eyes that she'd won. He'd do anything she asked. She could only hope she'd asked for the right thing. The thing that would keep him and her and their maybe-baby alive and give them all the future they deserved.

A real life. A real family.

Chapter 12

A brass bell tinkled over the deli door as Shane held it open and Gigi preceded him through. He breathed deep in appreciation as the smell of fresh bread and strong coffee greeted his rumbling stomach.

He would have stopped for food even before they'd paged her father and left instructions where to meet them, but there was the little problem of money. Fortunately for them, being stuck on the bad side of town had its advantages. Business was done the old fashioned way—the barter system.

Of course Shane didn't have much to trade except the clothes on his back, which technically didn't belong to him anyway, since he'd borrowed them from Fitz's closet.

That left his watch.

It was a little banged up, but it was one of those two-hundred-dollar jobs, waterproof down to a hundred feet; he got twenty bucks for it and considered himself lucky.

At least they would meet Gigi's father with food in their bellies. They both needed a good breakfast—her for the fortification and him for the time it would give him to talk her out of this crazy scheme.

They both chose bagels, juice and extralarge coffees and sat at a table near the window where they could keep an eye on Oliver, napping in the shade the storefront dropped over the sidewalk.

"Tell me about your father," he suggested casually, trying to find a way to ease her into the idea of him making the meet instead of her. "What does he look like?"

She smeared cream cheese on half her bagel and passed the plastic knife to him. "He's tall. Almost as tall as you, but heavier around the middle. His hair is gray, thinning on top. He looks like any man nearing his midsixties who's spent too much time behind a desk. Sometimes he stoops when he's tired."

"What about dress? What's he likely to have on?"

"My father always wears a suit. Even on weekends. At least he did before I left."

"Any distinguishing marks—scars, or a particular piece of jewelry he always wears?"

"Why the twenty questions?"

"I just want to be sure it's him."

"You think I won't recognize my own father?"

Shane took a long draft of coffee. "I was thinking about that," he said, trying to sound like he hadn't rehearsed this speech for the last four blocks of their walk over here. "Maybe it would be better if I was the one to talk to your father."

"You can talk to him all you want. After I've asked him why he's trying to kill me."

"You think he's going to tell you, just like that?"

"I'll find out."

"And if he answers you, do you think he's going to let you walk away?"

Gigi's chest expanded with a slow, deep breath. She set

her half-eaten bagel on her plate. "That's why you'll be there, right? To make sure he does."

Shane's nerves began to buzz. The caffeine from the coffee hitting his system, he told himself. "He might not be alone—we already know he has others working for him in Phoenix. I can't protect you from a sniper a block away or a shooter with an automatic weapon in a speeding car. It's better if I stash you someplace safe first—"

"You don't even want me to be there?" Her lips pressed into an ashen line. "I'm going, Shane. End of story. I have questions."

"Then let me call Margo. She can have him picked up at the meet site, then you can ask all the questions you want."

"No. We can't risk it."

"You'll trust your father but you won't trust Margo Maitland?"

"Shane, I know you don't think your friend is involved—I don't either, really. But someone found us at a DOJ safe house. They nearly blew us up. We don't know who the leak is or how he's getting his information. But you said it yourself last night—until we do, we're better off letting them think we're dead."

More than the caffeine from the coffee hit his system. The acid set his stomach on fire. She was right about not calling anyone in the DOJ, even Margo, for help. Someone way too close to this case wanted them dead. But he didn't want her anywhere near her father, either. "I should be the one to ask the questions. I'm a trained interrogator."

"I'm his daughter. His *family*."

She said it like that single word should make him understand. But it didn't. It made no sense to him at all. Never had; never would.

He hated that weakness in himself. Hated admitting to it even more. After all this time, you'd think he'd have accepted who and what he was.

Firming his jaw, he looked up at her. "Maybe someone should remind *him* of that."

The explosion of pain in her eyes shamed him into hanging his head. "I'm sorry," he told her. "But you said you and your father were never close. You haven't even seen him in three years. What does it matter if it's you that talks to him, or me, after all this time?"

Gradually she gathered her composure. When she met his gaze again, she locked on, steady, straight and true. "Did you ever try to find out about your parents, Shane? What happened to them? Why they gave you up?"

Shane squirmed subtly in his seat. Wherever she was going with that question, he doubted he was going to like it. Her blue eyes darkened mysteriously—like his mood—as she waited for his answer.

"Not until a few years ago," he said. "Margo got the records for me." He cleared his throat and continued. "My mother was seventeen when she had me, and she didn't list a father's name on the birth certificate. I told you she was a runaway. She gave me up so that she could go home. She didn't want her family to know she'd had a kid."

Gigi reached across the table and took his fingers. "Did you ever try to contact her?"

"She was killed in a car accident two years later. What does all this matter anyway?"

She answered his question with another of her own. "Why did you go to all the trouble to find out what happened to her? You were already grown, had a life of your own. And she had abandoned you—you knew that much."

"I guess the time came when I just had to know why." He shrugged, finally understanding where all this was leading. He'd been right before in thinking he wouldn't like it. He didn't. "She was my mother."

"That's how it is for me, too. The time has come when I just have to know."

"Know what?" Shane reined in his anger, struggling to understand. "What could he possibly tell you that would be worth risking your life to hear?"

"Why he pushed me away twenty years ago and never let me close again. Why he might be trying to kill me now. I'm looking for the same thing you were looking for with your mother." A ghostly smile feinted across her lips. "I want to know why my own father didn't love me enough to hold on to me."

Shane sunk in his chair, knowing she'd won. Gently he pulled his hand from hers and stacked his plate—uneaten bagel and all—on top of hers.

He might not know anything about family. But he knew just enough about love to recognize the sound of it in her voice. No matter what her father had done, she still loved him.

Loved him enough to let him kill her, maybe.

But Shane wouldn't—couldn't—let that happen. He'd sworn to protect her, and he planned to stand by his word. Even if it cost him her love.

He cupped his hand under her jaw. His pulse hammered at the silky-soft feel of her tender skin under his rough fingers. His groin hardened at the sight of her studying him.

How could he want her so much when he'd already decided to betray her? It was as if he thought that by joining himself to her in the most intimate way he could stave off time, keep her with him forever.

Her breath accelerated. Her lips parted, and he saw the same need shining from her eyes.

But they didn't have time. It was tough to tell without a watch, but he figured they had about twenty-five minutes before they were supposed to meet her father, and the ball-park they'd selected for the reunion was four blocks away.

Plus, he had business to attend to before they left.

Deadening his mind to his desire, he rubbed the pad of his

thumb over her chin. "Why don't you take a minute to freshen up in the washroom?"

The spell broken, she answered, "Are you trying to tell me I look like hell?"

"No." He smiled, pulling his hand away to show her the white blob on his thumb. "I just didn't think you wanted to see your father for the first time in three years with cream cheese on your face."

Gigi hurried to the rear of the deli while Shane hurried outside and collected Oliver. With any luck, he could finish his phone calls before she caught up to him.

Gigi caught up to Shane outside the deli with Oliver. The recreation department little league baseball fields were only a few blocks away, but by the time they got there her heart was pounding—and not from the exertion of the walk.

In a way, her physical reaction irritated her. It had been like that since she was a little girl, standing in front of her father's massive oak desk trying to muster the courage to ask him not to send her back to boarding school, or summer camp or bible retreat. To beg him, if necessary.

But she'd never been able to get the words out. She'd never begged.

Shane pointed to a players' dugout across the farthest ball diamond and led the way. The cinder blocks provided some relief from the sun, but Gigi's skin still prickled with sweat. Damp strands of hair stuck to the back of Shane's neck as he waited in the dugout, scanning the park.

Minutes ticked by monotonously.

A car pulled into the far lot. Before the man was all the way out its door, she knew it was him. He approached with the same daunting strides he'd taken as a younger man, only a little slower. She'd been right about the suit—it looked like a pinstripe gray from here—although he'd left the jacket in the car. His hair had thinned beyond what she remembered, and gone from charcoal to silver in the years since she'd seen him last.

But he was still her father.

She made no sound creeping up behind Shane in the shadows, but he must have known she was there. He put out an arm to hold her back.

"Wait," he said quietly, and she obeyed, for now, without question.

As much as she needed to talk to her father, she felt out of her element at a cloak-and-dagger rendezvous such as this. She had to trust Shane's experience.

More minutes passed. Her father paced restlessly under the broiling sun of center field, pausing now and again to mop his brow with a white handkerchief. His once-crisp white shirt began to stick to his chest and back. He loosened his tie with two fingers.

The shadows of the dugout that had once cooled and soothed now pressed against her, cloistering her.

"Why are we waiting so long?" she hissed.

"I want to make sure he's alone."

"It's been ten minutes. Maybe more."

His head never turned. He watched her father as he spoke. "Right. If he's got help, eventually they'll make contact to figure out what to do next."

She planted her hands on her hips, stepping around in front of him and demanding eye contact. "When? Next week?"

He graced her with a flickering glance, then turned his attention back to the field. Only then did she notice the tension in his shoulders and neck. He was leaning against the side of the dugout casually, but his body was lit like a stick of dynamite, ready to explode.

Did he really think they were that close to danger?

"Give it a few more minutes," he said. "It's best to be sure."

She stepped around to his other side, and he avoided her

gaze again. Every third second or so, his look left her father and darted to the streets at either end of the ball field.

She had a very bad feeling about this. It was like he knew something was going to happen. But how could he?

He couldn't. Could he?

Despite the heat, chill bumps burst over her skin. She put a foot on the first stair of the dugout. "I'm going."

"Wait!" The desperation in his voice made her certain that something was very, very wrong.

He reached for her, but she dodged his grasp. Her first steps were tentative. Then her father turned to her, recognition flashed across his aristocratic features. Something softer flooded his eyes. Something she remembered, barely, from many years ago.

Her feet flew across the dry grass of the infield. "Daddy?"

Two dark vans turned onto the block.

She ran faster. Her father took a step toward her, then fixed his gaze on something over her shoulder and retreated a step. She heard Shane closing in behind her.

Glancing side to side at the vans at either end of the street and behind her to Shane, her father opened his arms.

She flattened her stride into a dead run and hit him square in the chest. The impact reeled them both backward, off balance a moment.

Before she had a chance to recover, Shane passed in a flying leap, ripping her from her father's arms and propelling her to the ground in a tangled heap. Over his shoulder she saw her father turn, wide-eyed as men in black poured from the vans, rifles at the ready.

Shane covered her body with his, pinning her to the ground. "Stay down," he yelled in her ear.

Any moment she expected bullets to slam into his body, and eventually into hers. She clenched him to her and ground her forehead into his shoulder praying please, God, no. Not Shane.

But the bullets never came.

Eventually she opened her eyes and saw that the men in black had surrounded her father. He was on his knees with his hands behind his head and a dozen rifles circled around him.

It struck her that the men in black holding the rifles weren't just all dressed in black. They were dressed exactly the same, in black. Like uniforms.

Realization set in like icy water flooding her heart one chamber at a time, sinking it slowly in her chest.

"Shane?" she asked, her voice shaking.

He turned his head to one of the armed men, who nodded to him. "All secure."

Shane rolled off her and tried to help her to her feet. She jerked away from the brush of his hand like he was poison ivy.

"Daddy?"

Her father stared at the ground. Even from that angle, Gigi could see the flood barely retained in his eyes.

She turned to Shane, the same flood rising in her eyes. "Shane?" she asked, daring him to come up with any explanation other than the obvious.

He'd used her. Betrayed her. Set her up to get to her father.

"Was this the plan all along, Shane? Did you know who I was even back in Utah, or did you just decide to use me to get to my father after we got here and Margo found out he was a suspect in the murder of a DOJ employee?"

"Neither."

She wheeled away, afraid she wouldn't be able to contain her rising tears if she had to look at him a second longer.

"Gigi." He capped her shoulder with his hand and his touched burned. How could she ever have let him touch her other places, other ways?

"I couldn't let him hurt you," he said.

The men in black—officers or agents of some sort or

other—had handcuffed her father and were walking him to one of the vans.

"He could have killed you, Gigi!" Frustration rang clear in Shane's words.

She turned to face him. "But he didn't. He didn't have a gun, or anything else, did he? And there is no one else here— no sniper or drive-by shooter. So what does that do to your theory, big-shot DEA?"

Neither of them bothered to raise the fact that he wasn't DEA any longer.

"He was here to talk." She advanced on Shane with venom boiling in her blood. At least the anger drove back the tears. "He opened his arms to me for the first time since I was eight years old, and you *arrested* him!"

"He's not under arrest. They're just taking him in for questioning."

A technicality, in her opinion.

"I only wanted to keep you safe, sweetheart. I was afraid—"

The black warriors had moved out of earshot and his voice had dropped to a seductive tone that grated instead of soothed.

"You just couldn't do it, could you? Couldn't trust that I wouldn't betray you, like she did."

She struggled for control over her rampaging emotions. Struggled and lost as her father stopped outside one of the black vans and looked pleadingly back her way before being forced inside by one of the warriors. "Next time you look in a mirror, Shane, you ask yourself who you were really protecting. Me, or yourself?"

His foul oath colored the air as she spun on her heel and marched away, determined to get into that van with her father.

And just as determined not to look over her shoulder. She didn't care if the crust of his frustration had cracked and the soft underbelly of his hurt showed on his face. She didn't care about the vulnerability that bloomed in his eyes at her words. Or the rage that followed it.

She didn't care.

She wouldn't.

Shane sat on a hard bench in the hallway outside the Justice Department offices, just as he'd sat for the last four hours, his hands hung between his knees, his head hung between his shoulders.

Through the curtain of hair veiling his eyes, he saw two pair of legs approach—female legs in a dark skirt, hose and conservative pumps and male legs in navy blue wool trousers and wingtips.

He looked up to face Margo and the man he recognized as District Attorney Branson from New York.

"We got a full confession," Margo announced. "The money laundering, the murders in New York." Her voice softened. "And the attempts on Gigi's life."

A lump rounded out Shane's throat. "And Gigi?"

"He swears she knew nothing about it," D.A. Branson said. "Frankly, I have my doubts. But with the confession from him, there's no need to pursue it."

Numbly, Shane nodded, then hung his head. As she passed, Margo dropped a hand on his shoulder. "Come by the house this weekend. Bill will be out of the hospital, and I know he'd like to see you."

Shane swallowed hard. "I'll try."

Margo moved on, down the hallway and through another door. Shane thought about leaving, but couldn't seem to lift himself from the seat. He was tired. So damn tired.

The door Margo had come through opened again and Gigi walked through. Her red eyes and nose stood out against pale cheeks. Her impossibly long lashes looked even longer and heavier, weighted by recent tears.

"I guess you heard," she said stiffly. "I suppose you're happy."

He should be happy, at least about the case. A murderer would be brought to justice. But looking into her eyes, once as full of life as the teaming seas, now dead like a stagnant pond, he found no joy. The case wasn't the only thing over here. He didn't know why he'd even waited around. Why he'd bothered to hold out hope. "Nothing about this makes me happy."

"Good."

Shane schooled himself not to react. The barb was no more than he'd expected, no less than he deserved.

She lifted her chin, even if it did wobble a bit, and strode down the hall. He couldn't tear his eyes away from the taunting sway of her hips or swing of her arms. He had no doubt she wasn't trying to be sexy. She just couldn't help it. Everything about her appealed to him. Even her stinging remarks.

He'd earned them.

Dammit, he couldn't let go of what they had without a fight. He had to try one more time.

His footsteps echoed with hers on the tile walkway.

"Gigi," he called. To his surprise, she stopped just inside the door without pushing it open. The fact that she didn't run from him sparked hope in his chest.

He caught up to her in three steps and stopped behind her. His palms itched to settle on her hips, to stroke up from there, soothing her and seducing her until she remembered something besides the pain he'd caused. Until she remembered the way he could make her cry out in pleasure instead of hurt.

"I wanted to give this back." He pulled her Taurus from the back of his waistband.

She turned slowly to face him. His hope flickered out like a wick in a windstorm at the lack of emotion in her expression.

"I don't need it anymore."

He pulled her pack around to her side and stuffed the gun in the front zipper pocket. "Take it anyway. You never know."

She twisted toward the door.

He couldn't stand to see her go. "What will you do now?" he asked, intent on delaying the inevitable, even if only for a few more seconds.

"I'll go home again, I guess."

"New York?"

"No. There's nothing there for me now."

In a way, he was relieved. He knew she'd grown up in New York, but he hated to think of her going back there, all alone. There was only one place he could picture her being happy. "Utah?"

She nodded. "Pine Valley is my home now. If my friends there will forgive me for deceiving them."

"There's nothing to forgive. They'll understand."

"I hope so."

"I know so. I wasn't exactly honest with everyone when I came there, either. They didn't hold it against me."

She didn't look so certain. She glanced at the door as if she wanted nothing more than escape.

Shane shifted his feet, desperate for something else to say. Anything to keep her there. "The mountains will be good for you." He knew well the healing power of their peace and beauty, the way old doubts seemed to get lost in the sheer vastness of the wilderness.

She nodded again, then turned to leave. This time he couldn't think of a single other thing to say to make her stay.

With the door halfway open she angled her head back over her shoulder until he could just see the corner of one eye, and the teardrop that fell out of it. "I hope you find your mountains someday, too, Shane."

Then she left. The latch on the door caught softly behind her.

He could have stopped her again, but what would he have said? He'd already found his mountains, and he'd let them get away.

Chapter 13

Shane stretched out on the couch in his living room the next day, one hand thrown behind his head in place of a pillow and Oliver snoring on the floor beside him. Freshly showered and shaven, he should have felt more human than he had in days. Instead he just felt numb.

Dust coated his television screen, but not so thick that he couldn't see that nothing had changed on *Bonanza* in the weeks he'd been away. Even with the sound down, he could tell Little Joe was in trouble again. And Pa Cartwright and the older boys, Adam and Hoss, were hell-bent on rescuing him.

Shane flicked the TV off with the remote control. He wasn't worried about Little Joe. His family wouldn't let him down; they never did.

Wasn't that how family was supposed to be? Some unshakable, unbreakable tie that bound lives together, no matter what? Made one brother hurt when the other fell? Made the father die to protect the child?

Groaning, he pulled his arm from behind his head and let the back of his wrist fall over his eyes. He'd never pretended to know much about family, but what John Ferrar had done contradicted the few principles Shane thought he understood.

Shane's mother had abandoned him so she could go back to her family. Sure, he was her son, her family, too. But she'd been too young to start a family of her own, especially all alone, and he'd been an accident, so the rules didn't really apply. She needed her old family; Shane didn't begrudge her choice.

Lucia had betrayed him to protect her brother. As much as that hurt him, at least her motives were clear.

But what motive drove a man to kill his own daughter? Money? Power? The thrill of getting away with murder?

Just contemplating John Ferrar not loving his daughter— anyone who knew her not loving her—was like trying to make sense out of one of those confounded inkblots. No matter how hard he tried, he couldn't see the butterfly.

And he knew Gigi couldn't, either. Hurting and confused, she'd refused to see her father before she left for Utah. The questions she'd once wanted so badly to ask just didn't matter anymore.

Or so she said. Shane knew differently. He knew from experience how those kinds of questions could fester in the mind, infect the heart. Until she knew why, her father's betrayal would destroy her from the inside out. By God, she deserved to know why he did what he did.

If she wouldn't ask her father what the hell was wrong with him, Shane would.

Much as he hated to take advantage of Margo's influence again—not having a badge to flash limited Shane's access to prisoners—he called his longtime friend and convinced her to clear him into the lockup.

Two hours later, an officer escorted John Ferrar through the door of a plain interrogation room that smelled of old sweat and fear, and removed the prisoner's handcuffs. An orange jumpsuit replaced Ferrar's tailored clothes. His gray hair was rumpled and uncombed. But his eyes were bright. Intensely blue, like Gigi's.

Ferrar scanned the empty chairs at the table. "Where is my lawyer?"

"If you mean that low-rent public defender assigned to you, you don't need him. This isn't an official meeting," Shane replied. He'd been wondering why a man with the resources of Ferrar Industries at his disposal had settled for a public defender. But that wasn't his mission today. "I'm here on a personal matter."

Ferrar looked nonplussed, though his eyes darkened a shade as he studied Shane. Another characteristic he had in common with Gigi. "You're the man who was with my daughter," he said, sitting.

"That's right."

"What do you want?"

"I came to see for myself."

"See what?"

"What a man who could kill his own daughter looks like up close."

Ferrar's chest spasmed like he'd been struck. He recovered quickly enough, though. "Now you've seen," he said quietly. "Is there anything else I can do for you?"

He almost managed to sound dignified, and for some reason that scraped at Shane's last raw nerve. The man had no right to dignity.

Shane stood, propped his fists on the table and loomed over Ferrar. "Tell me, John. How did it feel when you ordered the hit on her? What were you thinking about? Were you remembering how tiny she was when she was born? How cute she looked riding her first pony? Or were you thinking about how you were better off rid of her, just like you were when she was a little girl missing her dead mother and you sent her away to live with strangers?''

Ferrar's chest rattled as he breathed. ''I did what I had to do.''

Shane made a rude sound. ''You had to rip your eight-year-old daughter's heart out?''

''I had to send her away.''

''Why?'' Shane asked.

Ferrar reached for his back pocket, stopped as if suddenly remembering he didn't have one, then used his sleeve to mop the beads of sweat from his forehead. No more linen handkerchiefs for John Ferrar.

''I loved her mother very much,'' he said. ''When she died, grief ate me alive. What kind of life would that have been for a little girl, living in an old mausoleum of a house with a corpse for a father?''

''But you were her family. The only family she had left.''

Ferrar's eyes dulled to matte blue. ''Family is just people, Mr. Hightower. People who love each other, but still people. And people make mistakes.''

Shane checked his fury. This wasn't what he wanted to hear. He didn't want to think of John Ferrar as anything other than a monster. ''Is that what this is, now? All a big mistake?''

''No. This is penance. I made my mistake twenty years ago when I sent my baby girl away. By the time I was ready to take her back, I found I—I didn't know how. I've waited a long time to make that up to her. This is my chance.''

Shane slammed his fist into the table so hard one of his knuckles split. He let the blood run. ''What is that supposed to mean?''

Heaving in a ragged breath, Ferrar raised his head. ''Tell my daughter to pick up my calls. I need to talk to her.''

At least now Shane knew that his phone calls weren't the

only ones left ringing. "You tried to kill her for God's sake. Why would she talk to you?"

Ferrar made a choking sound. "It's important that I speak to her," he said, his voice strangled.

"Speak to *me*."

"I can't."

"Why not? You've already signed a statement admitting you tried to kill her. All I want is to be able to tell her why. She deserves to know that at least, doesn't she?"

Still struggling for an even breath, Ferrar's gaze darted around the room, at ceiling level, and settled on a small grate that Shane knew covered the sound and video recording equipment in the wall.

Shane followed his gaze, a knot of apprehension tied up in his chest. "I told you this is an unofficial conversation. We're not being taped. You can say what you want."

"You love my daughter, don't you?" Ferrar asked out of the blue.

Shane reeled backward. "Yes," he admitted hoarsely when he'd found his balance, and his voice.

"And yet you used her to get to me."

"Yes." The frog in his throat had to be a great horny toad.

Ferrar's eyes shone with a feral gleam. "Then we're not so different, the two of us."

"But I'm not her family," Shane defended himself. "Not her blood."

"Blood doesn't make a family, Hightower," Ferrar said, his voice dropping to a surprisingly soft tone. "Love is what makes a family. And love is why we both did what we did. We had to keep her safe. Even if it meant giving her up."

Shane fell into his chair. There had been times, during his years with the DEA, when he'd fisted his hand in the shirt of some lowlife he was about to bust and hauled the man close so he could look down into his glazed eyes…and he'd wondered. Wondered if the man had known, way back when he'd lit his first joint or sold his first bag of little colored pills, how badly he was screwing up. Or that he would spend the rest of his life paying for that mistake.

Shane knew.

He knew he'd screwed up royally. Richly. Only he wasn't the one who was going to pay for his mistake. Gigi was.

He looked up slowly. "It's not over, is it?" he asked her father. "My God. You didn't do it."

Ferrar glanced around the room nervously. "I love my daughter, Hightower. Love her enough to give up my freedom—my life—for her. But it might not be enough. Do you understand?"

"I understand."

Shane was out of the building and in his car in less than thirty seconds. It was a six-hour drive to Utah. He could make it in three and a half, running his Mustang flat out. In the meanwhile, he'd call Bailey and send him to Gigi's house.

Her father's confession had bought Gigi time. Shane just prayed it had bought her enough.

Gigi packed a couple of apples and a granola bar along with bottled water in her canvas backpack. She had to get away from the phone. Away from the memories of Phoenix and the voices that reached across the wires from there to here.

Shane had called three times last night. She hadn't answered any of them. Hearing his voice on the recorder hurt enough; she couldn't imagine the pain actually speaking to him would cause.

Her father had called ten times or more. He'd blatantly admitted he'd bribed the guards for phone privileges and didn't know how many more chances he could buy, probably as a way to goad her into picking up. His disregard for the system, the law, anyone's rules but his, only made him that much more repulsive to her.

Finally, she'd unplugged the phone.

But even that wasn't enough. She had to get out. Away. Where she didn't have to look at it. Where she didn't have to think about it. Them. Shane and her father.

Somewhere away from the temptation to pick up the phone and let them both back into her life, to admit how much she missed them.

Her backpack hefted over her shoulder, she turned to the door, ready for a brisk hike in the mountains to clear her mind.

Just as she turned the doorknob, a car pulled in the drive. She forced herself to relax, taking seconds to uncoil the muscles that had stiffened at the sight of the strange car. Her reaction was understandable, she told herself, with all that had happened recently. But she didn't need to be afraid anymore.

District Attorney Branson sauntered to the house, a lazy smile on his too perfect face. "Julia," he called.

"Mr. Branson. What are you doing here?"

"I came to check on my favorite witness."

"Then you wasted a trip. I'm not your witness anymore. You don't need one. You've got a signed confession."

"Guilty as charged." He reached the front stoop and kept coming. "May I come in?"

He rested his hand on the small of her back in a touch more intimate than she was comfortable with, and steered her through the door and into the living room.

She turned inside the entryway. "I was on my way out."

"So I see." He lifted the pack from her shoulder and set it on the floor.

She jerked, about to protest, but something in his gray eyes stopped her. "Mr. Branson…" Her voice trailed off on the last syllable. She cleared her throat and continued. "What are you really doing here?"

"I was worried about you." He stroked her jaw.

Gigi couldn't suppress her shudder. His steel eyes shimmered threateningly, like a knife, reflecting the light as it fell to the throat.

Adrenaline coursed through her bloodstream. "No need to worry. The danger is over now." She raised her chin and poured her heart into her voice to keep it from breaking. "The case is closed."

"Yes, I suppose. But that isn't what I was worried about. You seemed upset when you left Phoenix. I wanted to be sure you were all right. I know this has all been hard on you, and I thought you might like some company—someone who understands, to talk it out with."

"You?"

His smile reminded her of a barracuda. "I don't have to be back in New York for a few days. Maybe we could…get to know each other."

Gigi forced oxygen in and out of her lungs. He was just being nice. He'd treated her decently in New York. More than decently. The way a few of his touches had lingered, the way his stares had weighed on her, she'd thought once that he was trying to seduce her, but she'd never been sure.

He raised his hand again, this time to tuck a curl behind her ear. His fingers caressed the sensitive skin behind her earlobe. Fire flared, white-hot flames, in his pale eyes.

This time, she was sure. He definitely wanted to seduce her. The question was, did she want to be seduced?

At the moment, she hurt so bad it was hard to know what she wanted. She knew only that she *wanted*.

He cupped his hand around the back of her neck, and for a fraction of a second, she swayed into the support. Paul Branson's head lowered slowly to hers, his mouth open and wet. She didn't move. Didn't breathe. Couldn't.

Her brain commanded her hands to push him away.

Before she could, the front door crashed open. Shane surged through like a host of demons and skidded to a halt at the entrance to the living room. His face was flushed. His eyes burned like he had a fever.

Gigi skittered backward as Shane's hot stare burned a path from her to Branson and back.

"Well, isn't this awkward?" the D.A. said, straightening his collar.

"What are you doing here, Branson?"

"I should think that's obvious. I came to comfort Julia after her ordeal."

"Comfort, hell," Shane growled.

Gigi stepped between the two men before the testosterone in the room reached an explosive level. "What are you doing here, Shane?"

He glanced her way. "You didn't answer the phone," he said, as if that explained everything.

"Maybe you should take the hint," Branson piped in. "She doesn't want to talk to you."

"Where's Bailey?" Shane asked, taking the conversation in yet another direction and leaving her in the dust.

"Who?" she asked, frowning.

"The damn state trooper I sent to keep an eye on you. I just talked to him on the cell phone fifteen minutes ago, he was in his car down the block. Now he's gone."

"I don't know what you're talking about."

Shane looked to Branson. "What did you do to him?"

Branson rocked onto his toes and back as if he were enjoying himself mightily. "Why, I coldcocked him and dragged him into the bushes, of course. What did you expect I'd done to him?"

For a moment, Gigi thought Branson was making a bad joke. When she realized he was serious, her heart went still. "You—you *what?*"

"Don't worry. He'll have quite a headache in the morning, but he'll live." Branson put on an exaggerated sigh, shaking his head at Shane. "It's really a pity you showed up, Hightower. I did have high hopes for an enjoyable evening with Ms. Ferrar. Until I had to kill her, of course."

He reached inside his jacket. In the same instant, Shane dived toward her, knocking her to the floor. Something whizzed past her ear, and she recognized it as a bullet even before the gun's retort blasted across the room.

Shane never stopped moving. He rolled to a squat and tackled Paul Branson at the knees, shoving the gun up with one hand, as the D.A. rounded the couch. The two men grappled on the floor like pro wrestlers. Except this event was all too real.

Shane's grip slipped from Paul's wrist and the butt of the pistol swung toward Shane's skull. Shane twisted his neck back just in time to prevent a crushing blow. The gun glanced off his temple. Blood splashed over both men.

Shane found new purchase on Branson's gun hand. "Run Gigi," he grunted.

Gigi scrambled toward the door on hands and knees. Behind her, the sounds of thrashing and thumping told her the fight continued.

She stopped in the entryway and looked over her shoulder. Shane still had hold of Branson's gun hand, but the pair had rolled until Branson was on top of Shane, his forearm crushing Shane's throat. Shane's complexion had changed color, from angry red to violent purple.

She could no more leave him than the mountains could leave Utah.

Why had he come here? Why didn't he bring a gun? God, he couldn't. He didn't have one anymore, and he'd given hers back to her. Her pack.

She crabbed across the entryway and snagged her pack,

relieved at the hard lump in the outer pocket. The Taurus was still there, right where he'd put it.

She yanked the zipper back and closed her hand around the pistol. Turning and shouting all at once, she pointed the weapon at the tangled mass of males grunting and gouging on the floor.

"Stop it!" she shouted. "Now."

The fray continued.

She fired a shot into the ceiling. The shot thundered through the room and the recoil of the gun kicked her arm backward. At least now she knew how it felt to fire it with the bullets in it. Her arm was numb.

She quickly brought the pistol level again.

The men had split apart, Shane swiping blood from his eyes with one hand while grabbing blindly for Branson with the other, Branson backpeddling out of his reach. Before she could sort out one man from the other, Branson had his gun up again, leveled at Shane.

"Drop it!" Branson commanded, his gaze flicking across her then back to Shane. "Or I'll kill him."

"You drop it!" she answered, the barrel of her weapon pointed square at his chest.

Shane lurched forward, furiously blinking blood out of his eyes. "Stay put, Hightower."

"You shoot him and you'll be dead before he hits the ground, Branson," she said.

Branson spared her a glance. "Then maybe I should take you out first."

"You move that gun toward her and I'll be on you before you can get a bullet out of the barrel," Shane warned.

"Well, well." Branson's head swiveled back and forth between Gigi and Shane. "It looks like we have quite a little standoff."

Gigi flexed her grip on the pistol's handle. "Will someone *please* tell me what is going on?"

After a moment of heavy silence, Shane spoke up. "You were right about someone inside the investigation being crooked. Only it wasn't in the police department or any of the DOJ's agencies like we thought. It had to be someone higher to have access to information about me. To track me back to Bill."

"There's very little about *anyone* that a New York D.A. can't find out, one way or another."

"So you were on the crook's payroll all along?"

"Is that what you think?" Branson laughed crazily. "I'm not on anybody's payroll, you idiot. I *am* the payroll."

Gigi flinched. "You..."

"All that money being cleaned at Ferrar Industries had to come from somewhere," he said gleefully.

Gigi tightened her grip on the gun. She knew he was trying to distract her. "So you killed Uncle Ben because he was going to expose your operation."

Another short bark of laughter escaped from Branson. "Poor bastard had no idea that when he called the D.A.'s office to turn over evidence he was calling the very man he was looking to bring down."

"So you played along, set up a meet and used it to kill him," Shane concluded.

Gigi frowned. "But an assistant district attorney was killed, too."

Branson raised his eyebrows and chuckled gleefully. "One of my best moves, don't you think? It made for a splashier headline, and all that press coverage just a few weeks before the election didn't hurt, you know?"

"You sacrificed one of your own for a few votes?" Shane snarled.

"I wasn't doing so well in the polls until I raised that public outrage at the loss of one of my dear, dedicated co-workers. Besides," Branson added, his voice going flat, "someone had to make sure Ben Carlisle had the book before all the shooting started. I couldn't risk taking him out until I was sure he had it with him.''

"The book incriminated you," Shane said.

Branson shrugged. "Carlisle was a fanatic about record-keeping. I never could break him of that ugly habit."

Shane shook his head in disgust. "Not a bad plan, except for one thing. You didn't plan on a witness. You were going to get rid of the book, weren't you? Pretend it didn't exist. But Gigi saw it. That's why you had her taken into protective custody, even though she never saw the killer—so you could keep her from talking about it. You even leaked the story of an eyewitness to the press so you could legitimize her murder. How many extra votes did *that* get you, huh, Branson?''

Branson's face pulled into a scowl. "I didn't care that she saw it. Or talked about it. I had an imitation all made up and ready to go. One that pointed the finger at her father instead of me. I couldn't be sure of all those votes unless I brought the killer to justice now, could I? Otherwise I'd look like a fool."

"Then why kill her? Especially now that her father has confessed."

"Because sooner or later, even with her father's confession, I'd have to produce the book. And when I did, she would know it was a fake."

"How?"

"Tell him." Hatred drilled from Branson's eyes into her. "Tell him what you left behind on the book, before I switched it for the imitation, that I couldn't reproduce."

Gigi searched her mind for the details of that night. Details she might have forgotten, or thought unimportant. Painful as it was, she relived it step by step. Like a movie, frame by frame. The shots. The blood. The bodies. Checking for pulses and finding none.

Then picking up the book. Opening it. Touching that first page, the Ferrar Industries logo.

"Fingerprints," she said shakily, looking at Shane. "Bloody fingerprints, from when I looked at the book. My hands were still coated. I smeared it all over."

Branson shook his head wearily. "All this trouble, because she had to pick up the damn book without even wiping her hands."

"I was in shock," she said as if she owed him an explanation. She looked to Shane for understanding, but his focus was on Branson, where hers ought to be.

"I'd love to stay and reminisce some more," Branson said, "But it really is time for me to be going. So what's it going to be, Ms. Ferrar? You seem to be the only one with a play here."

"Watch him, Gigi. I'll find something to tie him up with until we can get the law here."

"Don't move, Hightower. I'm an excellent shot. At this range, I can't miss."

"Don't do it, Shane." Her voice shook. Branson sidled toward the door.

"Don't let him go, Gigi," Shane urged. "He won't shoot me. He knows you'll kill him if he fires."

Branson laughed, a sickly sound. "She won't shoot me."

"Don't bet on it," Shane growled.

Branson sidled toward the door. "You can't do it, can you sweetheart? You can't shoot a man down like a dog."

"You tried to kill me."

"Yes." He smiled wickedly and took another step. "I did."

Gigi absorbed the evil gleam in Branson's eye. Studied the nervous contraction of his fingers around the handle of the gun. He was going to kill Shane before he left, and then he was going to kill her.

And she still couldn't make herself fire.

Frantically, she looked to Shane and saw understanding in

his eyes. More, she saw love. He knew she couldn't do it, and he forgave her for it. Loved her for it.

In that moment, it was like the sun rose for the first time after an Alaskan winter. Her whole muddled life suddenly became clear.

She loved him, too. Her heart burst with it; her mind rang with it. She loved Shane enough to die for him. She loved him enough to kill for him, if she had to.

She took a cleansing breath and imagined the penny on the barrel of the gun, just like he'd taught her. She wouldn't kill in cold blood, but she was ready to tell Shane to go ahead and find something to tie Branson up with. She'd protect him. If Branson so much as twitched when Shane moved, she would fire.

Branson must have sensed that she'd made her decision, and with it become the stronger threat. He swung his gun toward her.

Shane leaped into the air between them as two simultaneous gunshots boomed through the room.

The world spun and went dark. She was aware she fell, but she didn't know who was killed and who was alive.

Branson. Her. Or Shane.

Chapter 14

A cold mist swirled and danced in Gigi's head. Like the fog over the ice the first time she'd seen *Swan Lake*. It wasn't the real ballet, but one of those ice-skating productions put on for kids. Her father had taken her for her seventh birthday, and she'd been enchanted. With the ballet and with him.

For weeks afterward he'd called her his little ballerina and she'd pranced around the house, raising her arms over her head and twirling in clumsy, childish pirouettes, claiming to be Odette, the swan, waiting to be rescued by a man's undying love.

"Hey, beautiful." Shane's rich baritone voice cut through the fog. "Are you awake?"

Something warm and slightly rough—his fingers?—stroked her forearm, waking her nerve endings one by one.

"Mm, my prince," she murmured, her mind still half caught in her *Swan Lake* dream.

Shane's laughter vibrated inside her like a cello's low chord. "Hardly," he said.

The mist in her mind gradually cleared and she opened her eyes not to a cold ice rink, but to the searing heat of a lazy, heart-bursting, bone-melting, *trust-me-baby* blue-eyed smile.

She closed her eyes a second, but when she opened them again, he was still there. "Am I dreaming?" she murmured.

"No, darlin'. You're awake."

"Where am I?" Her gaze roamed the room, trying to place the utilitarian furniture, the sea-foam green tile floor, the emergency exit directions posted on the back of the door.

"In the hospital," Shane explained.

The memories crashed over her, sucked the breath from her chest. "Oh!" she gasped. Ignoring the lance of pain in her shoulder, she turned her head, scanning Shane's body frantically. "Are you all right?"

He soothed her forehead with his palm, gently pushing her head back to the pillow. "Shh. I'm fine. You were the one needing a doctor this time. I have to say, I *much* prefer being on the other end of the first-aid efforts. You scared the hell out of me, bleeding all over like that."

Her vision cleared enough to see the lines of exhaustion fanning out from his eyes. The bruise and butterfly bandage on his temple. "You're really okay? Really?"

"I'm fine."

"But you jumped in front of him! You—you—" She stopped resisting and fell back, gulping for breath, her eyes closed. "You weren't supposed to do that. You weren't supposed to die for me."

"And you weren't supposed to kill for me, remember?"

Her eyes flew open, suddenly heavy with tears. "Oh, God. Did I kill him?"

"No."

"But I shot him?"

"You didn't hit anything vital. Unfortunately."

Her heart rapped at her breastbone like a woodpecker. *Tap, tap, tap, tap.* Fast, sharp little beats.

"Don't feel badly for him, Gigi. He made his choice. You did what you had to do."

"You knew, didn't you?" she asked. "You knew it was him, and he was after me. That's why you came back to Utah."

Shane stroked the hair back from her temple, his expression turning somber as he nodded.

"How did you know?" she asked.

"Your father told me."

"My—?" A new pain knifed through her. She'd almost forgotten her father in all the confusion. She braced herself against the hurt that came with thinking of him in prison. "What did he do? Trade information for a lighter sentence?"

"No. He traded his sentence for the truth."

"You're not making sense."

A smile broke across Shane's face. "He didn't do it. Any of it. Ben Carlisle was the one laundering money, not your father. It seems *Uncle* Ben had racked up some sizable gambling debts and was working for the mob to pay them off, though he never actually saw any of the men he was working for, or knew their names. Your father caught him and convinced him to turn himself in. Your dad figured it would go easier for Carlisle if he gave himself up than if someone else reported him.

"But then, the next thing he knew, Carlisle was dead and you were missing. There were rumors that someone in law enforcement was involved in the whole scam. Your father didn't dare come forward with what he knew, at least not until he was sure you were safe. So he put his top security men—along with a dozen private investigators across the country—to work finding you. They tracked us to Phoenix by following Branson's moves."

Gigi absorbed Shane's statement for several long moments, hardly daring to believe it. "But he confessed."

"To buy you time. He bribed the guards at the jail, tried to call you and warn you."

A rock fell to the pit of her stomach. "And I wouldn't pick up the phone."

Shane cocked his head in subtle confirmation.

"Why would he do it? Why would he protect me after all these years."

"Maybe he was protecting you all along."

Gigi frowned. Shane was still talking in riddles, and her head ached too much to solve puzzles.

Her confusion must have been obvious, because he took her hand and explained before she'd had a chance to ask. He told her about his talk with her father. About her father's grief after her mother's death, and how he thought his bitterness would taint Gigi, so he sent her away. He told her about wanting to change it later and not knowing how.

By the time he finished, fresh tears had spilled over her eyelids and burned tracks down her cheeks.

"All those years," she said. "All the time I spent hating him and loving him at the same time. He needed me, and I didn't see it."

"You were just a kid."

"Maybe at first. But later I should have seen what he was going through. What he was doing. But I just thought he didn't love me."

"He loves you, Gigi. He always has. He just didn't know how to show it."

She squeezed her eyes shut against the leakage. "I should have tried harder. When he pulled back, I shouldn't have given up. I should have held on. But I just let him slip away."

"There was nothing you could have done."

She turned her grief into anger to stop the tears. "I should have tried. I was his family. His only family."

Shane stiffened like he was expecting a blow, then slowly

relaxed as he blew out a long breath. "Family is just people, Gigi—people who love each other, but still people. And people make mistakes."

"I thought you didn't know anything about family," she grumbled.

A hint of a smile curled up the corners of his mouth. "I don't. But your father does. Those are his words. Not mine. He was talking about himself, and the mistakes he made when you were eight."

Her shoulders shook. The movement jarred her shoulder painfully, and it took her a long time to push the pain aside. "Then he's free?" she finally asked.

"Margo sprung him this morning. He's on his way here."

Her father. Coming here. To see her. He'd never come to see her, in all the years she'd been away. She raised her hand to smooth her hair, stopping short when she felt the pull on the tube taped to her arm. "I—I can't see him like this."

Vanity was ridiculous at that point, but she couldn't help it. She didn't know what else to feel.

Shane patted a curl down on the side of her head. "You look fine. Gorgeous as ever."

"I don't know what to say."

"Start with hello and let him take it from there."

She picked at the fuzz on the blanket. She darted a look up at Shane, then lowered her eyes. "He really wants to see me? After I betrayed him?"

"You didn't betray him," he said firmly. "I did."

"You couldn't have known he was innocent." She looked at him, fighting back her own anguish to quench his. "I didn't. And I'm his daughter."

"But you gave him a chance to explain. Or at least you tried."

"Don't blame yourself Shane. Blame Branson. You were just protecting me."

"No. I was protecting *me*. You were right about me. I was

afraid.'' He shook his head, twining his fingers with hers and holding on tight enough to hurt. But his voice seemed to draw strength from the bond, so she didn't struggle. ''I was afraid you'd choose him over me.''

''Oh, Shane,'' she said, her eyes misting up again. To hell with the pain in her shoulder. She reached up and caressed his jaw. His short, golden growth of beard stubble rasped her knuckles. ''I choose you both.''

''Smart girl,'' a familiar baritone voice rumbled from the doorway.

Shane and Gigi both jumped. Gigi looked up, her breath a wisp. ''Hi, Daddy.''

John Ferrar stepped into the room and hugged her—a gentle cupping of her shoulders and peck on the cheek, as if he thought she might crumble in his grasp.

''How are you feeling, princess?'' His voice was gruff, whether from years of use, or emotion, she couldn't be sure.

He'd aged. The crevasses beside his eyes were twice as deep as she remembered. Then he tweaked her nose and winked, and he was thirty-five again, with burnished hair and a crooked grin.

She blinked, and the vision disappeared.

Shane stood. ''I'll give you two some time.''

''Stay put,'' her father ordered. ''You two were in the middle of a serious conversation, it sounded like.'' He looked at Shane. ''This the conversation we talked about on the phone this morning?''

''Yessir.'' Shane grinned.

Gigi looked from one to the other, trying to decipher the messages passing silently between them and finally giving up.

Men. Who could understand them?

''Then I'm definitely in the way here right now. I believe I'll head down to the cafeteria for a cup of coffee,'' her father said. "But when you're finished, I'll take my turn. My daughter and I have a lot of catching up to do."

"Yessir," Shane said again, still grinning as her father closed the door behind him. When he'd gone, Shane turned back to Gigi. "I think I like your father."

"I think I'm going to like him, too, once I get to know him." She drew a breath as deep as her injuries would allow. "It's going to be strange, having a dad again. I'm not sure I know how. But I'm looking forward to trying."

Shane turned serious. "You'll be moving back to New York, then?"

"No." She answered before she really thought about it, but she knew it was the right answer. "I want to spend some time with him. But I told you before, my home is here now."

Did he look relieved, or was it her imagination?

"How about you? Will you try to get your job back with the DEA?"

He sighed. "No. I meant it when I said I was tired of trying to save the whole world." He looked up at her through a golden forest of lashes. That sexy lock of hair fell over his eyes, hooding them even more. "But I think maybe I could handle saving one small piece of it."

A slow smile broke across her face as she guessed his meaning. "Maybe a piece in southwest Utah?"

"Maybe." He chuckled and flung the hair back out of his eyes. For a moment she wasn't sure which she preferred, the sexy, roguish look, or a clear view of his cornflower blues.

"I think I could get myself appointed interim sheriff. But sooner or later there'd have to be an election for the permanent position."

"You'd get my vote."

"I'd better," he said. "How would it look if my own wife didn't vote for me?"

Gigi's jaw fell slack. Her throat swelled shut and she couldn't speak.

Shane cleared his throat. "Something else your father said about family is that it's about second chances. And third and fourth and fifth if that's what it takes, but I'm hoping I won't need that many."

"Sounds like you and my father had quite a talk," she nearly croaked.

"Several."

"Really?" She was intrigued. And outnumbered. The men in her life were ganging up on her already, she suspected.

"In our first talk, he straightened me out on all this family stuff. In the second one, I straightened him out about it not being too late for the two of you and him getting his butt up here to see you. And in the third…"

"Yes?" All this talk about her father was interesting, but she wanted him to get back to that wife thing…

"In the third, I asked his permission to marry you." Shane took a deep breath and slipped down to one knee beside the bed. "I love you, Gigi. Will you be my wife?"

"Yes," she croaked. "I love you, too. And yes."

He leaned over the bed, held her and kissed her. He was careful, but this was no fragile hug and peck. It was a full-blown, on-the-mouth, open, wet, hot, lovers' embrace hug and kiss. A kiss that stole the last of her breath and left her dizzy.

A kiss that promised to last a lifetime.

Epilogue

Careful not to snag the train of her gown, Gigi walked across the bedroom she and Shane had been sharing for nearly a month and sat before the oak dresser. Last week, Shane had bought the cabin he'd been renting during his stay in Pine Valley, and they planned to make it their home.

Out in the great room, she could hear voices, people milling about, laughter. A wedding should be a happy occasion. Until this morning, she had been certain hers would be.

Now she wasn't so sure.

Nerves buzzing in her stomach like a honeybee hive, Gigi straightened the pins that held her veil in place and studied her reflection in the dresser mirror one last time. Only the woman's image reflected back to her wasn't Gigi McCowan. She hadn't been Gigi since news of all that had happened spread through the town after the shooting.

But she didn't feel like Julia Ferrar, either. She wasn't the same woman who had left New York three years ago; she'd changed too much. Though she was happy to have her father in her life again, she couldn't go back to the person she had been.

Who she was wasn't important anyway. Who she was going to be, *Shane's wife*, was what mattered. So she'd put her energy into planning this wedding. But now that was in jeopardy, too.

Before she could say her vows, she had to break the news to Shane.

Three raps sounded on the door, and Shane poked his head in. "You wanted to see me? I thought it was bad luck or something."

Bad luck. She hoped not. She worried the strands of pearls her father had given her. They'd been her mother's and were serving as the "something old" for the ceremony. The pearls had been a surprise this morning. She thought her father had given her all her mother's jewelry years ago. He said he'd saved these just for this occasion.

Shane came into the room, breathtaking in his black tux and tie, and closed the door behind him. "Is something wrong? If it's about the chairs, don't worry. I brought a few more in from the kitchen. Everyone will have a place to sit."

She'd almost forgotten about the chairs. She'd miscounted the number of guests and ordered too few from the rental agency. She'd been bustling about figuring out where everyone was going to sit when the call came in. After the call, she'd forgotten just about everything.

There was no way through this except straight ahead. Setting her hands in her lap, she lifted her chin and squared her shoulders. "It's not about the chairs. The doctor's office called this morning."

"The doctor?" He was at her side in two long strides, squatting in front of her. "Are you all right?"

"That night in the train car...I thought it wasn't the right time. I don't know what happened. I must have miscalculated. Numbers are not my strong suit, as you can tell since

I didn't even get the number of chairs right at my own wedding.'' She chewed her lower lip, knowing she must be messing up her lipstick, and not caring. "I'm pregnant."

His body went still. She couldn't even see his chest rise and fall. In the long moment that stretched between them, her thumb and forefinger found the pearls again and rubbed them, comforted by their smooth warmth and the fact that they were her mother's.

It seemed like days, though she knew it couldn't have been more than seconds, before his big body relaxed. "Well, then." He drew a deep breath and smiled, even if it did look a little forced. Or was it just stunned? "No champagne toast for you after the ceremony."

The tears she'd been biting back sprang forth, and she figured now her mascara was ruined, too. "Then you still want to marry me?"

He rested his arm across the back of her chair, just touching her shoulders. "Of course I want to marry you. I love you and we're having a baby."

He'd recovered quickly—more quickly than she had. His smile was genuine now.

"I know how you feel about family," she tried to explain her doubts. "I...I was afraid this would just be too much. All at once."

He rocked back on his heels, his smile dimming. She couldn't tell if he was upset, or trying not to laugh.

"Oh, Shane. We're the two most clueless people in the world when it comes to family. How will we ever make it work?"

He raised up, scooted her over on the chair with his hip and pulled her into his lap. Looking at his handsome face, she realized he wasn't mad or laughing. In fact, she thought maybe his eyes were as glossy as hers.

"Scared?" he asked.

"Yeah." Elation warred with sheer terror.

"About the wedding or the baby?"

"Both."

"Do you love me?"

"Yes."

"Good. Because I love you too. And that's all it takes to make a family work."

She squinted at him through her drying tears. "My father again?" Shane and her dad had become close faster than she would have imagined.

"He's a very smart man."

"He'll be a great grandpa, huh?" She sniffed.

He nodded. "So let's go get married so we can tell him the good news."

She checked her reflection in the mirror. Heavens, the damage was worse than she thought. "You go stall," she said, smiling as she pushed Shane away. "Tell Dad I'll be there in a few minutes."

A few minutes turned out to be fifteen, but Shane didn't care. He'd wait a lifetime for her. Nothing could have made his heart expand the way seeing her, as a vision of a beautiful woman in white lace, her cheeks as lustrous as the pearls around her neck, did.

Watching her walk down the aisle on her father's arm, he realized he loved her even more than before. He wouldn't have thought it possible, but knowing she was carrying his baby, their baby, deepened his feelings in a way he'd never have imagined.

It was like a desert creature contemplating life in the sea. Until the moment she'd told him she was pregnant, he'd simply had no frame of reference for what he felt.

His family. The words suddenly had meaning. It was an awesome responsibility, and an incredible gift. Quite some wedding present his soon-to-be wife had given him. Nothing could have been more perfect.

The ceremony passed by in a flash, and was over too soon.

He kissed his bride as instructed, standing in the cove of his great room with the world laid out behind them and their friends, old and new, seated before them. With all his heart he tried to imbue the love and commitment of a lifetime into that one touch of his lips to hers.

When he finally lifted his head, the minister gave him a short nod, and Shane knew the man would remember to introduce them to the guests exactly as Shane had requested.

His wife couldn't be Gigi McCowan any longer, especially with the original Gigi, flown in from Ocala that morning, dabbing at her eyes with a hanky in the second row beside Eric Randall and Mariah, his bride of a week. But she'd said she didn't want to go back to being Julia Ferrar, either.

That was fine by him. He had a new name for her, anyway. His.

The minister closed his bible and opened his arms to the crowd. Shane squeezed his wife's hand.

"Ladies and gentlemen," the minister pronounced. "I present to you Mr. and Mrs. Shane and *Julia Hightower*."

Shane slid his gaze sideways to check her reaction. From the look on her face, she liked the sound of it.

He knew he sure did.

*   *   *   *   *

If you enjoyed what you just read,
then we've got an offer you can't resist!

Take 2 bestselling
love stories FREE!
Plus get a FREE surprise gift!

Clip this page and mail it to Silhouette Reader Service™

YES! Please send me 2 free Silhouette Intimate Moments® novels and my free surprise gift. Then send me 6 brand-new novels every month, which I will receive months before they're available in stores. In the U.S.A., bill me at the bargain price of $3.80 plus 25¢ delivery per book and applicable sales tax, if any*. In Canada, bill me at the bargain price of $4.21 plus 25¢ delivery per book and applicable taxes**. That's the complete price and a savings of at least 10% off the cover prices—what a great deal! I understand that accepting the 2 free books and gift places me under no obligation ever to buy any books. I can always return a shipment and cancel at any time. Even if I never buy another book from Silhouette, the 2 free books and gift are mine to keep forever. So why not take us up on our invitation. You'll be glad you did!

245 SEN C226
345 SEN C227

Name	(PLEASE PRINT)	
Address	Apt.#	
City	State/Prov.	Zip/Postal Code

* Terms and prices subject to change without notice. Sales tax applicable in N.Y.
** Canadian residents will be charged applicable provincial taxes and GST.
  All orders subject to approval. Offer limited to one per household.
  ® are registered trademarks of Harlequin Enterprises Limited.

INMOM00   ©1998 Harlequin Enterprises Limited

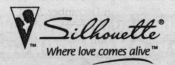